"You felt a woman's p... was the one who gave it to you."

Belle turned to face him. "Am I . . . am I truly your love?" she asked tentatively.

He nodded and didn't hesitate to reply. "Yes, Belle. I love you with every fiber of my being." Kissing her brow, he drew her into his embrace. "No matter what happens, always remember that I love you."

She rubbed her cheek against his shoulder and sighed. "Of course I shall never forget that. And remember that I love you, too, Trelane."

Pain ripped through Eric far worse than any of the tortures he had suffered during his hellish imprisonment in Venice. *She calls me Trelane. Hell, I would give the world if she would love me instead of my brother. But that's never going to happen.*

His determination shielded him like armor as he lifted Belle onto the sofa beside him. "I can't stay for tea, Belle. The House has called a special meeting of one of my committees at Westminster. As a matter of fact, I might not be available to visit you for several days. I hope you understand."

Belle smiled, yet sadness clearly shone in her eyes. "Of course I understand, Trelane. Isn't that what a good politician's wife is supposed to do?"

Eric swallowed against the tightness in his throat and nodded. "Yes, love, exactly that." Closing his eyes, he kissed her brow and gave her a final hug. *Goodbye, my dearest love. The next time we meet, I'll find a way to tell you the truth. Then you will never want to see me again.*

Dear Romance Readers,

In July of 1999, we launched the Ballad line with four new series, and each month we present both new and continuing stories set everywhere from medieval England to the American West—the kind of passionate, romantic stories you love best, written by the most gifted authors. At the back of each book, we tell you when you can find subsequent books in the series that have captured your heart.

First up this month is **Moonlight on Water,** the second book in the fabulous new *Haven* series by beloved author Jo Ann Ferguson. Will a young woman leave her familiar community behind for a steamboat's dashing captian? Next, talented Annette Blair takes us back to Regency England to meet **An Undeniable Rogue,** the first irresistible hero in her new series *The Rogues Club.* Marrying a fallen friend's sister is a simple matter of honor for one dashing rake newly returned from the war, until he meets the wildly tempting—and very pregnant—woman in question!

The MacInness Legacy continues with new author Sandy Moffett's **Call Down the Night,** as the second of three sisters separated at birth discovers her gift of second sight may lead her to a strange heritage— and keep her from the man she loves. Finally, talented Susan Grace begins the new series *Reluctant Heroes* with **The Prodigal Son** as one of the infamous Lady Cat's twin sons masquerades as the other—and finds himself falling for his brother's beloved . . .

These are stories we know you'll love! Why not try them all this month?

Kate Duffy
Editorial Director

RELUCTANT HEROES

THE PRODIGAL SON

SUSAN GRACE

ZEBRA BOOKS
KENSINGTON PUBLISHING CORP.
http://www.kensingtonbooks.com

ZEBRA BOOKS are published by

Kensington Publishing Corp.
850 Third Avenue
New York, NY 10022

Copyright © 2002 by Susan Grace

All rights reserved. No part of this book may be reproduced in any form or by any means without the prior written consent of the Publisher, excepting brief quotes used in reviews.

If you purchased this book without a cover you should be aware that this book is stolen property. It was reported as "unsold and destroyed" to the Publisher and neither the Author nor the Publisher has received any payment for this "stripped book."

All Kensington titles, imprints and distributed lines are available at special quantity discounts for bulk purchases for sales promotion, premiums, fund-raising, educational or institutional use.

Special book excerpts or customized printings can also be created to fit specific needs. For details, write or phone the office of the Kensington Special Sales Manager: Kensington Publishing Corp., 850 Third Avenue, New York, NY 10022. Attn. Special Sales Department. Phone: 1-800-221-2647.

Zebra and the Z logo Reg. U.S. Pat. & TM Off.

First Printing: July 2002
10 9 8 7 6 5 4 3 2 1

Printed in the United States of America

I dedicate this book to the real hero and heroines in my life.

To Peter DeCicco, my best friend and adopted little brother, who inspired me to create Eric and Trelane Grayson with his good looks, intelligence, and sense of humor, and allowed his handsome image to be used on the cover.

To Suzanne Koski Fioto, who helped me get my work done and wouldn't let me forget that a good story had to be told.

To Ann LaFarge, the greatest editor in the entire world, who believed in me and gave me the extra time I needed to complete my work.

And to Sophia Duffy, the art director who didn't scoff when a crazy lady author said that she'd found the perfect man for the cover of her book, and made the impossible happen.

My thanks to you all! Without you, this book never would have been written.

PROLOGUE

London
February 1, 1840

"Bloody hell! If I'm not careful, I'll break my neck climbing over this damned garden wall in the dark," he muttered, pulling himself up onto the high, slate-covered ledge. "There really should be an easier way to sneak into a house during a party."

Dried grass crackled beneath his feet as he dropped to the ground, then turned to look at the house. It appeared to shimmer in the moonlight. Grayson Manor had been the town residence of the Earl of Foxwood for five generations. The regal house was four stories high and filled with all the trappings of great wealth. Works of art, priceless antiques, Persian rugs, and silk brocade draperies filled its rooms.

But this wasn't the time to ruminate over such things. The air was bitter cold and made him shiver. He needed to get inside. Winter was a despicable season, one that no one should have to endure. A snifter of brandy and a blazing hearth would take the icy chill from his bones. Knowing where to find both, he crept around the evergreen hedge to the French doors of the library.

He was pleased to find the large, book-laden retreat devoid of people. Thankfully, the party guests had not found their way to the room. The glass-paned doors were locked, but that didn't deter him. Removing the specially made stickpin from his cravat, he performed a task he had done many times in his chosen career. The clicking sound of the lock disengaging was music to his ears.

With a triumphant chuckle, he kissed the jeweled head of the pin. "Ruby sweetheart, you never let me down. Now I can get into the house without anyone being the wiser." He put the pin back in his cravat and entered the library.

Warm air washed over his cheeks as he went to the liquor tray on the desk. He filled a glass with brandy and took a hefty swallow. The potent beverage felt like liquid fire going down his chilled throat. In a matter of moments, he was feeling warmed, inside and out. Tossing his greatcoat onto a chair, he began walking around the room. As he picked up a jade statue from one of the shelves, a soft, feminine voice called out behind him.

"Here you are, late as usual! Shame on you, Trelane Grayson. Have you lost your pocket watch or did you simply forget about the ball tonight?"

The woman's words held no rebuke. He found the humor in her tone quite beguiling. Without answering her question, he set down the statue and turned to face her.

In spite of her angelic beauty, there was no mistaking the mischievous glint in the lady's hazel eyes when she crossed the room to stand in front of him. Wearing a gown of pale blue satin, she shook her head and caused her burnished gold curls to fall over her left shoulder in a stylish disarray.

"Not only are you late, sir, but you haven't taken the time to dress properly."

He bit back a smile and gave her his most offended frown. "You don't like my new coat and vest? I picked them up from my tailor on Bond Street this afternoon. The man claimed these were the finest quality to be found in the city."

Tiny brass bells on her bracelet jingled when she reached up to stroke the lapel of his blue wool coat. "You look quite handsome in your new clothes, Trelane, but tonight is a formal occasion. Surely you've brought along your evening attire for the party."

Ignoring the last part of her query, he grinned. "Do you really think I'm handsome?"

"Of course I do, you silly man. Why do you sound so surprised?"

He shrugged. "No real reason. Even a gentleman enjoys a compliment on occasion."

She smiled up at him. "Then I shall compliment you on a regular basis, sir. I mustn't let the hardest-working man in Parliament feel neglected."

"Am I also forgiven for being late this evening?"

"Why . . . yes, of course," she replied as he put his arms around her and drew her against him. A nervous laugh escaped her lips. "You're certainly in a strange mood tonight, Trelane. First, looking for compliments and now this unguarded display of affection." She cast a quick glance toward the open door to the corridor. "Aren't you afraid someone will come in and find us like this?"

Gazing down at her flushed cheeks, he smiled. "The only thing I'm afraid of is not being allowed to do this."

His lips touched hers in a gentle, seeking kiss. Her initial tension receded when he kissed her again and soon she was soft and pliant in his arms. Though the top of her head barely reached his chin, she felt exceptionally right in his embrace. He was about to deepen his kiss and sample the sweetness of her mouth when an all-too-familiar voice drew his attention to the door.

"Good evening, son. Forgive the interruption, but Belle's father has been looking all over for her."

His head jerked up. "Ah . . . hello, Mother."

Belle tried to pull away from him, but was stopped when the clasp on her bracelet caught on the buttons of his silver-gray waistcoat. Blushing with embarrassment, Belle quickly freed herself and dropped into a curtsey. "I'm sorry you had to come searching for me, my lady. Trelane and I . . . well, we were talking and . . ."

The Countess of Foxwood, Catherine Grayson, entered the library and put her arm around Belle's shoulders. "No need to explain yourself to me, my dear. I remember well how impetuous young men can be with a beautiful lady."

"But this wasn't all Trelane's fault," Belle objected. "I was teasing him about being late and then . . . well . . . he surprised me by kissing me . . . and I kissed him back. I'm sorry you found us like that."

Catherine shook her head. "Just be happy it was I and not one of those gossips of the *ton* who came upon you. The last thing Trelane needs in his quest to retain his seat in the House is any sort of impropriety. I think it would be for the best if none of us ever discussed this little incident ever again. It shall be our secret. All right?" She walked Belle to the door. "You go on now, and find your father. I have a few matters to discuss with my son."

Belle nodded. "Certainly, my lady. Thank you very much for understanding."

Catherine closed the door and locked it. Turning around, she glared at the man across the room. "So, what do you have to say for yourself, Catlin Eric Grayson?"

"Bloody hell, Mama! How did you know?"

She rolled her eyes. "From the day I gave birth to you boys, I've always been able to tell you and

Trelane apart. Mirrored twins or not, you could never fool *me*, Catlin. Besides, your frugal brother would never waste the funds to purchase that fine ruby stickpin on your cravat or that expensive silk waistcoat.''

''Would you please stop calling me *Catlin*. You know very well I prefer using my middle name.''

Dressed in a gown of claret-red velvet and as regal as a queen, Catherine moved toward him. Eric was pleased to see that his mother was still a very beautiful woman. With a trim figure, she didn't look old enough to be the mother of five and the grandmother of six. The only toll time had taken on her appearance was the tiny laugh lines around her bright green eyes and the pale flaxen color of her once-golden blond hair.

Eric jerked back in surprise when she stepped in front of him and briskly slapped his cheek. ''You might be a man full grown, but that doesn't give you leave to swear in front of your mother. Now, give me a kiss and a proper greeting, and perhaps I'll forgive you for not writing or coming home all these years.''

Suddenly feeling like a little boy, Eric kissed his mother's cheek and hugged her. ''I am sorry, Mama. I know I should have written more often, but it's difficult to post letters from a country that's engaged in a civil war or under siege.''

Catherine leaned back and shook her head. ''You don't have to explain, *Eric*,'' she replied, carefully using his middle name. ''You come from parents who did more than their share of fighting for political causes in their youth. I'm grateful you were the only one of my children who inherited those noble and dangerous traits.'' She kissed his cheek. ''Welcome home, my son.''

Eric smiled. ''Thank you, Mama.''

Looking around the room, she frowned. ''You didn't come in the front door and I don't see any luggage lying about. Are your things arriving later on or are you planning on leaving soon?''

''I wanted to get home quickly, so I made arrangements to send my baggage here next week. I put Papa's name and title on the bill of lading. Perhaps having it addressed to an earl will get it here safely.''

She shook her head in disbelief. ''For someone so anxious to be home, you certainly have an odd way of showing it, son. What did you do, climb over the garden wall and pick the lock on the door? If I hadn't come looking for Belle, I wouldn't have known that you were here.''

Eric shied under his mother's scrutiny and nervously brushed at a non-existent bit of lint on his deep-blue coat. ''I'm sorry I crept into the house without seeking you out, Mama, but when I arrived and saw that you had a party under way, I decided it would be best if I waited. What's the celebration for anyway? I heard you say something about Trelane being a member of the House. So, my brother the good barrister is now in Parliament. Is the ball to celebrate his winning an election?''

''No. Trelane was appointed to his seat in the House of Commons when Sir Wilbur Zachary passed away several months ago. This evening, we are celebrating your brother's engagement. Trelane is getting married."

Eric chuckled. "Well, that should please you, Mama. I'd wager you doubted if either of your younger sons would ever settle down long enough to take a wife. Tell me, who is he marrying? Is she pretty?"

Catherine's brow arched. "You tell me, Eric. When I walked in here a few minutes ago, you were kissing her."

"You don't mean to say—"

She nodded. "Oh, but I do, son. The pretty little blond lady you were holding in your arms and trying to seduce is your brother's fiancée, Belle Kingsley."

Closing his eyes, Eric sighed. "Bloody hell. . . ."

CHAPTER 1

"There you are, Belle! Your father is driving me insane looking for you!"

Stepping into the ballroom, Belle smiled at her irrepressible American cousin, Paris Mackenzie. "I was gone only a few minutes. Surely Papa wasn't that bad."

Paris sniffed and patted the bright red curls of her upswept hair. "That's what you think! Uncle Francis is as nervous as a Christmas goose on December twenty-fourth! Rushing about, talking himself into a frenzy. You weren't here to listen, so he spouted off at me. If I hear him rant on about the importance of his new expedition one more time, I swear I'm going to scream!"

Belle bit back her laughter and tried to console

her irritated cousin. "Forgive me for putting you through that. I went to find the ladies' withdrawing room and managed to get lost. In a house this size, it's an easy thing to do."

"You wouldn't have gotten lost if you were wearing your spectacles," Paris snickered. "I love you dearly, Belle, but you *are* a tad nearsighted. Why on God's green earth did you let that idiot fiancé of yours talk you into leaving your spectacles at home?"

"Trelane says I shouldn't wear them at parties or social functions. He doesn't want people thinking his future wife is a bluestocking who wastes her days with her nose in a book."

Rolling her eyes, Paris shook her head. "Trelane says no spectacles. Trelane says I should wear only pastels. Trelane says this, Trelane says that. The man's a bloody tyrant, Belle! Why do you let him dictate to you like this?"

Belle sighed. "Don't carry on so, Paris. Trelane is merely concerned with his future in politics. Everything about his life, including me, should be conservative and above reproach. If wearing certain colors and leaving my spectacles off helps his career, then so be it."

"Rather you than I, cousin." Paris shook out the full skirts of her emerald-green gown. "If my late husband had made such demands, he would have been laid to rest a great deal sooner than he was."

"Ian loved you to distraction and wouldn't have cared what you wore."

Paris got misty-eyed as she laughed with the memory. "Yes, Ian Mackenzie loved me and I absolutely adored him. We were very happy together for ten years and I miss him. That's the trouble with marrying a man twenty-five years older than oneself. He goes off to his Great Reward and you're left alone."

Belle shook her finger at Paris, causing the tiny bells on her bracelet to jingle. "Stop casting about for sympathy, cousin. You are alone by choice, and well you know it. You're beautiful, barely thirty-two years old, and have more money than you'll ever spend. If you were truly looking for male companionship, all you'd have to do is crook your finger at a man and he'd come running."

"Well, I wouldn't waste the effort here in England," Paris replied tartly. "Most men are too stodgy and pompous for my liking. And if they're titled, it's even worse. I've never met such snobs. All this bowing and groveling to titles curdles my cream!"

Belle knew where this conversation was going and pulled her outspoken cousin away from the finely dressed people grouped around them. "Paris, I'm parched. Why don't we go to the dining room for a glass of lemonade?"

Paris followed her lead, but continued to complain. "If it wasn't for spending time with you, Belle, I would never have come to England. By God, it's the nineteenth century and people still prostrate themselves to this lord or that like it's the Middle Ages. I swear I shall never bow down to anyone but my God!"

As Belle was about to congratulate herself for her successful retreat from the crowded ballroom with Paris, a cultured male voice called out to her. Smiling to mask her grimace, she turned to greet the tall, attractive man coming toward her.

"Good evening, Your Grace," she said, dipping into a curtsey. "I'm pleased you came to our party this evening."

Jonathan Carlisle chuckled and kissed her hand. "If I hadn't, your future mother-in-law would have come after me with weapons drawn. No one ignores an invitation from my sister. Not even me. My being a duke doesn't impress Catherine at all."

Belle found much to like in Trelane's uncle. Besides his boyish good looks and tawny blond hair, Jonathan Carlisle was an astute businessman and politician. He'd become the Duke of Chatham when his father died five years before, and had reportedly taken on the responsibilities with a determination few could match. And his efforts didn't go unnoticed. The past spring he had become a member of the Queen's Privy Council. Quite an accomplishment for a thirty-five-year-old nobleman.

Belle smiled. "Well, under duress or by choice, I am delighted you could join us, Your Grace." Recalling that Paris was standing beside her, Belle sighed and turned to introduce her. "Your Grace, may I introduce my cousin, Mrs. Mackenzie, newly arrived from—"

Paris reached over and shook the duke's hand. "No need for introductions, Belle. Jon and I met last week at the races. Well, Jon, I trust you'll take my advice next time and not wager on another gray horse. Remember, gray horses only run well in the rain."

Belle wished the floor beneath her feet would open up and drag her beneath it. If Trelane had heard her cousin address his uncle with such familiarity, he would have found another reason to despise Paris. Heavens above, she was tired of being the peacemaker between them.

Jonathan was unaware of her distress. He kissed Paris's hand and laughed. "Oh, yes, my delightful new friend from America. I thank you again for your help, my dear. As I told you, I usually don't attend races, but my niece Diana owned the sorrel in the third contest, so I had to attend. Having you there to explain things certainly made the event far more pleasant."

"Save the flattery, Jon," Paris countered with a sassy grin. "You promised to teach me how to play whist and I'm not going to let you get out of it. Are you available tomorrow afternoon or would later in the week be better for you?"

"Paris," Belle interrupted, "His Grace is a very busy man. If you want to learn how to play whist, I'd be happy to teach you."

Jonathan shook his head. "That's quite all right, my dear. I'm quite looking forward to it. Perhaps you and Trelane will join us. We can make a day of it. First dinner, then an hour or two of playing cards. Spending a Sunday afternoon with my nephew and two such lovely ladies will be a rare treat.''

"I would love to, Your Grace, but I can't speak for Trelane. He mentioned going to the government offices on Sunday afternoon to prepare his schedule for the week.''

The duke smiled. "Since I aided Trelane in getting his appointment to the House, I shall insist that he set aside his duties until Monday morning and join us. A few hours relaxing over food, cards, and pleasant conversation will do him a world of good.''

Belle felt her stomach churn. She knew there would be no relaxing of any kind if Trelane and Paris were there together. Her usually calm and levelheaded fiancé had no forbearance when it came to Paris. Trelane constantly lost his temper with her and Paris enjoyed goading him. Before she could think of a way to turn down the duke's invitation without revealing this, her father rushed over and grabbed her arm.

"Here you are at last, Bella!" Sir Francis declared in a near shout. "I've been searching all over for you. Where is Trelane? I need to talk to him immediately.''

Hearing the desperation in her father's voice, Belle sent Paris and Jonathan on to the dining room for refreshments. Then she led her father to a small, deserted drawing room near the foyer for a private chat.

"Trelane hasn't arrived at the party yet. Why do you wish to speak with him?''

Sir Francis raked his fingers through his tangled white hair. "It's about my work. With Trelane's new committee position in the House, he could be of great help to me with my next expedition."

Belle frowned. "What new committee position? I haven't the faintest idea what you're talking about, Papa."

Sir Francis threw up his hands and began to pace the room. "God's blood, daughter! How could you not know? Your intended has been appointed to the very committee in Parliament that oversees archaeological quests such as mine. His support will help me gain the government's permission to search through the bowels of that old church that's built on the Scottish border."

"Oh, Papa, don't tell me you're going to proceed with that insane idea that the Templars hid the Holy Grail in Great Britain. I thought you abandoned that notion months ago."

"I most certainly did not," he sniffed. "The theory is sound and I mean to investigate it thoroughly. With luck and a lot of hard work, this could very well be the greatest accomplishment of my professional life."

Closing her eyes for a moment, Belle sighed. Being the only child of a famous archaeologist and explorer like Sir Francis Kingsley wasn't easy. The man was a genius who had written a dozen books and been knighted by the king for his efforts. But his work and continuing success had always ruled their family's existence. Their lovely town house had never really been home for their family, just a stopping-off place between journeys.

From the time she was born, Belle had been dragged about the world with her mother as Sir Francis hunted for artifacts and historical treasures to confirm his theories about the past. By the time she was eleven, she'd seen the snow-covered Alps, the jungles of South America, the sandy deserts of Africa, and the Great Wall of China. Not even her mother's death the following year slowed the pace of her father's quest for knowledge. In fact, without his wife to temper his actions, he seemed more driven than ever.

Though still a child, Belle quickly realized her father was using his work to mask his pain over his beloved wife's death. It was then that she took it upon herself to help him in any way she could. For the next thirteen years, Belle aided him with his research, took notes, and handled his correspondence. She enjoyed the excitement of his work, but longed for the serenity of setting down roots and having a real home of her own.

"Papa, after those heart seizures you suffered in Egypt last summer, the physicians said you should stop your explorations and consider retirement. That's why we returned to England."

"Bah! I would prefer death to such an arrangement," Sir Francis scoffed. "As long as there is life in this body and blood flowing through these veins, I intend to continue my work."

"I'm not suggesting that you stop working entirely, Papa. You could write a new book or accept the chair you were offered at Oxford last week. With your experience and expertise, you would make an excellent professor."

Shaking his head, Sir Francis sighed. "My girl, I have been a 'doer' all my life. I can hardly sit back now and change my ways."

"But, Papa, you don't understand—"

Sir Francis put his arm around her shoulders. "I understand all too well that you are worried about me, and I appreciate your concern. You've taken very good care of me since your mother's passing, but now it's time for me to fend for myself and for you to have a life of your own." He dropped a quick kiss on her forehead before leading her toward the door. "Now enough of this prattle. Let's return to the party. Perhaps Trelane has arrived. I really must speak with him tonight."

Belle winced at the noisy jingling sound her bracelet made as her father hurried her past groups of guests and into the crowded ballroom. "Papa, this is my engagement party. Can't you wait and speak to Trelane tomorrow?"

"Oh, no, that won't do at all. I have a meeting in the morning with my investors. They won't pledge a half pence to the expedition unless I can assure them that your betrothed will be casting his vote to approve my request."

"But Papa, how much difference can Trelane's one vote make?"

"All the difference in the world, my girl. The other six members of the committee are evenly split on whether my application should be granted.

Trelane's vote will give me the majority that I need." Stopping near the dance floor, Sir Francis looked about the room and frowned. "I don't see Trelane. You remain here while I look for him in the other rooms. If you locate him first, Bella, keep him occupied until I return."

"Papa, I don't think—" Belle's objection died on her lips while she helplessly watched her father push his way through the crowd. *Why must Papa always do things like this to me? I'm a grown woman and he still finds ways to drive me insane with his far-fetched ideas.*

Recalling the vehemence in her father's demands and knowing how Trelane prided himself on making his own decisions, a shudder passed through her. *Trelane isn't going to like this at all. Thank God he isn't here yet. If given a few quiet moments to think, perhaps I can come up with a way to get him to consider listening to my father's request.*

"Good evening, my dear. I pray my late arrival isn't causing that dreadful frown."

Belle's spine stiffened in surprise. *Well, so much for a few quiet moments alone. I may as well get on with it.*

She turned to smile at her future husband. Although they'd been engaged for several weeks, Belle still couldn't believe that she was going to marry Trelane Grayson.

Single at six and twenty, Belle had totally given up on the idea of ever getting married. When most girls her age were making their debuts into society and being courted by young men, she'd been busy traveling with her father and helping him do his research. She enjoyed the excitement and challenge of her father's work, but a part of her yearned for the kind of happiness she'd seen her parents share. Yet one could hardly hope to meet a proper suitor while riding a camel along the Nile or digging in a cave on an island in the South Pacific. She'd accepted her lot as a spinster and would likely have remained "on the shelf" if her father's heart seizures hadn't forced the family back to London for treatment.

While her father was examined by his physician, Belle nervously sat in the doctor's crowded anteroom and tried to concentrate on the book she'd brought along to pass the time. Reading *The Iliad* usually kept her attention, but not this time. Her hands quaked and the pages were sticking together. Embarrassed by her fidgeting, she avoided looking at the people around her. When she attempted to clean her spectacles with a handkerchief, they slipped from her fingers and fell to the floor. The man sitting beside her retrieved them for her. As he placed them in her hand, she turned to thank him for his aid and her world slipped off its axis.

The handsome gentleman apologized for being forward and introduced himself. His name was Trelane Grayson, a barrister and the nephew of her father's physician, Justin Prescott. He had arrived early for a lunch appointment with his uncle when he noticed the book she was reading. Very few people of his acquaintance enjoyed reading

Homer, he explained, and he was intrigued by her choice. Chatting for the better part of an hour, they quickly discovered their tastes in literature, history, and philosophy were quite the same.

Over the next month, Belle and Trelane were nearly inseparable. When he wasn't working, they visited museums, attended lectures, and spent countless hours talking. He was everything she had ever wanted in a man: intelligent, well-mannered, financially sound, and honorable. That he was handsome and from an excellent family only added to his worth and her utter disbelief when he proposed marriage. Surely her guardian angel must have been watching over her to have brought this paragon into her life.

"My frown has naught to do with you, sir. But I do have something important to tell you. Before the dancing begins, can we step outside onto the terrace so we can talk without being interrupted?"

Pristine as usual in his elegant evening attire, Trelane nodded to a passing colleague and acknowledged another as he offered her his arm and led her toward the door. "Certainly, my dear, so long as it doesn't pertain to your father's latest quest. Searching for the Holy Grail is a pipe dream. I won't cast my vote for his application and that's final."

Belle stopped and pulled him to a halt. "Then you already know about Papa's next expedition?"

"Of course I do, my dear. I learned of his request two weeks ago."

"But you never mentioned a word about it to me."

Trelane smiled indulgently. "Why would I do that? His application is strictly a government affair. I saw no sense in worrying you over such matters."

Belle bit back her retort over his high-handed attitude and tried to be pleasant. "I appreciate your consideration, sir, but I've handled Papa's expeditions and business dealings for years. I think you should have told me about this."

"Your father's work is no longer your concern, my dear. We're engaged to be married in four months. Why, that's hardly enough time to make all the necessary arrangements for the ceremony and reception, let alone furnish our new home and hire a suitable staff." He patted her hand. "By the by, all the papers were signed today for the house. As of one o'clock this afternoon, that magnificent town house we found in Mayfair officially became mine. I hope this pleases you, my dear."

Without being told, Belle knew the discussion about her father's application was over. Trelane had summarily changed the topic and no amount of cajoling or polite insistence would make it otherwise. Rather than argue with her stubborn fiancé, she smiled and, as usual, acquiesced to his wishes.

"Of course I'm pleased, sir. I really didn't think Lord Drummond was going to accept your offer."

Preening with importance, Trelane grinned. "I didn't doubt it for a moment. Thanks to his spend-thrift child bride, Drummond's in dire need of cash to pay all the debts she's incurred remodeling his country estate. The girl's but seventeen and knows naught about the value of money. Poor Drummond's going to the poorhouse if he doesn't rein her in."

Belle felt awkward at the turn of their conversation. When a footman stopped before them with a tray of filled wineglasses, she waved him away, causing the bracelet on her wrist to jingle. "None for me, thank you."

Trelane scowled at her. "You're wearing that old bracelet again. Besides being noisy, it's tarnished and singularly unattractive. If you want to wear jewelry, permit me to buy you a decent bauble or two."

She sighed. "I happen to like this bracelet. It's a good luck charm for me."

"Good luck piece or not, I'm buying you a new bracelet first thing in the morning. As my intended wife, you should be wearing gold or silver, not a tasteless piece of junk on your wrist. I won't have my friends or colleagues thinking I treat you shabbily, my dear. It just isn't done."

Belle nodded and smiled, but deep inside she was hurt. *I understand that appearances need to be maintained, but why must Trelane be so controlling and overbearing? First he dictates the colors of my gowns, then has me abandon my spectacles, and now it's my jewelry he wants to get rid of. What will he insist on next? Stilts because I should be taller? Why can't he just loosen up a bit and be sweet? Like he was a short while ago when we were alone in the library.* Recalling his unexpected kiss, she sighed. *Yes indeed, that would be lovely.*

* * *

Catherine stood at the top of the back stairs and looked down the deserted corridor. "There's not a soul in sight, Eric. If we hurry, perhaps we can get you safely ensconced in your room without anyone seeing you."

The countess and her son had nearly reached the family's private wing on the second floor when they heard voices coming toward them. Eric pulled his mother into a small salon and shut the door.

"All this subterfuge," Catherine scoffed as they stood together in the dark room. "I haven't had to creep about like this since I outwitted Napoleon Bonaparte some thirty-odd years ago. Why don't you simply make an appearance at the party and be done with it? Everyone will know soon enough that you're home, Eric."

"That's true, Mama. But doing so wouldn't be fair to my brother and his young lady. This is their celebration, not mine. My surprise arrival would only detract attention from them."

Catherine sighed. "Of course you're correct. Trelane would be quite perturbed by that."

Eric pressed his ear to the door and grinned. "Not to mention my encounter with Miss Kingsley in the library. She truly believed I was Trelane. My saintly brother would likely shoot me between the eyes or have an attack of apoplexy if he knew that I'd been kissing his fiancée. You don't think she will say anything to Trelane about what transpired between us, do you?"

"Not Belle. She goes out of her way to accommodate your brother's need for utter propriety. I assured her that discussing the incident further would be wrong and she believed me." Catherine nudged Eric with her elbow. "Your father is going to be wondering where I am. Can you hear if anyone's out there?"

"The voices are muffled, but close by. Perhaps from the nursery across the hall." He turned and looked around. "I wish it wasn't so bloody dark in here. Any idea where the flint and candles are?"

"No. But perhaps this will help." Catherine carefully crossed the salon and ran her fingers along the edge of the large framed painting on the far wall. Hinged like a door, it swung back, letting in the light and noise from the ballroom below.

Eric hurried to her side and looked down at the party. "I'd nearly forgotten about this. The carved scrollwork on the ballroom wall disguises the opening."

"And as long as you don't light any candles, no one knows you're here in the salon. Your great grandfather installed this years ago so the children of the household could see what was transpiring at the parties in the ballroom. With the exception of Sarah, all of my children took advantage of his gift."

"Sarah is a great deal younger than the rest of us. Wasn't she told about the viewing window?"

Catherine frowned. "Of course she was, but Sarah thought it wasn't right to spy on people without their knowledge. The girl's propensity for proper social conduct has become legendary in this family.''

Leaning forward, Eric perused the crowd below. ''Where is she? Sarah's eighteen now. I'm curious to see how she's grown up.''

''She's not here. Last year, she insisted that she be sent to Lady Pritchard's Academy for Young Gentlewomen in Devonshire. I tried to talk her out of it, but your father said yes.''

''I can't believe he let her go. Sarah's always been his precious baby.''

Catherine sniffed. ''After the debacle your older sister Diana caused years ago by running off on her own, your father was quite pleased by Sarah's request. Once Trelane voiced his approval, the matter was settled in spite of my objections.''

Heaving a sigh, she turned to Eric. ''Well, enough talk about that now. Give me a hug and I'll do what I can to keep everyone away from this part of the house. Once it's quiet, make your way to your room and get some sleep. I will see you in the morning.'' Catherine kissed his cheek. ''Good night, son, and welcome home.''

''Thank you, Mama. I'm really very glad to be here.''

Catherine brushed back a lock of hair from his brow and studied his face for a moment. ''I can see you are, Eric. I also believe that you've had your fill of racing about the world and are thinking about coming home for good.''

''Now, Mama, I'm not making any promises—''

She smiled. ''Of course not, son. But I understand you. Of my five children, you and I are the most alike in temperament. We're kindred souls who thrive upon adventure. But eventually even that changes, and you grow weary. You begin to crave the simpler joys that come with hearth and home, and family. I just want you to know that it's all here waiting for you when you're ready.'' She kissed him again. ''Good night, my impatient warrior.''

As the door closed behind her, Eric pulled off his stickpin and cravat and stuffed them into his coat pocket. *Mama's always been able to read me so well. Even after all my time away, she can see through my defenses. But I can't allow her to delve too deeply. My memories of these past two years are mine alone to dwell upon.*

At that moment, the door opened and a little girl wearing a long, white nightgown stole quietly into the room. When she saw Eric's face illuminated from the light coming from the ballroom, she stopped in her tracks and curtsied.

''I beg pardon, Uncle Trelane. I didn't know you would—'' A frown creased her young brow and she moved closer to him. ''You're not Uncle Trelane.''

The child's defiant observation made Eric chuckle. ''Oh, really? And how can you be sure that I'm not Trelane?''

Looking up at him, the little girl's bright red curls fell away from her face. ''It's quite simple. Besides never going about without his perfectly tied cravat, Uncle Trelane doesn't smile at me as you do. He pretends to be pleasant, of course, but his smile is stiff and looks almost painful. I know he doesn't like children, most especially intelligent ones like me. I am your niece, India, sir. Your brother James is my father. I will be seven years old on my next birthday. I also have a baby brother named Bryce who is only a few months old. You must be my other uncle. The one Grandmama calls her prodigal son. You know, like the one in the Bible story. I daresay, she's been quite worried about you, sir. Staying away without a letter to your dearest mama isn't a very nice thing to do, you know. But I am most happy to make your acquaintance at long last, Uncle Eric."

By the time India paused, Eric's head was reeling. He couldn't believe anyone so young could say so much so quickly, and on a single breath of air. Rather than mock the child's exuberance, he took her tiny hand in his and bowed respectfully.

"I am delighted to meet you as well, Lady India. I knew James and his lovely Miranda had a daughter, but I never imagined her to be so pretty, mature, and well-informed. However did you learn so much about me?"

India beamed with pride. "Because I'm a child, adults seldom guard their words around me, so I learn many things. You see, I'm very observant and an excellent listener. Why, I know a secret or two about Uncle Trelane that even Grandmama doesn't know about." Although they were alone, she beckoned him close with her finger and waited for Eric to bend down before she whispered, "Uncle Trelane stole Lord Drummond's town house in Mayfair. Offered him a fraction of his asking price and poor Drummond accepted. Uncle Trelane's moving from his rented flat into the town house tomorrow.''

"I thought my brother still lived here at home.''

India rolled her eyes. "Of course Uncle Trelane has a room here at Grandmama's that he uses on occasion, but he also has an apartment not far from the Parliament buildings and his law office. He says its location is most convenient when the Houses are in session or if he has to plead a case before the courts.''

Straightening to his full height, Eric chuckled. "My word, you are a veritable fount of information, my lady.''

"I know a great many things,'' she boasted. "Pull that footstool over to the opening on the wall for me and I'll show you.''

Amused and intrigued by her claim, Eric placed the footstool beneath the window overlooking the ballroom and lifted India onto it. Barely a second passed before she began pointing out people of interest below.

"See the pretty, red-haired lady talking to my father? She is Paris Mackenzie, the widowed cousin of Miss Kingsley. Uncle Trelane says she's an American with more money than common sense, but I think he's wrong. She's funny and ever so clever. She insists that I call her by her first name. I like her very much.''

With his brother James nearly a head taller than most men in the room, Eric found him quickly and surveyed the woman in the emerald-green satin at his side. "A widow, you say? Does she live here in London?"

India shook her head. "Oh no, she's only visiting Miss Kingsley. She has a home in Philadelphia and an estate in Scotland not far from her late husband's distillery. Mr. Mackenzie was a great deal older than Paris and made his fortune by manufacturing and exporting his family's whiskey. He also built two more distilleries in America before he died. Apparently there's a lot of profit to be made in . . ." Perusing the room, the child suddenly gasped. "Uh-oh! Uncle Trelane looks angry enough to explode. Poor Belle!"

India's words and grave tone had Eric quickly scanning the crowd. "What do you mean 'poor Belle'?" *Where are they? I don't see them anywhere.*

"Over there, just coming in from the east terrace. See the old man with the white hair tugging on Uncle Trelane's coat? He's Sir Francis Kingsley, Belle's father. The men seem to be arguing and she's wringing her hands."

Even from a distance, Eric could see the distress on Belle's flushed face. *Good grief! This is all my fault. She probably mentioned what took place in the library and Trelane knows something's amiss.*

The little girl sighed. "Sir Francis really should have waited until tomorrow to confront Uncle Trelane about his application. This is going to spoil the party for everyone."

Her remark garnered Eric's attention. "An application for what?"

"Sir Francis needs government permission for his next expedition and Uncle Trelane's committee must approve his application. Sir Francis is an arc . . . arche . . ." India sputtered in exasperation. "You know, a scientist who digs up dead people and all their stuff."

Eric fought not to smile. "You mean an archaeologist?"

"Yes, an archaeologist. Sir Francis wants to search for the Holy Grail in some old church in the north country and Uncle Trelane will not cast his vote for it. Uncle Trelane told Grandfather that the quest for the icon was a fool's errand and a waste of money better spent elsewhere."

Eric nodded. *Now that sounds like my ever penny-wise brother.* "Are you sure that's what they're discussing, India?"

"I'm positive. I heard Paris lamenting just the other day how Sir Francis pays scant attention to his daughter and only gets riled up about his work."

Wracked with frustration at not being able to help, Eric watched helplessly as the two men argued below. Belle kept trying to intercede, but they ignored her. Trelane looked implacable and throughly unimpressed while Sir Francis appeared more and more agitated. Their debate grew in intensity and began garnering lots of interest from the guests around them.

"Bloody hell! If someone doesn't stop those two, they're going to come to blows."

India leaned forward and scanned the crowded reception. "Grandfather is across the room talking to my parents now and isn't aware of their spat. But don't worry. I see Uncle Trelane's friends, Lord Beekham and Mr. Townsend, rushing toward him. They'll set things right straightaway."

Though he hadn't seen him in years, Eric quickly recognized Neville Farnsworth, Lord Beekham. He and Trelane had attended Eton with Neville and spent several summers visiting his family's oceanfront home near Brighton. But the man with Neville was a stranger he had only learned about through his mother's letters. Eric could only surmise that the stocky fellow in the peacock-blue coat was Trelane's law partner, Henry Townsend.

"I certainly hope you're correct, India. Belle deserves better than being subjected to this sort of disgrace at her own party."

Neville Farnsworth put his hand on Sir Francis's shoulder. "Kingsley, calm down. Bickering over this in front of everyone isn't going to solve anything."

The older man pulled away from his touch. "How can I be calm, sir? This brash young pup is saying all my work is inconsequential and without merit."

"I made no such claim about your work," Trelane defended. "I merely said your current quest is without merit or proper forethought. Only a fool would consider searching for a treasure that only exists in ancient fables.''

Sir Francis pointed his finger at Trelane. "See there, he again calls me a fool! Of all the impertinence! Lord Beekham, we are men of similar interests, members of the same antiquities society. Surely you can help me dissuade your friend into giving me his vote for the approval of my application.''

Shaking his head, Neville held up his hands in surrender. "Not I, sir. While I may give credence to the possibility of your theory, I learned long ago that Grayson is a man who knows his own mind. Once he makes a decision he adheres to it.''

"B-b-but that's not fair! A representative of our government shouldn't be so closed minded," Sir Francis insisted. "He's going to vote against my application without giving me a chance to state my case.''

Trelane frowned. "For your information, sir, I wasn't going to vote against it. In fairness to our pending familial connection, I intended to abstain from casting my ballot—''

"Abstaining isn't going to help me, Grayson! The committee is deadlocked.''

"I know. And until you assailed me this evening, I was going to allow my fellow committee members to vote without my interference, but no longer. Tomorrow, I'm going to call on each of them and see to it that all the votes are cast against your application. What you're proposing to do is totally abhorrent to me. Tearing apart a holy building for personal or professional gain is a sacrilege and a sin against God.''

"Why, you sanctimonious prig!" Sir Francis countered. "I'll stop you. I'll file suit against you for slander and libel. And for—for defaming my character.''

Henry Townsend, who'd been quietly standing beside Trelane during the heated debate, started laughing. "Slander, libel, and defamation aren't quite the same things, Sir Francis. You would have to file two separate lawsuits, perhaps three, and you'd have no chance of winning. Trelane is a member of Parliament and an authorized part of this committee. As such, he has the right to voice his opinions and to try to sway the others to vote as he sees fit. Sir Francis, you don't look well at all. I implore you to please calm down before you do yourself a mischief. Surely there must be some other missing relic or lost civilization you can concentrate your efforts on besides this one.''

Belle was torn by her loyalties. She loved her father and wanted him to be happy, but she agreed with Trelane. Destroying a church on the slim hope of finding an icon that might not exist was wrong. Based more on medieval Christian legend than fact, the Holy Grail, reported to be the cup Jesus Christ used at the Last Supper, was heavily surrounded by mystery.

Countless people had searched for the Holy Grail without success since the Crusades. Besides the difficulty of locating its hiding place, no one could say exactly what it looked like. Some claimed it was a gold chalice encrusted with gems, while others swore it was a cup of a simpler design, carved of wood or possibly cast from brass or lead. A few other historians even believed that the Holy Grail wasn't a cup at all. Depending on whose text you read, it was described as a silver dish, a broken sword, a lance, or a book written by Jesus himself.

For Belle, the most fascinating aspect of the fanciful legend was not the Holy Grail itself but its caretakers, the Templar Knights. Also called the Warrior Monks, these devout men fought to defend the Holy Land and supposedly kept the Grail safely hidden from the world. According to the story, when the Grand Master of the Knights Templar was unjustly burned at the stake in 1314, the order was disbanded, forcing its followers into a secret society that still existed hundreds of years later. Belle knew it was a silly, romantic notion to think that a group of brave, dedicated men continued to pledge their lives to protecting the cherished relic.

She took her father's arm. "Papa, Mr. Townsend is right. You don't look well. Perhaps we should go home—"

Sir Francis slapped her hand away with such force, the clasp on her bracelet popped open and sent the piece of jewelry falling to the floor. "Don't touch me, Belle," he snapped. "You're siding with that man and I want nothing to do with you. From this moment, I have no daughter." The old man waved his fist at Trelane. "You're at fault for this, Grayson. You deny me my work and rob me of my only child. Well, I'll get you for this, you heartless brigand!"

Sir Francis began pushing his way through the crowd, nearly knocking people over in the process. As Trelane drew a sobbing Belle into his arms, he noticed his law partner was bent over, looking at the floor. "Henry, what are you doing?"

"Miss Kingsley's bracelet came off and I was trying to retrieve it. Oh, here it is." Henry held it up and frowned. "The clasp seems to be broken. If you wish, I could drop it off to my jeweler in the morning to be repaired."

"Don't bother, Henry. I'll do it myself." Trelane took the bracelet and put it in his pocket. "What I really need you to do at this moment is find my mother and tell her that I want the dancing to begin immediately. Perhaps some spirited tunes will amuse our guests and stop them from gaping at us."

"Of course, Trelane. You can count on me." Henry nodded and hurried away.

Trelane turned to Lord Beekham. "Neville, go after Sir Francis and see if you can reason with the man. He's a bit overwrought and I don't want Belle to worry about her father being alone while he's in such a state."

Neville nodded. "Not a problem, Trelane. I'll do what I can."

Just as Lord Beekham went off to find Sir Francis,

Paris appeared at Trelane's side. Seeing Belle in tears, she scowled at him. "Why is my cousin crying, Lane? If you've hurt Belle's feelings again, I'll pull every hair out of your foul head and punch you in the nose!"

Trelane battled to contain his anger. "Mrs. Mackenzie, would you kindly lower your voice and refrain from making innocuous threats against my person? Belle is upset because of her father. If you had half a brain in that addled head of yours, you would be comforting your cousin instead of accusing me of hurting her."

Paris snickered. "It's because I have a brain and two very good eyes, Lane, that I know how much your careless remarks have injured her in the past."

"That's not true. I'm a gentleman, courteous and well-mannered. In spite of your low opinion of me, Mrs. Mackenzie, I know very well how to treat a lady."

"Ha! What you know about dealing with a woman's tender sensibilities could be engraved on the head of a pin, Lane!"

"Stop calling me 'Lane'," he hissed through clenched teeth. "My name is Trelane, nothing more, nothing less. If that's too difficult for you to remember, madam, you can refer to me as 'sir' or even 'my lord'."

Paris folded her arms across her chest. "Call you 'my lord'? Unless the church suddenly deems you the son of God, that's never going to happen, Lane."

"Well, at least my name is a good and noble one

that has been used proudly by my family for many years," he countered. "Your name, on the other hand, represents naught but a filthy city over-crowded with the very dregs of humanity, Paris."

"True, I was named for the city of Paris, but it was chosen for the most romantic of reasons. My parents did it to commemorate the place where they met and fell in love."

Trelane chuckled. "Then you should thank God that He brought your parents together in France and not in Sweden or Spain. In that event your name might have been Stockholm or Barcelona."

Belle suddenly raised her head. "Stop this infernal squabbling, both of you! If you can't be civil with one another, then say nothing. Can't you see that your constant battles are tearing me apart?"

Trelane took the handkerchief from inside his coat and gave it to Belle. "Pray forgive us, my dear. We won't do it again."

Paris sniffed indignantly. "I can apologize for myself, Lane. I don't need you pleading my case . . ." Her voice faded. She closed her eyes for a second and sighed. "Drat, I'm doing it again. I'm sorry, Belle. Old habits are hard to break, but I'll do my best to change for your sake, honey."

Dabbing the tears from her eyes, Belle smiled. "Thank you, Paris. After my father's rash behavior this evening, I would truly appreciate that."

"Uncle Francis ran past me a few moments ago. His face was red and he looked angry enough to kill anyone who got in his way. What happened to set him off?"

"Papa learned his next proposed expedition wasn't going to get the government approval he needed."

Paris frowned at Trelane. "You're a member of Parliament, sir. With all your friends and influence, can't you do anything to help Uncle Francis?"

Knowing Trelane's reply would only increase Paris's dislike, Belle quickly interrupted. "Paris, you don't understand. I don't want Papa to go on this quest. Besides his health being at risk, this expedition would be doomed to failure. My father will simply have to accept that fact and concentrate his efforts on some other search. Once he does that, Papa will be fine."

The sound of musicians tuning their instruments garnered Paris's attention. She nodded to Belle and Trelane. "If you two will excuse me. Apparently the dancing is about to commence. I promised your darling Uncle Jon the first waltz and I never keep handsome men waiting. See you later, cousin." In a flurry of emerald silk, she disappeared into the crowd.

Belle braced herself for Trelane's outburst at Paris's lack of decorum, but it never came. She looked up at his face and saw him gazing toward the dance floor, a crease of confusion deeply etched in his brow.

"I am sorry that Paris upsets you. I sometimes think my cousin acts that way simply to tease you, sir."

Trelane frowned down at her. "Forgive me. My

mind was wandering a bit. What were you saying, my dear?"

"Well, ah . . . nothing of any great importance. Shouldn't we be making our way to the front of the dance floor? Your mother said that we have to lead off the first dance."

He nodded and took hold of her hand. "I know. But there's something I need to tell you first, Belle. I was wrong to speak to your father in that manner. It was rude and disrespectful. Tomorrow morning, I'll stop by and apologize for my actions."

"You haven't changed your mind about voting for his application, have you?"

With a wry smile, Trelane shook his head. "No. I am still going to abstain, but I won't try to dissuade my colleagues. If your father wants to meet with the committee to present his theory and perhaps gain their votes, I'll not interfere. Even if he doesn't win, your father's pride will be restored. And to a man like Sir Francis, that means more than gold. Does that please you, my dear?"

Tears of happiness glittered in her eyes. Ignoring the curious stares of those around them, Belle threw her arms around his neck and hugged him. "Oh, yes, Trelane, it does. Thank you so very much for understanding."

Watching them from the upper salon, Eric felt alone and envious of his twin. *A wonderful career, a new home, and a beautiful, loving wife to share it all.*

Perfection such as this is rare in life. Don't waste a minute of it, Trelane.

India patted his arm. "Uncle Eric, I'm going to bed now. Mama said we're leaving for home first thing in the morning, so I have to get some sleep."

He lifted her down from the footstool. "You sound as if you're looking forward to going home. Don't you enjoy coming to London and visiting the rest of the family?"

She nodded, causing her curls to bounce. "Of course I do, but I have to get home to Sidra. Papa wouldn't let me bring her to town and I miss her terribly."

"Is Sidra a friend of yours?"

India sighed in obvious exasperation. "Sidra's a great deal more than just my friend, Uncle Eric. She's my protector and the very best companion to have when trouble's afoot. Come visit us at home, and I'll introduce you to her."

He smiled at her dramatic description. "Well, I'll look forward to it, India. I certainly hope your Sidra likes me."

"Oh, she will, Uncle Eric. Sidra's a wonderful judge of character."

India stopped at the door and turned back to him. "One more thing, Uncle Eric. I wouldn't be mentioning Sidra to Uncle Trelane if I were you. The poor man still turns a bit pale when he hears her name."

"Why does he do that?"

"The one and only time he saw her, Uncle Trelane made the mistake of stepping on her tail. Sidra took out the seat of his pants with her teeth.''

Eric laughed. ''Now I understand. You've been talking about a dog.''

India scowled at him. ''What gave you that idea?''

''You said Sidra had a tail and tore Trelane's pants with her teeth, so I assumed that your Sidra was a dog.''

''Well, you are wrong, Uncle Eric. I don't even like dogs.''

''Most children love having a dog as a pet. I had several when I was a boy.''

''Not me. Why would I want a dog when I have a tiger?''

''A what?'' Eric gasped.

But India didn't hear him. She called ''good night'' and was out the door.

Eric fell back against the wall and shook his head. ''She said a tiger! Bloody hell, I have been away far too long indeed! I'll ask James about it in the morning.''

Drawn back to the window by the melodious strains of a waltz, he looked down at the ballroom. Dozens of couples were dancing, but his eyes narrowed on just one.

That could have been me down there. Smiling and happy, looking forward to the future. But no, I had to be a rebel. I had to be the gallant soldier, defending those who couldn't fight for themselves. Selling my expertise as a warrior to others who could well afford my price. Eighteen years and what do I have to show for my efforts? I've got a stash of gold and money to burn in the bank.

I've traveled the world, had adventures enough for a dozen men, but I have no friends, no home to call my own. And no one to love me like Belle.

Suddenly feeling weighed down with sadness and regret, Eric closed the viewing window and went off to bed.

CHAPTER 2

"Bloody hell! Where the deuce did this blasted headache come from?" Throwing off the covers, Eric sat up in bed and rubbed the back of his throbbing head. The glare from the six candles burning on his bedside table made him wince and shut his eyes. "I only had one glass of brandy. That's hardly enough to . . ."

Bits and pieces of a dream began sifting through his mind. More of a nightmare than a fanciful vision, he saw himself being attacked by a group of men. He tried to fight back, but was badly outnumbered. His assailants were shabbily dressed and their bodies smelled of dirt, sweat, and cheap ale. The tallest of them, a thin, bearded man with a jagged scar on his cheekbone, wielded a pistol and shouted at his companions.

"Watch 'im, lads. His lordship ain't payin' us a pence of the hundred quid he promised us if Grayson 'ere gets away."

"Are ya sure we got us the right one, Harry?" one of the men asked.

"Aye, that's the bloke we was hired to get rid of. Drag him down this alley behind Westminster Hall, where no one will see what we're about."

A scuffle ensued and just as Eric thought freedom would be his, one of the thugs clouted him on the back of his head with a wooden club. As he fell to his knees from the blow, the men surrounded him and beat him mercilessly to the ground.

Eric's recollections of the dream were suddenly interrupted by the sound of his mother's voice. She was standing beside his bed wearing a dressing gown and slippers.

"Eric, are you all right? I was just going down to the kitchen for some warm milk when I spied the light shining beneath your door. I knocked, but you didn't hear me."

Suddenly embarrassed by his bared chest in front of his mother, he pulled at the blankets to cover his midriff. "I'm fine, Mama. Just a bit of a headache and the remnants of a bad dream."

Catherine stepped closer and brushed back the mussed locks of hair from his brow. "I haven't had much luck falling asleep myself. The excitement of the party and Trelane's disagreement with Belle's father had me at sixes and sevens all evening."

Looking at the burning candles, she frowned. "From the amount of wax dripping from those tapers, it appears you fell asleep with them lit. Trelane picked up that dangerous habit a while back. Claimed some awful dreams plagued him every night, making him too uncomfortable to sleep in the dark. Thank God those wretched dreams and his need for constant light ceased last spring before he moved into his own apartment across town or I would have worried about him burning down the building with all those candles while he slept."

Eric swallowed hard and carefully schooled his reactions to his mother's words. He wasn't merely afraid of being in the dark, he was petrified of it. Too many long days and nights imprisoned in a dungeon, devoid of light and simple human contact, had taken their toll. Black as pitch, the air in his shuttered jail cell had been cold and damp, the silence deafening. His heartbeat pounded in his ears and his breathing sounded like a windstorm to his acute hearing. The only other sounds were those of water dripping in a fetid puddle and the occasional scurrying of rats across his cell. The sensory deprivation he suffered surely was a form of hell here on earth.

Since his escape, Eric's senses had almost returned to normal. Once again, he could laugh and talk to anyone. Sounds didn't startle him. Being alone in a room with only his wits for company no longer bothered him either. Only the darkness taunted him and robbed him of his peace of mind.

He could only pray that in time, this fear and discomfort would fade as well.

Catherine walked around to straighten the quilt
at the foot of his bed. "You know, I never could
understand why Trelane would be having dreams
about being imprisoned in a dungeon cell.
Although he prosecuted many criminals when he
was working for the Crown, I doubt if he's ever set
foot inside any kind of prison."

"When did Trelane begin having these dreams
about the dungeon?" Eric asked, trying not to
sound too alarmed.

"Almost two years ago. The dreams kept returning and Trelane was so upset by them, he seldom slept for more than a couple of hours at a
time." She looked up at Eric and frowned. "What's
troubling you, son? You've suddenly gone pale."

He closed his eyes for a moment and took a deep
breath before he continued. "Mama, long ago you
told me how you and your twin sister used to have
visions of one another when you were apart. You
and Aunt Victoria even knew when the other was
in pain because you would feel it at the same time."

"Yes, I recall telling you that. I also remember
you complaining about how you felt cheated
because you had never experienced such magical
connections with . . ." Her voice faded. "Saints
above, Eric! Are you telling me that Trelane was
actually having visions about you? That you were
being held prisoner in some godforsaken dungeon
all that time?"

He nodded. "That's precisely what I'm saying, Mama."

Hurrying to his side, Catherine drew him into her arms. "My poor, dear baby! The injustice of it all," she said, kissing his cheek and holding him close. "Are you all right? Why didn't you send word to me? How did you escape? Tell me who did this dreadful thing. As God is my witness, I vow I'll find a way to make them pay for what they've done to you, son. They won't get away with this travesty, I swear it!"

Though tears threatened to spill from his eyes, Eric bit his lip to avoid laughing. His mother was an original! While most people would ask what he had done wrong to deserve imprisonment, she never questioned his innocence. Her only response was to retaliate against the ones responsible for his captivity. The world saw Catherine Grayson as a grand lady and a leader of the aristocracy, but deep inside she was still the rebellious Lady Cat. Like him, a part of her would always be a warrior.

Catherine began to search his face and upper body for signs of injury. "Your jailer was clever enough not to scar your handsome face, but you're a bit leaner than I imagined beneath your clothes. First thing in the morning, I'll instruct Cook to have all your favorite foods prepared. A few weeks of good meat, fish, and poultry will help build you up again. I'll even have Cook use Tilly's recipe for that vanilla egg custard that you always liked so well."

"Mama, stop fussing over me. I'm a grown man, not a babe in arms."

She scowled. "No matter how old you are, Catlin Eric Grayson, you will always be my youngest son and the child of my soul. If I want to fuss over you, then it's my right." As she playfully ruffled her fingers through his thick hair, he gasped in pain. "Sorry, dear. I forgot about your headache. Any idea what brought it on?"

Eric used his left hand to smooth back his hair. "Not a clue. I only had—"

Catherine snatched his hand from his head and stared at the large, red mark below his wrist. "What's this? Some kind of tattoo? It looks like a dark pink lightning bolt. I didn't know you were interested in adorning your body with tattoos."

Easing his arm from her, he shook his head. "It isn't a tattoo, Mama. The Italian noble who jailed me in his dungeon had me branded like an animal as a part of my punishment. The lightning bolt is on his family crest."

"Why, that despicable bastard! How dare he . . ." A frown creased her brow. "Good grief! I'd nearly forgotten. When Trelane began having those dreams, he also developed an odd rash on his left arm. It looked like a red 'W' and was sore, like a burn. Your Uncle Justin and the other physicians at his hospital were quite mystified by it."

The enormity of his twin brother actually sharing his pain and turmoil caused Eric to shake his head in amazement. "I never would have imagined that such things were truly possible. I wonder why I haven't felt similar things for Trelane."

Suddenly, bits of his earlier dream flooded his mind. Oddities of the vision and the lingering pain in his head began making sense to him now. "Bloody hell! That wasn't a dream at all. I've got to go and find him. He needs my help." Forgetting his lack of clothing, he threw back his covers and stood up.

Catherine gasped in surprise and turned her back to him as he pulled his trousers on. "Eric, what are you rambling about? Who needs your help?"

"The dream that woke me up was about Trelane. Some men have brutally attacked him and dragged him behind Westminster Hall. My head is throbbing because one of the villains struck him on the head with a club."

Catherine spun around. "If Trelane's been hurt, then I'm going with you. I won't allow two of my sons to be harmed."

Eric sat on the bed to put on his boots. "I can protect myself, Mama. I've dealt with far worse miscreants than the scum who hurt my brother."

"But you can't go alone. Let me wake your father and James so they can go with you."

"Mama, what happens if my vision was wrong? That my dream was nothing more than a nightmare and Trelane hasn't been hurt at all. Is it fair to get Father and the rest of the family all upset for nothing?"

Catherine picked up his shirt from the chair and

gave it to him. "I know you're right about this, Eric. I've had too many of my own experiences with Victoria to doubt what you're feeling about your twin is true. Please, I'm begging you. Don't go alone," she implored him. "Take Jake, the coachman, and his two sons with you. They're big, strapping young men who could help you in a fight if the need arises."

From the determined look on his mother's face, Eric knew arguing with her would be a waste of time. "Fine, Mama. I'll take them along. While I'm gone, get Trelane's room ready and send one of the footmen for Uncle Justin. If my vision was correct, my brother is going to need a physician right away."

As he hurried down the back stairs to the servants' quarters a few minutes later, Eric realized the throbbing pain in his head had disappeared. That could mean one of two things: either the vision was only a dream or Trelane was no longer in pain. And if that was the case, was he unconscious or already dead? That possibility caused him to shudder to the very depths of his soul.

Bloody hell! I haven't come home after all this time to lose you now, Trelane. Hang on, brother. I'm coming to help you as quickly as I can. I only pray that I'm not too late.

The sun was coming up over the horizon as Eric paced across his room deep in thought and seething with rage. His vision of the attack on Trelane had been all too correct, making him curse its accuracy. Questions filled his mind to battle with logic. Why would anyone want to hurt his brother? Did Trelane have enemies? What was he doing coming out of his offices at that late hour? Who knew he would be there? Was someone following him? Who hired the thugs and sent them to kill Trelane?

Eric cast a quick glance at the pile of his blood-stained clothes thrown in the corner and memories of kneeling in the dark alley cradling his twin to his chest assailed him anew. At first he'd thought Trelane was dead, but the sounds of his brother's labored breathing proved he was still alive, but just barely. His face was almost unrecognizable, severely bruised with both eyes swollen shut. Blood was flowing from his nose, ears, and a gash on the back of his head. His right arm and leg were bent at odd angles and damp with blood as well, suggesting they were badly fractured.

Fighting as a mercenary the past eighteen years, Eric had seen more than his share of wounded and dying men. He'd aided his comrades and even many of his enemies by binding their wounds and getting them to a field hospital or a local physician. But nothing had prepared him for dealing with this. He knew he should get Trelane treatment as quickly as possible, but he couldn't move. He was numb with grief and anger. His ability to bury his emotions, and do what had to be done, was gone.

Thankfully, the coachman, Jake, and his sons were only steps behind him. It was their presence that forced him into action. Between them, they carefully lifted Trelane inside the carriage and placed him on the soft leather seat. The ride back to the house and getting his brother into his room down the hall was a blur of time and movement to Eric. He was oddly relieved when his mother sent him back to his own room with orders to remain there while Justin and his medical assistants tended to Trelane's injuries.

Hours had passed without a word from anyone. He bathed, donned new clothes, and ignored the tray of food a servant had silently delivered to his room. Eric went to the washstand, and once again scrubbed his hands with soap and water. No matter how many times he cleaned them, in his mind's eye he could still see the dark stains of his brother's blood on his hands.

Rubbing his damp hands across his eyes, Eric sighed. "Don't die, Trelane. Please don't die. We're a part of one another and there's so much I need to tell you. I can't abide losing you now."

There was a short, clipped knock on his door. Before he could respond, it opened and his parents hurried into his room. Though he wanted to ask them about Trelane, Eric couldn't speak as his father embraced him for the first time in many years. In his youth, his father had been his hero. Larger than life itself, Miles Grayson was brave, courageous, and respected by all who knew him. Where most noblemen were a spoiled and cosseted lot who abhorred hard work and knew nothing of loyalty, the Earl of Foxwood thrived on it. Besides overseeing his many prosperous holdings, he built and maintained one of the most successful shipping companies in Europe, with trading routes set up around the world. His political views were entirely his own. He was a strong advocate of Irish independence, and apologized to no one for his unpopular views on the issue.

Miles hugged Eric tightly. "It's good to have you home, son. I'm only sorry your arrival has been overshadowed by this tragedy."

Suddenly alarmed, Eric pulled away from his father. "Tragedy? Has Trelane . . . has he died? I should go to him. Why didn't you send for me?"

Catherine patted his back. "No, your brother is alive, but he hasn't regained consciousness yet. He has compound fractures in his right arm and leg, and some internal injuries. His lung was punctured by a broken rib. Justin performed surgery to correct the damage and set his broken bones in splints. Of course, he'll have to be watched closely for signs of infection. You can see him after Justin finishes dressing his wounds."

"But what about his head, Mama? I felt the blow from that damned club. It was powerful and knocked Trelane off his feet."

"Justin cleaned the wound and found no damage to the bones in Trelane's skull, but the brain may have been injured. We won't know for sure until he wakes up and . . . and . . ." Catherine closed her eyes and struggled to control her tattered emotions. "I swore I wouldn't cry again. Tears are for people who've given up and accepted defeat. But not me. Trelane will recover, I know he will. And while he's getting better, the rest of us are going to find out who did this to him—"

"And make them pay," Eric added, putting his arm around her shoulder. "I don't know who hired those men to hurt Trelane, Mama, but I'll do whatever's necessary to find the bloody culprit."

Miles cleared his throat. "I'm rather glad you feel that way. Because your mother and I were talking out in the hall, and we may have come up with a way to trap the villain responsible for the attack on your brother. But the success of our plan will rest entirely on you, Eric."

"Fine. You can count on me, Father." Eric paced across the floor and rubbed his hands together in anticipation. "So, what do you need me to do? Go through Trelane's files? Look for a list of his business acquaintances or possible enemies? I'm quite good at getting past locked doors, you know. Anyone you want me to abduct and coerce into giving us some information? I learned a few tricks about torture from the Turks that are guaranteed to get the truth out of anyone."

Shaking his head, Miles gave his wife a knowing smile before he turned back to Eric. "No. Though I applaud your enthusiasm, that's not exactly what we had in mind."

Eric was perplexed. "Then what do you want me to do?"

"It's actually quite simple. We want you to be your brother."

Looking from his father to his mother, Eric

frowned. "I know I haven't been the best of sons or the easiest of children to raise, but I'm not my brother. And no amount of wishing is going to change that."

Catherine scowled at her husband. "Miles, you've got him more confused than ever. Let me explain it to him." She sat on the bed and patted the place beside her. "Sit with me a moment, Eric, and I'll tell you what we have in mind."

After Eric reluctantly did as she asked, Catherine reached over and took his hand. "Your father and I aren't asking you to change or take your brother's place in our lives. We want you to portray Trelane in a ruse to fool the person who tried to have him killed. You will live in his house, wear his clothes, and attend functions in his stead. When the guilty party sees 'Trelane' is still up and about, and not dead as he planned, he will reveal his hand and we shall be there to catch him."

Eric shook his head. "It will never work, Mama. Everyone knows that Trelane has an identical twin brother."

"You've been away a long time, son. No one has seen you for years. With the exception of your father and me, only your Uncle Justin and a few of our trusted servants know that you've returned home."

Eric felt uncomfortable at the prospect of portraying his brother and began looking for ways to dissuade his mother from her plan. "Other people have seen me, Mama. The tailor on Bond Street, the barber where I was shaved and had my hair cut, and the hackney driver who brought me to the house. They could identify me.''

Catherine's brow arched. ''Did you give them your name and get a written receipt?''

''Well, no, but—''

''Then they are of no consequence. You needn't worry about them. Was there anyone else? How about the ship you arrived on? Any chance that you might run into a member of the crew or one of the passengers here in town?''

He considered lying to his mother, but knew better. The woman had the most uncanny ability to know when he wasn't telling the truth. Heaving a sigh, he shook his head. ''No. The ship left me in Dover and then departed the next day for America. I wanted my homecoming to be a surprise for you and Father, so I never told anyone my real name and altered my appearance by keeping my hair long and growing a beard.''

She nodded. ''Excellent. Then there's no one else to worry about.''

''I suppose not.'' Suddenly, a tiny face surrounded by bright auburn curls flashed in his mind. ''I nearly forgot. I met James's daughter, India, in the salon overlooking the ballroom and she knows who I am. As a matter of fact, she was the one who told me that I wasn't Trelane. If I can't fool a little girl with my charade, how will I convince a lot of adults?''

Winking at her husband, Catherine smiled. ''I always told you that granddaughter of ours is too much like me to ignore. Poor James and Randy are going to have their hands filled when that one grows up, just wait and see.'' She turned back to Eric. ''Don't worry about India. She wasn't supposed to be out of her room last night, so I doubt if she'll say a word to her parents about meeting you. But just to be on the safe side, I'll have a word with her before she leaves this morning.''

Eric saw his opportunities to escape this plan were quickly being eliminated, but couldn't resist trying a few more. ''Mama, I'm not a barrister and I'm definitely not a politician. Hell, I've never even voted in an election! How on earth will I ever be able to convince Trelane's law partner and his associates in Parliament that I am Trelane? I have no idea what his duties entail and I don't know any of these men. I can hardly have you or Father with me all the time, coaching me. People would grow suspicious.''

Catherine nodded. ''I quite agree. That's precisely why I thought we should include my brother in our plan. Jonathan and Trelane have grown quite close in the past few years. Besides being friends, Jonathan is one of Trelane's clients. They share many of the same acquaintances socially and in Parliament. He could tell you who these people are and aid you. No one would question Jonathan's presence at your brother's office or at Westminster Hall.''

''But Jonathan is a duke, with duties of his own. He won't be able to spend all his time coaching me.''

Miles pulled up a chair and sat next to them.

"You're intelligent and an excellent actor, Eric. What you don't know, you can bluff your way through. Skirt the issues, don't commit yourself to anything. Members of Parliament do it all the time. It's the politician's way," he scoffed.

"Impersonating a government official is against the law, Father. I could be arrested for taking his seat in the House of Commons."

"The House isn't in open session at this time, because of the construction work going on with the new government buildings. Trelane told me last evening that he only had a few committee meetings to attend during the coming month. If we are able to find the man responsible for the attack on your brother quickly, you'll be able to cease the charade and won't have to worry about attending those meetings either."

Catherine squeezed Eric's hand. "I know portraying Trelane won't be easy, son, but it's the best way to find out who tried to murder your brother. Please, Eric, say yes. You're the only one who can do this."

His mother's entreaties found their mark. Taking a deep breath and letting it out, he nodded. "All right, I'll do it. But what happens if Belle doesn't go along with this plan? She's engaged to marry Trelane. Surely we're going to tell her that he's been hurt and that we are trying to trap the man responsible."

Glancing at Catherine, Miles scratched his chin. "Well, that's the crux of the matter, Eric. We can't tell Belle about any of this."

"Why not? You don't think Belle had anything to do with this, do you?"

"Not at all. But you see, Eric, the man we're looking for, the one with a grudge against your brother, could very well be her father, Sir Francis Kingsley. Half the *ton* witnessed their altercation during the party. We simply have no proof that he hired those men to kill Trelane."

Eric leaned forward and covered his face with his hands. *Bloody hell! I came home because I've had my fill of sneaking about and intrigue. Now they want me to pretend that I'm my brother. Living his life as though it were my own is bad enough, but lying to Belle, letting her believe that I'm Trelane, is going to be the most difficult part of this deception. How can I look into that lovely, trusting face and lie to her? And what about me? How can I portray the role of a doting fiancé and not be drawn to her? If her father is proven to be innocent in all this, when she learns of our ruse, Belle will likely be hurt. She will hate me, despise our family, and decide not to marry Trelane. Is that being fair to either of them?*

Catherine rubbed his back. "I don't doubt for a minute that Belle's an innocent in all this. But she does love her father. If she learned of our suspicions, she would be forced to take sides. I don't want to do that to her."

Looking at his mother, Eric sighed. "But is Belle's father the only person who could have done this? Doesn't my brother have any other enemies? Someone he's angered or crossed in his endeavors?"

"Of course," Miles replied. "Everyone has enemies. Trelane spent a bit of time working as a prosecutor before he set up his law practice and got involved in politics. Lord knows he had a hand in sending quite a few unsavory characters to prison during his tenure. But that was several years ago. It's hardly likely that one of them waited all this time to exact revenge on him, though I could be wrong."

"How does Trelane get along with his law partner?" Eric asked. "I've never met him. What kind of a fellow is he?"

"Henry Townsend is a likable chap. He and your brother have been close friends since they met at Cambridge. His father taught history at the school. While he doesn't have Trelane's ambition to take on social issues and politics, Henry is an excellent barrister and businessman. They seem to have a perfect blend for their partnership."

Catherine smiled. "Henry also has a delightful sense of humor. He may be a tad plain in looks, but his charming wit and his ability to make people laugh by reciting a silly rhyme or an amusing anecdote make him a very popular choice on everyone's guest lists. Even Neville Farnsworth likes him. And you know how particular Neville has always been about making friends with people."

"Hold on a moment," Miles suddenly cut in. "I just thought of someone who might have cause to be angry with Trelane. Yesterday morning, your brother purchased Lord Drummond's town house in Mayfair. From what Trelane told me about the negotiations, they were hardly amicable."

Catherine snickered. "Seeing how Trelane

played on Drummond's desperation and only paid him a third of his asking price, I can well understand the man being upset."

Miles gaped at her. "You know about that?"

She winked. "Of course. I have my ways of learning things, even when certain people try to keep secrets from me."

"Well, I ... ah ... it wasn't my idea to keep it from you," Miles hurried to explain. "Trelane didn't mind boasting to me about his success, but he didn't want you to think he was some kind of a thief for taking advantage of Drummond's situation as he did."

"Being a clever thief runs in our blood," she countered with a coy smile. "The only difference is that I did it with a ship and a sword, while Trelane does it by manipulating people with words and numbers."

"Cat, I thought we weren't going to discuss the past anymore. You know I don't like being reminded of such things."

She waved a finger at her chagrined husband. "Don't fault me because you were caught, English. Accept your part in this and don't do it again. And the next time you close yourself off in the library to discuss things you want kept secret, be sure to check behind the tall, upholstered chair in the corner."

"Who would have ... ?" Understanding lit Miles's eyes. "India was in there, wasn't she? That child is too smart for her own good."

Catherine preened. "I told you our granddaughter was exactly like me. I wonder if India's too young to begin training with a sword?"

Miles frowned at her. "Cat, that isn't funny!"

She leaned over and kissed him. "I know, English. I simply enjoy teasing you."

Eric silently watched the loving interplay between his parents. *Married all these years and they still use pet names and act like young lovers. I'd give half the fortune I've stowed away to experience such feelings with someone.*

The corners of his mouth turned up in a secretive smile. *Bloody hell! Who am I kidding? I'd abandon it all for a chance to have a love like theirs. Well, thinking about such things isn't going to be enough. The moment Trelane has recovered and everything is settled, I'm going to find a love of my own and really start living my life.*

But his smile faded when Belle's face entered his thoughts. He shook his head at the memory. *No matter how drawn I am to her, I must remember that Belle loves my brother, not me.*

Dealing with villains and assassins was easy, he decided. For the battle he'd soon engage in would be the most difficult struggle he would ever fight. Because his enemy in this war was his own heart.

CHAPTER 3

"Your future husband is a damned toad!" Paris slammed her coffee cup into its saucer. "Yesterday, Lane got his uncle to cancel our lovely Sunday afternoon of cards and dinner. Now, you receive a note saying they're both stopping by this morning. Here I am, dressed in this frumpy old dress with no time to change into something decent. I swear that man goes out of his way just to aggravate me."

Belle adjusted her spectacles and set the folded piece of parchment beside her untouched plate of fried eggs and bacon. "Stop complaining, Paris. You look quite lovely in that blue gown and well you know it. If you'd rather not see His Grace this morning, you can go up to your room and I'll make your apologies."

Looking dutifully chagrined, Paris shrugged. "No, that won't be necessary, Belle. Forgive me for losing my temper and taking it out on you, but I was really looking forward to visiting Jon's home yesterday."

"And naturally you assumed Trelane caused the postponement." When her cousin's cheeks grew nearly as red as her hair, Belle sighed. "For your information, Paris, I was the one who begged off our appointment yesterday. I sent word to Trelane that my father had gone out of town, and I had things to take care of here at home. Trelane notified the duke, who, in turn, sent his regrets."

Paris pointed at Belle's plate. "You're not eating again. Admit it, Belle. You have no appetite because you're worried about your father."

Belle walked across the morning room to gaze out the window. "Of course I'm worried. Papa left town the other night after the ball without a word to me. If our housekeeper hadn't helped him pack his bags, I never would have known what became of him."

"Uncle Francis just needed time to calm down. He probably realized what a terrible mistake he made confronting Lane like that in front of everyone and now he's off trying to come up with a way to apologize."

Belle pulled the lace curtain back to view the street below. "Papa will never apologize because he wholeheartedly believes he's right. Without a doubt, my father is the most stubborn man I know."

Paris sniffed. "He's a rank amateur when compared to La—"

"Don't say it, Paris. For you're wrong. Trelane was very sorry he provoked Papa's anger and injured his pride. He fully intended to apologize to him yesterday. But with Papa away somewhere, sulking or licking his wounds, I'm left behind to sort it all out on my own."

At that moment, a carriage bearing a ducal crest pulled up at the front door. Belle leaned forward, her breath fogging the chilled pane of glass. "If you intend to primp before our guests arrive, you'd best move quickly, cousin. Apparently His Grace isn't one to arrive fashionably late for his appointments."

"Late? The silly man is early!" Paris hurried to stand behind her at the window. "Even in America, civilized callers don't show up at your home until at least midday. Why it isn't even nine o'clock in the morning! Only fishmongers and tradesmen would dare show up at such an ungodly hour."

Watching the two men in the beaver hats and fine wool topcoats alight from the carriage, Belle couldn't resist teasing her cousin. "Well, if you really feel that way about it, I could have Mrs. Tuttle send them away and ask them back later for tea. I wouldn't want to offend your tender sensibilities, cousin."

"Absolutely not," Paris insisted. "They're here and we'll see them." A wistful sigh escaped her lips. "He really is quite handsome."

Belle stepped away from the window and nodded. "Oh, yes, Jonathan Carlisle certainly is that. With his good looks and wealth, His Grace is the most sought-after bachelor in England. I'm not surprised that he caught your eye, Paris."

Her cousin seemed oddly distracted. She turned to Belle and frowned. "I'm sorry. My thoughts were wandering. What did you just say?"

"You said the duke was quite handsome and I was merely agreeing with you, that's all."

"I said the duke was handsome?" A second later, Paris tittered nervously and shook her head. "My goodness! I hadn't meant to say such a thing out loud. I really must watch what I'm saying around here. The last thing I want to do is shame you or give Lane more cause to find fault with me."

"You'd never shame me, Paris. You are more dear to me than a sister and I'm very grateful that you're here."

"Thank you, sweetie. I feel the same way about you." Smiling, Paris removed Belle's spectacles and placed them in her hand. "Better put these in your pocket for now. We wouldn't want to spoil a certain man's opinion of perfection."

Before Belle could respond, Paris took her arm and urged her out of the room.

Eric frowned as the elderly housekeeper hurried away with their hats and coats. He closed the drawing room door before turning to Jonathan. "I think she knows that I'm not Trelane. Did you see the way she was looking at me?"

Standing beside the fireplace to warm himself, Jonathan chuckled. "You're allowing your imagination to run amok, sir. It wasn't you she was staring at, but that ruby stickpin you're wearing in your cravat. That's quite a stunning piece. Where did you get it? In the Orient?"

"Bloody hell!" Eric removed the jeweled pin and put it in his coat pocket. "I never meant to use it at all, but I couldn't find an appropriate substitute among my brother's things at his apartment." Using the mirror over the mantel, he straightened the fit of his cravat. "For a man of means and intelligence, Trelane is sorely lacking in fashion sense. By God, everything in his wardrobe is black, brown, or white."

"He is a bit reserved in his tastes, but Trelane's always been that way." Jonathan's smiling countenance sobered. "Has there been any change in his condition?"

Eric shook his head. "Not that I know of. I sat with him several hours yesterday, but he never moved. Justin said he might not regain full consciousness for several days, maybe even a week."

"Considering the amount of pain he would be in if he was awake, perhaps sleep is the best medicine."

"That's true," Eric conceded, "but I want Trelane to know that I'm here, willing to do whatever I can to help him."

"Then you're feeling better about deceiving Belle?"

"Hell, no! But with her father's hasty departure,

I have no choice but to go through with this plan my parents devised." Eric nervously began to prowl the neatly appointed drawing room. "I don't know how long I'll be able to fool her, Jonathan. Belle might have mistaken me for Trelane the other evening, but that was only for a few minutes in a dimly lit room. There's still so much I don't know about her."

"You told me that you found Trelane's diary among his things and spent most of the night reading it. Surely he must have written something about Belle in his daily entries."

Eric's frown deepened. "Of course he did. But his entries about her were more like a list one would keep about a business endeavor. Nothing truly personal about Belle, just her assets and worth as the proper wife, and appointments they had to keep during the coming weeks. Though I was surprised how often Trelane mentioned her American cousin in his journal. Apparently, he and Paris were constantly bickering, and he worried that Belle was being hurt by that. He wrote something about mending his ways and getting along with the woman to please Belle. Have you any suggestions—"

"Good morning!" Smiling, Paris stood in the open doorway with Belle. "I hope you fellows will excuse our shabby appearance. We only received your message a few minutes ago, so there was little time to prepare ourselves for your visit."

"Paris, that will be enough," Belle warned. She dropped into a proper curtsey before entering the room. "Good morning, gentlemen. Please forgive my cousin's indirect rebuke and exaggeration. She tends to be a bit waspish if she hasn't had at least four cups of coffee at breakfast."

Jonathan laughed as he took Belle's hand and bowed. "I can't fault her for that, my dear. Though I prefer tea later in the day, I begin every morning with a pot of strong coffee myself. A nasty habit I acquired while visiting my niece, Diana, in Baltimore a few years ago. Isn't that right, Trelane?"

Eric was about to respond when Belle turned to face him. The memory of holding her in his arms and kissing her two nights before flooded his mind. She was shorter than the women he was usually drawn to, but Belle Kingsley had felt perfect in his embrace. The morning sun coming in the window revealed that she was quite pretty, without need of adornment or cosmetics. Her wavy blond hair was gathered back with a ribbon at the nape of her neck. There were a few freckles across the bridge of her nose and long, dark lashes framed her hazel-green eyes.

As he inwardly cursed his stray thoughts and tried to recall what Jonathan had said, Paris stepped beside him. "Why are you frowning, Lane? A person would think you were angry about something by that look at your face."

Eric fell into character and smiled at her. "I'm not angry at all. I simply realized how rude it was to arrive so early in the day, Paris. I'm afraid my concern for Sir Francis got the better of me. I beg your indulgence and pray that you and Belle will forgive my lack of manners."

Easing away from him, Paris's brow knitted in confusion. "Why . . . ah . . . of course. We really didn't have anything else planned for this morning, did we, Belle?"

"No, not a thing." Belle touched Eric's arm. "And you need not apologize for coming by, Trelane. We're going to be married in a few months. You and any member of your family are always welcome in this house."

"Thank you, Belle." Eric kissed her cheek and fought to ignore the satiny feel of her skin beneath his lips. Taking her arm, he led her to the sofa in front of the hearth and sat down beside her. "Has there been any word from your father?"

She stared down at her clenched hands in her lap. "No, and I'm worried about him. As I mentioned in my letter yesterday, Papa was gone by the time you brought us home from the ball. My housekeeper said he arrived home around midnight, all flushed and out of breath. He had her pack him a bag for an extended trip while he gathered things from his study. Minutes later, he left with our coach and driver, and no one's heard from him since."

Paris moved to the end of the sofa beside her cousin and patted her shoulder. "I think Uncle Francis was embarrassed by what he did at the party and simply needs some time away. He will be back in a few days—you'll see."

Belle shook her head. "I don't think so, Paris.

I checked the safe in his study and discovered that the thousand pounds he usually kept there for emergencies was missing. Papa wouldn't have needed that much cash if he were only going away for a short while."

"Well, I still think you're worrying over nothing, honey. Uncle Francis will be in touch with you soon, I'm sure. He loves you and wouldn't want to distress you. I bet he sends you a letter by the end of the week, just begging for your forgiveness."

Belle sighed. "I can only pray that you're right, Paris."

As the two cousins spoke to one another, Eric looked up at Jonathan and nodded. Their suspicions that Sir Francis was the one responsible for hiring the men who attacked Trelane seemed more likely than ever. The information they gleaned from this visit would be given to the private investigators his parents hired that morning along with the description of the men he had seen in his vision.

Eric was determined to find Sir Francis Kingsley. And the best way to trap the man was to stay close to Belle. If that meant spending a lot of time with her in the guise of his twin over the coming days, then so be it. No matter how difficult the task would be for his conscience and his heart, it had to be done.

But days grew into weeks, and Eric was soon cursing his optimism and burning with frustration.

"Conversing with politicians all day, exchanging clever platitudes, attending meetings where nothing is solved! Remembering to use my right hand when my natural inclination is to use my left! Jonathan, I don't know how much longer I can keep up this bloody charade. Three weeks have gone by and we aren't any closer to finding out who was responsible for the attack on Trelane than we were the night it happened!"

Looking out of his coach window as they rode away from Westminster Hall, Jonathan shrugged. "I don't see why you're so upset, Eric. Investigations like this take time. At least your brother is showing signs of recovering. After nearly losing him to that fever and those nasty bouts of pneumonia, it's a miracle Trelane's even alive."

Eric took off his hat and tossed it on the seat beside him. "If you call lapsing in and out of consciousness recovering, I suppose you're right. But I need more. I want to talk to Trelane, tell him what I've been doing on his behalf, and see if he knows of anyone else who would have wanted him killed. As much as we all believe that Sir Francis is the man behind this dastardly plot, I can't help thinking it might be someone else entirely."

Turning toward him, Jonathan cocked his brow. "Having a villain besides Belle's father to pursue would surely make things easier on the family. But are your thoughts about this fueled by your instincts or are they merely a product of wishful thinking?"

"What are you really asking, Jonathan?"

"Have you fallen in love with Belle Kingsley?"

Masking his true feelings, Eric chuckled. "You must be jesting. Miss Kingsley is a sweet young lady, but she's hardly the sort of woman that would interest me. Why on earth would you even ask such a silly question?"

"You and I have spent a great deal of time together these past few weeks. I've seen firsthand how you act when you're around Belle. You're attentive and adoring. You go out of your way to make her laugh and please her."

Eric snickered. "Why does any of this surprise you? It's a part of the role I'm playing. I'm supposed to be Trelane, her concerned and devoted fiancé. I could hardly treat her like a strumpet from the streets."

The duke frowned. "It's more than that. There's a warmth in your eyes and a gentleness in your demeanor that's only present when you're with Belle."

"Of course there is. I've worked very hard to perfect those particular traits. How else am I to convince everyone that I'm Trelane?"

"But I've seen you watching Belle when you thought no one was looking. You follow her every movement with such open adulation, so sincere, so loving. How can you deny that you're in love with her?"

Shaking his head, Eric rolled his eyes. "And this from a thirty-five-year-old man who's never been married or engaged. If I didn't know about the string of beautiful mistresses you've been keeping in high style since you were twenty, I would certainly wonder about your disinclination to have a relationship with a woman, Your Grace."

"This isn't about me, Eric, and well you know it. Stop ducking the issue and tell me straight out. Are you in love with Belle Kingsley?"

The tone of Jonathan's voice broached no argument and wiped the sardonic smile from Eric's face. "No, absolutely not. What you've witnessed has nothing to do with genuine feelings on my part. I was merely acting, playing a role in this tedious melodrama. If I fooled you with my portrayal, then I should be commended for doing a fine job, not taken to task for making it believable."

Jonathan turned back toward the window. "Well, if your acting ability is that good, perhaps you should have been treading the boards doing Shakespeare all these years instead of selling your proficiency as a soldier. With your talent, you'd probably own Covent Garden by now."

Closing his eyes, Eric carefully assumed a pose of bored reticence as a battle of conscience and tattered emotions warred inside him. *Bloody hell! I despise lying to Jonathan, but there's no help for it. I've tried not to care, not to have these feelings for Belle, but it's too late. I love her. I love everything about her. She's pretty and intelligent. Her sense of humor is a delight and her honest approach to life is so appealing. How could I not fall in love with her?*

He wearily rubbed his brow. *But Belle's engaged to my brother and will never be mine. Perhaps it would be best for all concerned if I put some distance between us for a while. God knows I could better use the time to concentrate on getting to know more about Trelane's friends and associates. There's still a possibility that one of them could have hired those cretins to kill him. All I have to do is figure out why.*

"Paris, would you kindly stop pacing around my bedroom like a candidate for Bedlam and button my dress for me? Trelane will be here soon and I don't want to keep him waiting."

Though she was still frowning, Paris hurried over and secured the buttons on the back of Belle's rose-pink gown. "I'm telling you something is definitely amiss with that fiancé of yours, Belle. He's being much too nice to me."

Looking over the top of her spectacles at Paris, Belle laughed. "A month ago you were complaining that Trelane was being overbearing and mean. Now you're ranting over the fact that he's being too nice. I'd best keep my eye on you, cousin. I fear you are suffering some odd sort of dementia."

Paris yanked the ribbons that formed the belt on Belle's gown and tied them into a bow. "I am not the one you should be wary of, Belle. There is something drastically different about Trelane."

Belle sighed and dropped into the chair in front of her mirrored vanity to brush her hair. "I really have no idea what you're talking about, Paris. What exactly are you implying?"

"Well, first of all, have you noticed how much time he's spent with you recently? Every night a party or a concert. Afternoon teas and visits to parks or museums. He even went to the dressmaker with you and picked out the fabric for that gown. Why, he's barely let you out of his sight in weeks."

"And I should be worried about that?" Belle saw her cousin's glower reflected on her mirror. "Paris, is it so hard to believe that Trelane simply enjoys being with me? We are going to be married, you know."

Letting out a sigh, Paris picked up the brush and vigorously began brushing Belle's hair. "Of course, honey. But you've been engaged for months and never before has Lane exhibited such ... such tenderness, such caring. It just seems strange that he's suddenly acting like a ... a ..."

"Man in love?" Belle turned to face her cousin and took hold of her hand. "Oh, Paris, I know when I accepted Trelane's proposal, there weren't any declarations of love between us. We were friends who shared many of the same interests. He needed a proper wife and I wanted a husband and a home to call my own. It was a good match for both of us. Of course, in time, I hoped a love would develop between us. I simply never expected it to be this soon."

Paris smiled as unspent tears glistened in her eyes. "So, you've fallen in love with him. My ever-efficient, very levelheaded cousin has finally let her heart rule her mind."

Belle stood up and swallowed hard against the emotional knot gathering in her throat. "Yes, I have. During these past few weeks, I've grown to love him very much. To imagine that he might feel the same for me is like a dream come true. Please be happy for me, Paris.''

Paris put her arms around Belle and hugged her. "I am happy for you, honey. Really, I am. Trelane wouldn't have been my first choice for you, but if you love that boorish Englishman and you're determined to marry him, then I'll support your decision. Above all, I want you to be happy.''

Belle pulled back to look at her cousin. "And no more silly talk about something being wrong with Trelane. Perhaps he's being pleasant to you out of consideration for me. Or maybe he actually likes you.''

"Ha! Trelane likes me as much as he would a rash from poison ivy. I'm red, I'm prickly, and eventually I'll go away!''

"Now, Paris—''

Paris held up her hands in defeat. "Fine, fine. I'll behave and keep my opinions to myself regarding Trelane. But don't think I won't be watching him, Belle. I still think something isn't quite right about him. And why is he constantly with Jonathan Carlisle?''

Shaking her head, Belle sat down at her vanity. "The problem with you, Paris, is that you have too much time on your hands. Instead of worrying about Trelane, you should be thinking about Jonathan Carlisle. He's been quite attentive to you lately.''

Paris brushed her cousin's hair and pinned up her curls into a neat chignon as she considered her reply. *If I tell Belle that I think those two are up to no good, she'll say I'm imaging things. I'd best keep that suspicion to myself.* "Jon is handsome, charming, and wealthy, but he's not the kind of man that interests me, honey."

"Why ever not? What's the matter with him?"

Patting her own fiery curls in the mirror, Paris shrugged. "There's nothing the matter with Jon. Even though he's a duke, Jonathan Carlisle is probably the most perfect man I've ever met. I just don't deal well with perfection, I guess."

Belle was perplexed. "I don't understand. Are you saying that you can only be happy with a man who is riddled with flaws?"

"Not riddled with them exactly, but a few would make him more human and easier to live with." Noting Belle's frown in the mirror, Paris turned around to explain. "I want a man who doesn't always agree with me. Who questions my choices and makes me fight a bit to get what I want. Compliments are lovely to hear, but I need to know that they are genuine, and not merely a way to placate me or be polite. I need to earn them. Do you understand?"

Belle smiled and nodded. "Yes. In an odd way, I think I do. Being with a man who constantly gives you your way would bore you to tears. You enjoy challenges in life, and having a man who can bring that kind of excitement to your relationship is even better. Am I right?"

A sad smile curved the edges of Paris's mouth. "Close enough, honey." Shaking out the folds of her gold velvet gown, she hurried across the room. "I've got the perfect necklace and earrings for you to wear this evening. Lane wouldn't dare complain about a few tasteful pearls. I'll be back in a minute." As she got to the door, Paris turned back to Belle. "I certainly hope your maid, Sylvia, gets better soon. The poor dear's been gone for days and I could use the rest."

"Sylvia isn't sick. Her mother was hurt . . ." Belle didn't bother to finish what she was saying, because Paris was already halfway down the hall. "Oh, well. I'll just tell her about it later."

Checking her appearance a final time in the mirror, Belle took off her spectacles and slipped them into her pink satin reticule. *Better take these with me. I wouldn't want to get lost roaming around Lord Neville's home while I was looking for the ladies' retiring room. The last time I did that during a party, I wandered about for a half hour before I found Trelane in his father's library.*

The memory of that night made her smile. It was the first time Trelane had ever flirted with her. He had teased and baited her, and playfully asked for a compliment. He'd also abandoned his usually vigilant attitude and drew her into his arms for a kiss. Just the thought of that one special kiss sent shivers over her skin.

Belle rubbed her arms and sighed. *Maybe I can get Trelane to kiss me like that again. I know he's adamant about waiting until our wedding night, but that's still weeks away and I want to feel that sort of excitement tonight. I wonder if he'd find me too bold if I tried kissing him first.*

She laughed to herself. The thought of actually doing such a thing never would have occurred to her before their encounter in the Graysons' library. Though they never discussed it, she couldn't help noticing another side of Trelane had emerged since that night. He seemed more relaxed and far less critical of things, including her outspoken American cousin. There even was a trace of playfulness in him that she'd never noticed before.

Yet in spite of all these changes, Trelane had never stopped being a gentleman. With the exception of an occasional kiss on the cheek, he never attempted more.

Well, I've experienced a taste of your passionate nature, Mr. Grayson. I think it's past time for another sample and I mean to get it tonight, right after Lord Beekham's little party. I can hardly wait!

Lord Beekham's little party turned out to be a sit-down dinner for forty of his most intimate friends. Before the meal was served, the guests were gathered in the grand salon of his palatial home to admire his newest artifacts from the Far East.

Neville nudged Eric with his elbow and pointed to the carved figurine on his mantel. ''Paid a king's ransom for that piece, Trelane. The dealer who acquired it for me in Peking says it's the only one of its kind. Once I learned that, I didn't mind the outrageous price. The piece fits perfectly into my private collection of rare and ancient things.''

His old friend's excited tone and his interest in artifacts surprised Eric. It seemed out of character for the Neville Farnsworth he'd known from childhood. "Oh, really? I wasn't aware that history and antiquities had become such a passion for you. Aren't you afraid of draining your coffers by spending your cash on things of this nature?''

Neville shrugged. "Not really. As a point of fact, besides objects of beauty, I look on these treasures as an investment. Rather than keeping my fortune in a musty old bank, I can have it around me to look at and admire when I choose. If I need additional funds to purchase a more expensive, much sought-after relic, I'd merely sell off a few of the lesser pieces to other wealthy collectors. Why, Lord Rayburn's already offered me twice what I paid for this piece on the mantel. That jade dragon with the ruby eyes pre-dates the Ming Dynasty.''

Belle, who was standing beside Eric, squinted and leaned toward the piece. "Rubies? I didn't think such gems were used to decorate art in that time period.''

When she moved closer to the statue, she caught the toe of her slipper on the marble lip in front of the fireplace and was suddenly pitched toward the flaming hearth. She screamed, but Eric quickly caught her around the waist and pulled her into the safety of his arms. His heart was pounding almost out of his chest as he held her close and struggled to speak.

"Bloody hell, sweetheart! You could have fallen into the fire and been killed! Didn't you see that raised tile?"

Too shaken to look up, Belle clutched the lapels of his tailcoat with her trembling fingers and burrowed her face against his chest. "N-n-no, I d-didn't see it. I c-c-can't focus w-well without my spectacles."

Eric turned her away from the people who'd witnessed the mishap and were now crowding around them. "She's fine. No harm done. Paris, would you and Neville please lead everyone in to dinner now? Belle needs a chance to collect herself. We will join you momentarily."

Before Paris could reply, Neville took her by the arm and nodded to his remaining guests. "Of course, Trelane. My friends, if you will kindly accompany us in to the dining room, the meal is about to be served. Cook has prepared a veritable feast for us tonight that I'm sure will please you all."

After they were alone, Eric guided Belle onto a sofa and sat beside her. He put his hand beneath her chin and made her look at him. "Are you truly all right, sweetheart? We can leave now if you're not feeling up to staying. I pray I didn't crack one of your ribs when I yanked you away from the flames."

An embarrassed smile curved her mouth. "A cracked rib or two is a lot better than being turned into kindling. Why, if you hadn't rescued me as quickly as you did, I would have—"

Eric captured her lips in a kiss and wouldn't allow her to finish. He'd nearly lost her because he had been so involved in questioning Neville. The thought of her being hurt was more than he could bear. Only the warmth of her soft, pliant mouth beneath his and the feel of her safely ensconced in his arms eased the tension in his gut. Relief merged with desire, compelling him to deepen his kiss. His tongue teased the crease of her lips and she willingly parted them for him. The sweet taste of Belle and the satin smoothness of her tongue touching his as she responded were a heady and potent mix. Losing track of all else, he took his fill and gloried in his new-found euphoria.

The sound of the clock chiming in the corner suddenly reminded Eric of where he was and what he was doing. He cursed himself and reluctantly eased away from Belle. *Bloody hell! What's the matter with me? Belle's engaged to Trelane. I can't allow this to happen again.*

Ignoring the awakened passion he saw in Belle's eyes, Eric took on a stern expression and waved a warning finger at her. "Belle Kingsley, vanity be damned! From now on you are to wear your spectacles at all times."

She frowned. "Vanity has nothing to do with it. You were the one who insisted that I not wear my spectacles, Trelane. You didn't want your friends or constituents thinking I was a bluestocking."

Eric recognized his error and smiled to hide his mistake. *My brother is an idiot! When he wakes up, I'm going to tell him so.* "That was stupid and irresponsible, Belle, and I was wrong. What people think isn't as important as your safety." He nodded at the drawstring purse hanging on her arm. "Are your spectacles in your bag?"

With her cheeks flushed pinker than the color of her gown, she nodded. "Yes, I brought them along in case I got lost walking around Lord Beekham's house."

"Fine. Put them on."

"But what will people—"

He tapped his finger on her lips. "I insist." Eric removed her spectacles from her bag and put them on her. "You look quite lovely in these. I didn't think it was possible, but they actually make your eyes appear more bright and luminous."

Belle smiled at his praise. "Thank you, Trelane."

"Don't mention it, sweetheart."

Paris stood beside the doorway watching them. *Don't tell me nothing's amiss with that man! After months of insisting that she go without spectacles, now Lane wants her to wear her them. And that ego-driven prig would never admit to being wrong about anything! He's using pet names, being polite to me, and waxing poetic over my little cousin's eyes. A leopard doesn't change his spots and no one changes that drastically without a reason. You're up to something, Trelane Grayson. And until I find out what it is, I'm going to keep a close watch on you.*

CHAPTER 4

Dinner was indeed the sumptuous feast that Neville promised. The ten-course menu included tender cuts of beef, lamb, and fowl. Fresh fish, prawns, a dozen vegetable dishes, and crusty rolls still warm from the oven were served along with four different wines. Fruit tarts, trifle, and an assortment of pies and cakes were displayed on the long sideboard for their dessert.

But Paris was too busy watching her cousin's betrothed to notice. She'd been placed directly to his right and had spent the entire meal studying his every move.

God's teeth, Lane's eating enough for two men and that's not like him at all. Besides his constant complaints about too much rich food adding to his waistline, he usually spends most of his time spouting off about politics and ignores the meal. But tonight, other than speaking to Belle and Jonathan across the table, Lane's barely said a word to anyone. He's concentrating on eating his food like it's a chore he has to deal with carefully.

When she saw him using his fork with his left hand, Paris frowned. *That's odd. I thought Lane was right-handed.* With her attention drawn to his hand, she noticed a strange, dark-pink marking resembling a snake on his inner wrist just below the cuff when he set down his fork and reached for his water glass. *A tattoo? I never knew the saintly Trelane Grayson indulged in such lowborn things. Isn't he worried that his political career would be tainted by anything less than pristine in his perfect appearance?*

Paris tried to shrug off her questions and turned her interest back to her plate of food. She was chewing on a morsel of roasted beef when she looked up and saw him using his fork with his right hand. His left hand was in his lap, hidden from sight by the tablecloth. Catching her looking at him, he smiled at her and nodded.

Her curiosity was sparked by her growing annoyance. *Left hand, right hand, strange tattoos! Lane's being far too cordial to me! And why is he always head to head with Jonathan Carlisle, whispering when they think no one's about? Are the two of them up to something? In spite of what Belle says, I am not imagining any of this. Too many things about Lane aren't making sense. Tomorrow, I'm going to hire one of those investigators from Bow Street and have him followed. Something's afoot with this man and I'm going to find out what it is.*

* * *

Five days later, Belle bustled into the morning room with a stack of papers and called to her cousin. "Paris, I'm sorry to disturb your breakfast, but that odd little man, Mr. Nash, is downstairs asking for you again. Coming without an appointment at this early hour is quite an imposition. Will you see him or shall I have Mrs. Tuttle send him away?"

Paris set down her coffee cup. "No. I'll see him. But before I go, did you ever notice the reddish tattoo on Trelane's left arm, just above his wrist? It looks like a jagged bolt of lightning."

Belle put her papers on the table and filled her plate with scrambled eggs and a slice of toasted bread. "Don't be ridiculous, Paris. Trelane is much too worried about appearances to have a tattoo anywhere on his body. What you saw must have been an ink stain."

"Since when does Trelane use red ink?" When Belle shook her head and wouldn't reply, Paris sighed. "Fine. Forget I said anything. You go on and have your meal without me. I'll be back in a few minutes."

"Not a problem. I have to go over these estimates from the decorators for the work on the town house." Belle looked up from her plate to frown at Paris as she moved toward the door. "You told me Mr. Nash is doing some work for you, but you didn't explain any of the details. What trade is he in?"

"He . . . ah . . . gathers information for me," Paris replied, carefully keeping her tone light and her words guarded. "I was thinking about finding a factor here in London to handle the distribution and sales for my whiskey distillery in Glasgow. My solicitor recommended a few firms to handle the task, but they're all strangers to me. I hired Mr. Nash to investigate their backgrounds and credentials so I can see which one would be the best choice."

Belle nodded and began shuffling through the documents on the table. "That was a very wise decision, Paris. A woman alone can't be too careful when it comes to protecting herself."

Watching Belle for a moment, Paris sighed. *I know, little cousin. And right this moment, I'm doing all I can to protect you. I just pray that you'll understand and forgive me for interfering in your life.*

Minutes later, Paris ushered Silas Nash into her uncle's office and shut the door. Nash was a short, chubby man of mid-years with a pale face and graying dark hair. Everything about him was nondescript. In his brown attire and plain appearance, he was the type of fellow who wouldn't draw attention from anyone. In his line of work, Paris decided that this was a good thing. She sat behind the desk and nodded to him.

"All right, Nash, have a seat and tell me what you've discovered about Trelane Grayson."

Nash pulled a small notebook from his coat pocket and reviewed his notes. "Not much more than I reported to you three days ago, Mrs. Mackenzie. Lord Grayson leaves his town house every morning promptly at half past eight and visits his law office before going to Westminster. The last few evenings, he's frequented Slaton's, the private gentlemen's club where many of the MPs gather.''

"Is the Duke of Chatham still accompanying him everywhere?"

"Aye, he is. His Grace comes by coach and fetches him every day. Guess it can't be helped 'cause Lord Grayson doesn't own a conveyance of his own.''

Paris sniffed. "That doesn't surprise me. He's such a skinflint, the house probably doesn't have a suitable barn to store a carriage anyway.''

The runner's grizzled brow went up. "On the contrary, Mrs. Mackenzie. The home has a fine barn of its own, accessible through the service lane behind the houses. The only thing currently kept there is a handsome black stallion his lordship purchased a few weeks ago. 'Tis a fine animal indeed.''

"Lane bought a stallion? Whatever for? The man's so busy with his political career, he never has time to ride.''

Nash chuckled. "Well, he's been riding every night that I've been watching him. Handles that horse like a jockey in the derby, he does.''

That bit of information surprised Paris. "Where does he ride to?"

"The Earl of Foxwood's residence." The older man frowned. "The strange thing is, 'tis his parents' home, but he never rides up to the front door. He goes in through the kitchen, stays an hour, and then returns to his own house."

"Oh, really? What time of the night does he do this?"

"Well after midnight. 'Long about two in the morning. Can't help wondering what he's doing there at that time of night."

Paris shook her head. "Neither can I, Mr. Nash, but I'm determined to find out. Tonight when you follow Trelane Grayson, I'm going with you."

"B-b-but, 'tis not p-possible," Nash sputtered in surprise. "You're a lady. I can't be taking you with me."

"I'm also the one paying you, Nash, and you'll do what I say. If it will soothe your offended sensibilities, I'll triple your fees."

"You'll be in danger—"

"I'll quadruple the fee, and not a penny more. Do we have a deal, Mr. Nash?"

The man mopped his brow on the sleeve of his coat. "The money's a right temptation, Mrs. Mackenzie, but how can you come with me? We can't very well follow the man in a coach."

Paris rolled her eyes. "Mr. Nash, I know how to ride a horse. I'll also wear britches and ride astride as I do in America. The ladies in England might not do such things, but the women where I come from are made of sterner stuff, I assure you. I'll give you money to hire a proper mount for me."

"But, Mrs. Mackenzie—"

Paris held up her hand. "Not another word, Mr. Nash. Bring the horse to the side entrance of this house around eleven o'clock. Rather than follow Trelane to his parents' home, we'll wait for him there. When Trelane goes into their house tonight, I intend to be right behind him. Now what about that other job I hired you to do? Have you learned anything about my uncle? Sir Francis left several weeks ago without a word and we're anxious to locate him.''

Nash shrugged. ''Ain't got much to report on that quarter, Mrs. Mackenzie, though I have come up with one startling fact. We're not the only ones looking for your uncle. According to my sources, two nabobs have hired associates of mine to find Sir Francis as well.''

''Oh, really? Any idea who they are?''

''One is working through a go-between to hide his identity. And the other is the Earl of Foxwood, Miles Grayson. He's even offering a hefty bonus of five hundred pounds to the man who finds Sir Francis and brings him back to London.'' Frowning, Nash scratched his head. ''It's not like your uncle's a criminal or something. For the life of me, I can't figure out why his lordship would be spending all that blunt looking him.''

''I can't either, Mr. Nash. But I intend to find out. Possibly tonight.''

The air was bitter cold as the half moon peeked out from behind the small cluster of clouds in the sky. As he'd done every night since beginning his charade as Trelane, Eric rode up the path to the kitchen door of his family's home, where he dismounted and tied his horse to the hitching post.

Sleeping through the night was something he hadn't been able to do for a long time. When he did manage to drift off, nightmares of the hellish existence he endured in the dungeon in Italy haunted his dreams and woke him up. Only short naps in a brightly lit room sustained him and gave his body the rest it required. But even those naps were sporadic. Rather than toss and turn in bed, he would get up to read or stare into the fire, deep in thought. But the loneliness and silence of the night was a deeper torment. He couldn't stand being alone. That's why he returned home every night to spend time with his brother.

But Trelane was more than his brother. He was his twin, the mirror image of himself. No one could interfere with the bond they shared. Though they'd chosen different paths, they were very much alike. Both were stubborn, honorable men who wanted to make a difference in the world. They strove to help people who weren't capable of defending themselves. Their methods of doing it were the only things separating them. Where he had used his expertise and cunning as a soldier, Trelane had employed his talents as a barrister, and now a Member of Parliament, to achieve his goals.

Yes, Eric decided, they were very much alike in many things. But the most painful coincidence was their feelings for Belle. His brother had courted and proposed marriage to the lovely young woman. She was beautiful, intelligent, caring, and the perfect choice for his ambitious sibling. Portraying Trelane and being with Belle these past weeks had been both heaven and hell for Eric. He knew it was wrong to have tender feelings for his brother's betrothed, but he couldn't help it. Belle would have been the perfect spouse for him as well. Like him, she had traveled the world and now longed for the goodness of home. They were kindred souls searching for the simple happiness of having a loving marriage and a family to call their own.

He felt guilty about pretending to be Trelane. Belle valued honesty, and when she discovered his deception, she would hate him and never speak to him again, no matter how noble the cause. But he would make it up to her. He was going to prove that her father wasn't guilty of sending those men after Trelane. Sir Francis loved his daughter. Eric couldn't imagine the elderly archaeologist doing anything to harm her or the man she loved, no matter how desperate he was. With that in mind, he swore he would save Belle's father and destroy the man who had thrown them all into this dreadful situation.

And to do that he needed help. He had to talk to Trelane.

Eric peered into the kitchen window. The house was dark and locked up, the inhabitants all asleep. But none of this stood in his way. Removing the ruby stickpin from his coat, he knelt beside the door and manipulated the lock until it clicked free. He eased the door open and stepped inside, unaware that he wasn't alone.

* * *

"Did you see that, Mr. Nash?" Paris gasped from behind an evergreen bush in the earl's garden. "He picked the lock to get inside! Don't tell me there isn't something strange going on. You wait out here while I see what he's up to."

Nash grabbed her arm. "This idea to follow him inside could prove dangerous, Mrs. Mackenzie. Why don't you let me go in your place? In my line of work I've done things like this before."

"Not on your life, sir," Paris insisted, pulling herself free of his hold. "I want to see what Trelane Grayson is doing and no one is going to stop me." Flipping her hood over her head, she wrapped her cloak tightly around her and ran the short distance to the kitchen door. Finding the door unlatched, she silently went inside.

Silas Nash wearily sat back on his heels and shook his head. "If that balmy American chit ain't out of there in a few minutes, I'm going home. No amount of money is worth getting hung for."

"How's Trelane doing, Mama? Has there been any change?"

Catherine stood up from her seat next to the bed and embraced her youngest son. "Very little, I'm afraid. He's restless, mutters in his sleep, and groans in pain, but not much else. At least his fever has finally abated and he's breathing a lot easier tonight."

"That's good." Kissing his mother's cheek, Eric moved toward the bed and gazed down at his brother. "I wish he was awake, Mama. There are just so many things I want to say to him. But he doesn't even know that I'm here."

She patted his back. "Trelane knows you're here, Eric, I'm sure of it. Why don't you sit down beside him while I go down to the kitchen and fetch you something warm to drink? As cold as it is tonight, you could probably use a hot toddy or a cup of tea."

"Don't bother, Mama. I'm fine. But what are you doing up at this hour, sitting here in your nightgown and robe? Isn't the nurse Uncle Justin brought in to care for Trelane still here?"

Catherine pushed Eric into the chair. "I sent the woman to bed a couple of hours ago so I could have a bit of private time with both my boys. Other than these late-night visits you have with Trelane, I never get to see you. How are you doing, son?"

Eric sighed to himself. *I wonder what you would say if I told you the truth, Mama. I can't sleep because I'm tortured by the memories of the past two years and being alone in the dark scares the hell out of me. And if that's not bad enough, I've fallen hopelessly in love with my brother's fiancé.*

Instead of confiding these truths to her, he reached over and touched his brother's hand. "I'm all right, Mama, truly I am. Save your concern for Trelane. He's the one who needs it. Has Father received any word from the investigators about Sir Francis and where he's gone off to?"

"No. Though your father did learn yesterday that two other people are searching for him as well. Apparently, Paris Mackenzie and one of the members of Slaton's have hired investigators of their own to find Sir Francis, too."

Eric looked up at his mother and frowned. "Belle's beside herself with worry over her father's disappearance, so I can understand why Paris is looking for him, but who can this other person be? Why would a member of Trelane's private club be searching for Sir Francis? Slaton's members are all politicians, barristers, and high-ranking government officials."

Catherine shrugged. "We don't know. Our man said the gentleman wanted to remain anonymous, so he got George Miller, the manager of Slaton's, to make the arrangements with the investigator in his stead."

"Has Father been to see this Miller chap yet?"

"I don't believe so, but I'm not sure. Your father's been worried about me lately and doesn't tell me everything. Why don't we go ask him together? If you're with me, he'll have no choice but to tell you the truth."

"But it's the middle of the night, Mama. He's probably asleep."

Shaking her head, her thick blond braid fell over her shoulder. "Not your father. The man claims he can't sleep unless I'm lying in the bed beside him. He was catching up with his correspondence in our bedroom when I came in here to sit with Trelane."

"But what about Trelane? Is it safe to leave him alone?"

"We'll only be gone a few minutes and he will be fine. With the dose of laudanum the nurse administered around ten o'clock, Trelane should sleep peacefully through the night, but we will leave the door ajar so we can hear him if that will put your mind at ease." Tugging his arm, she pulled him from his seat and toward the door. "Come along, son. I'm suddenly very anxious to hear what your father has to say."

"Drat it all! Which way did he go?" Paris muttered to herself as she looked up and down the long, dimly lit corridor. "I followed him up the servants' staircase to this level and lost him. I never realized this house was so damn—" Hearing a woman's voice, she ducked behind a cabinet and braced her back against the wall. When it was silent again, Paris stuck out her head and saw light coming from a door that was left open at the far end of the hall. "I guess that's a good place to start looking for him."

Within seconds, Paris was standing in the doorway, looking inside the bedroom. The chamber's decor had a definite masculine feel to it, with dark wood furniture and oak paneled walls. A brass lantern on the nightstand barely illuminated the sole inhabitant of the room, who was sleeping on the wide bed. Forgetting her fear of being caught, Paris was inexplicably drawn toward the bandaged man on the bed. When she crossed the room and saw his face, she gasped.

"Dear God, it's you, Trelane! What have they done to you?" she said, caressing his pale, bruised cheek with her hand. "Who hurt you like this? I'll kill them, I swear it. Lane, please talk to me. I have to know that you're all right, Lane."

Trelane's lips twitched. His eyelids opened slightly as he struggled to focus his gaze on her. "M-my name's . . . n-not Lane, Paris. Stop c-calling m-me Lane."

Paris dashed the tears from her eyes with her hand and smiled. "I'll call you anything I choose, you insufferable man. But don't you dare die. I don't know what I would do if you died on me."

He frowned and shut his eyes. "Not dying, Paris. Just trying to sleep. We can talk later."

She nodded. "Of course we can, Lane. The moment you wake up, I'll be right here and we will talk then."

Trelane sniffed. "Always did talk too much . . . and Paris?"

She grabbed his hand and held it tightly. "Yes, Lane? What is it you want?"

He sighed. "Don't . . . call . . . me . . . Lane."

The even cadence of his breathing told Paris he was sleeping again. Cradling his hand against her breast, she leaned over and stroked the hair from his brow. "The other man obviously is your long-missing twin brother. He might look like you, Trelane, but I knew something was amiss. I knew he wasn't you. When I tell Belle—"

"Forgive the interruption, Mrs. Mackenzie," an imperious female voice called from behind her, "but you won't be telling Belle or anyone else what you found here tonight."

Paris leapt from her seat and spun around to face the Countess of Foxwood, who was standing in the doorway watching her. "Of course I'm going to tell my cousin what I discovered, Lady Catherine. She's engaged to marry Trelane and has the right to know that he's been hurt. Who did this to him?"

Keeping her hands in the pockets of her dressing gown, Catherine walked into the room. "A group of street toughs was hired to attack my son the night of his engagement ball. We don't know who employed those men, but we're searching for the culprit. And until the guilty party has been found, no one outside of this household is to know that Trelane was nearly killed or that his twin brother, Eric, has returned to England and is impersonating him."

"How long do you think you can get away with this charade? I noticed the differences right from the start," Paris boasted. "That's why I followed your other son into the house tonight. I didn't know exactly what was happening, but I knew something was wrong."

A cool smile curved Catherine's mouth. "Then you are a most observant lady, Mrs. Mackenzie. Or perhaps you've been blessed with extraordinary intuition. Either way, you won't be sharing your news about this with anyone."

"Oh, really? What are you going to do, Lady Catherine, make me a prisoner in your house?"

With a curt nod, Catherine took the pistol from her pocket and aimed it at Paris. "Whatever it takes, Mrs. Mackenzie. Whatever it takes."

Catherine stepped out of Trelane's room a half-hour later and locked the door with a key. Eric, who'd been listening to her conversation with Paris from the corridor, shook his head at her.

"Mama, you really wouldn't have shot Paris, would you?"

"Of course not," she scoffed, putting the gun back in her pocket. "The pistol wasn't even loaded. But Paris didn't know that."

Eric frowned. "I don't see how you're going to be able to keep her locked up in this house. Paris Mackenzie isn't a woman to be trifled with. She'll find a way to escape. You mark my words and see if she doesn't."

"Paris will try, but she won't succeed. I'll keep an eye on her myself," Catherine explained with a playful wink. "So, did Jake and the footmen find anyone else on the grounds? I can't imagine that young woman came out at this time of night without an escort. Paris is clever and brave, but she's not stupid."

"They searched, but no one was found. Jake's son reported hearing a couple of horses riding away from the back of the gardens while they were searching."

"Her hired man must have lost his nerve. Well, that's one less problem we'll have to deal with." She took a folded piece of parchment from her left pocket and gave it to Eric. "We don't want Belle worrying about her cousin, so please have a messenger deliver this to her in the morning. It's a note from Paris saying that she's been called away on urgent business regarding the construction of her new distillery in Scotland."

"I suppose you used the pistol to gain Paris's cooperation in writing this letter."

Catherine shrugged innocently. "Don't blame me because the woman couldn't discern whether the gun was loaded or not. 'Tis a lack in her education, not mine. Perhaps when all of this is over, I'll teach her the difference." She hooked her arm through Eric's and ushered him to the stairs. "Let's go down to the kitchen and have a cup of tea before you go."

Frowning, Eric looked back at Trelane's locked door. "Mama, you really shouldn't leave Paris alone in that room with Trelane. If given the chance, she's likely to smother him with a pillow. They hate one another—she utterly despises him."

"No, she doesn't. Though Paris balked quite outrageously when I informed her that she was going to help me nurse Trelane back to health, it was all bluster. I believe Paris Mackenzie is in love with your brother."

Eric rolled his eyes in disbelief. "I'm sorry, Mama, but you're wrong. Paris and Trelane have been battling constantly since they met. In his journal, Trelane even referred to Paris as the 'red-haired witch from Philadelphia.' If it weren't for pleasing Belle, the two of them would never be in the same room together.''

Catherine sighed. ''Be that as it may, I'm telling you Paris has a tender spot in her heart for Trelane. She even offered to sit with him while I had a room prepared for her. And she must be special to him as well. When I heard Trelane talking to her—''

Eric yanked his mother to a halt at the foot of the stairs. ''Trelane was talking to her? Was he making sense or just muttering in his sleep?''

Catherine chuckled. ''He was making plenty of sense. Trelane was scolding Paris for calling him 'Lane' and implied that she talked too much. The poor girl was begging him not to die and he tersely informed her that he wasn't dying, just trying to get some sleep. It appears your ever-laconic brother is nearly back to his old charming self. Isn't that wonderful, Eric? Trelane is truly going to be all right.''

Torn by his conscience, Eric hugged his mother. ''Yes, Mama, that's wonderful news indeed.'' *And once I can prove that Sir Francis wasn't the man who ordered the attack on my brother, Belle shall be reunited with Trelane, and I will be out of her life forever. Bloody hell! What will I do then?*

CHAPTER 5

Belle pulled off her gold-framed spectacles and tossed them on the desk. Working on her father's journals and cataloguing the artifacts they'd found on their expeditions had always been an enjoyable task. But now it was little more than a way to keep busy and allow her to forget how miserable and alone she felt. Her father had been gone a month and still there was no word from him.

Now Paris had deserted her as well.

Five days had passed since she received the note from Paris saying a problem had arisen at the site of her new distillery that required her immediate presence in Scotland. Her cousin was known for spur-of-the-moment decisions, but this trip had taken Belle totally by surprise. Not only did Paris leave during the night when no one was about, but she went without any of her clothing or personal things. If the letter hadn't been written in Paris's flowery style with its flourishes and bold script, she might have thought her cousin had been abducted. But the familiar handwriting was indeed hers and there weren't any signs of distress or alarm in her message.

Thinking about handwriting, Belle picked up the missive she'd received that morning from Trelane. Though she hadn't seen him since Neville's dinner party, he wrote her a personal letter every day, apologizing for his absence due to his work and begging her forgiveness. Laying the letters side by side, she noticed his penmanship had been slanting more and more to the left recently.

"Writing his own legal briefs, taking notes in meetings, signing bills. Poor dear must be tired. When Trelane comes to dinner tonight, I'll suggest he take a holiday. He deserves a respite and I would like to see my fiancé a little more often."

Mrs. Tuttle entered the study and handed Belle a calling card. "This gentleman's out in the foyer asking to see your father, Miss Kingsley. Said he made the appointment with Sir Francis two months ago."

Belle read the card. "Alexei Chernoff. Hmmm. I don't recall the name. He must be one of those elderly professors Papa befriended at the university in January. I suppose I'll have to see him." She stood up and began tidying up the desk. "Show

Mr. Chernoff in and please bring us some tea, Mrs. Tuttle.''

A few moments later, Belle knew her assumption about her visitor was definitely wrong. Alexei Chernoff was far from elderly, nor was he old enough to be a professor. With long, flaxen hair and pale gray eyes, the tall, broad shouldered man filled the open doorway looking like an ancient Viking. He was impeccably dressed all in black and was possibly the most beautiful man Belle had ever seen. When he stepped into the room, she was too stunned to do anything but stare up at him.

An odd thought crossed her mind. *Heavens above! If the Archangel Gabriel were to come to earth, he would probably look exactly like this man.*

Alexei took her hand and bowed. ''Good afternoon, Miss Kingsley. I appreciate you seeing me this afternoon. I hope I have not disturbed your work.''

His voice was deep and rich like a fine red wine. There was a slight accent to his English, but Belle couldn't quite place it and that intrigued her. His name suggested that he was Russian, yet there was a soft roll in his words more reminiscent of a Scotsman. Was that a hint of French or possibly Italian in his speech as well? Perhaps if she listened to this handsome man speak a bit more she'd be able to discern where he was from. Would an hour or two be enough time?

Looking at her face, Alexei frowned. ''Are you all right, Miss Kingsley? If you are not well or if I have arrived at an inopportune time, I could return at a later date.''

''Oh, no,'' she gasped in embarrassment, ''I'm fine. I was just a little distracted by your ah ... wonderful voice. Please forgive me.''

Alexei bowed his head and smiled. ''But of course, Miss Kingsley. Consider me your most humble servant.''

Feeling awkward because she'd been gaping at the man, Belle ignored the heat building in her cheeks and moved toward the upholstered chair and settee by the hearth. ''Why don't we sit down by the fire so we can be comfortable while we talk? Our tea should arrive in a few minutes.''

Seeing Alexei Chernoff sitting in her father's favorite chair did little to squelch her fascination. *But at least I won't get a stitch in my neck from looking up at him,* she mused as she primly folded her hands in her lap and cleared her throat.

''Well, Mr. Chernoff, I'm afraid I have some rather bad news for you. My father is out of town and I have no idea when he'll be returning. If you tell me why you've come to see him, perhaps I can assist you.''

He nodded. ''It has to do with artifacts, Miss Kingsley. One in particular that Sir Francis reportedly found several years ago. I wanted to examine it for a research paper I will be presenting to the Royal Antiquities Society in May.''

Belle was impressed. The Royal Antiquities Society was the most prestigious organization of its kind in England, and maybe even the world. Only the best-respected archaeologists, explorers, and scientists were ever permitted to address their membership. Evidently there was a great deal more to this man than just his incomparable good looks. "Mr. Chernoff, I personally catalogue all the relics and artifacts collected on my father's expeditions. Which one are you referring to?"

Alexei's brow arched for a second before he replied. "A mantle clasp, Miss Kingsley. One that dates back to the early Crusades. Knights used them to secure their cloaks around their necks."

Belle frowned. "I know very well what a mantle clasp is, Mr. Chernoff, but my father has no such item in his collection. Those kinds of things simply don't interest him. Maybe you have my father confused with—"

At that moment, Mrs. Tuttle knocked on the door and rushed into the study. "Miss Kingsley, I'm sorry to disturb you, but his lordship, Mr. Grayson, is here to see you."

Surprised and delighted by the news, Belle quickly got to her feet. "Trelane is here? Why, show him in immediately, Mrs. Tuttle. We mustn't leave Mr. Grayson waiting in the vestibule."

Alexei stood up and took her hand. "Apparently you have company and I am imposing on your time, Miss Kingsley. I am sorry that I troubled you."

"Oh, that's perfectly all right, Mr. Chernoff. Though I regret not being able to help you, I thoroughly enjoyed making your acquaintance. Perhaps you can come again and tell me all about the paper you'll be presenting to the Society."

A familiar male voice tinged with rancor called from the door. "I think not, my dear. If Mr. Chernoff wishes to speak to you again, he'll have to go through me first."

Belle turned to confront him when he crossed the room. "Trelane, what's the matter with you? That scowl would stop a clock. This gentleman had an appointment with my father. Since Papa wasn't here, I was merely trying to help him."

He put a proprietary arm around her and pulled her to his side as he glared at the tall, blond man. "Mr. Chernoff can bloody well help himself from now on. Isn't that right, Alexei?"

A hint of a smile tilted the corners of Alexei's mouth. "Whatever you say, sir." Boldly approaching Belle, he took her hand and kissed it. *"Adieu,* sweet lady. The pleasure of this meeting, though short in length, has been entirely mine." Looking at the man beside her, he nodded. *"Trelane,* we really should get together and talk about old times. I will be in touch."

As the door shut behind Alexei, Eric felt his spine easing a bit. Finding another man so close to Belle was difficult enough to accept. Seeing her with a man who'd been his sworn enemy for the past two years without killing him on the spot was torture. *What the hell is Alexei Chernoff doing in England and why is he trying to get close to Belle? Chernoff knows full well who I am, yet he calls me "Trelane." What sort of game is that bastard playing with me now?*

Belle pulled free from his embrace and glared up at him. "Trelane Grayson, I'm ashamed of you.

Evidently you knew that man and had issues with him, but that doesn't give you leave to growl at my guest."

Masking his distress, Eric held up his hands in surrender and tried to look contrite. "Forgive me, my dear. I was a brute and you deserve far better."

"What did Mr. Chernoff do to you that put you in such a state?"

Eric shook his head. "Nothing much, I assure you. If truth be told, I was jealous."

Belle's face was a portrait of shock and surprise. "You were jealous?"

"Of course I was. Chernoff's a handsome devil. When I saw him holding your hand, gazing into your eyes, I lost my temper. I wanted to hit him for touching you."

She reached up and cradled his face in her hands. "The only handsome devil I am interested in, Mr. Grayson, is you. Don't you know how much I love you?"

Eric was searching for the right words when Belle caught him unaware by stretching up on tiptoes to kiss him. He struggled to ignore how perfect and warm her mouth felt on his, but quickly lost the battle when her tongue met his. Logic abandoned, he opened his mouth and allowed their kiss the freedom he'd been denying himself. Their tongues touched and shivers of desire coursed through them both. All he could think of was having more of her.

Fueled by need, he lifted her from the floor. Her soft, feminine body was pressed fully against him.

Her arms entwined his neck and she returned his kisses with matching ardor. Dropping onto the settee, he held her on his lap and ravished her mouth with his own while his hand explored the gentle curve of her bosom. This was heaven; this was right, he decided. Yet seconds later, it wasn't enough.

His fingers urged the scooped neckline of her gown and camisole off her shoulder, exposing one of her breasts. It was firm and plump beneath his touch, her skin like satin. He rained kisses across her cheek and nuzzled the sensitive slope of her neck until his lips made their way to the pale pink nipple. He laved it with his tongue and drew it into his mouth. Belle's moan of pleasure and the way her nipple beaded when he suckled emboldened him to go for more.

His mouth returned to kissing hers while his hand found its way beneath the skirts of her gown. He was soon caressing the length of her legs and she didn't object. Caught up in her passion, Belle actually parted her thighs, inviting him to touch the most private part of her person. Eric didn't delay. Brushing past her underclothing, his fingers touched her woman's flesh. She was moist and warm. A shudder rushed through her as he found the small nub hidden within the slick folds and stroked it.

Belle gasped with pleasure, sucking his breath into her lungs as he gently rubbed the sensitive spot between his thumb and fingers. Her hips moved of their own volition. The feel of her buttocks rubbing suggestively against him caused his manhood to swell and harden beneath his clothing. It was heaven; it was hell, but he didn't care. At that moment all he wanted was for Belle to explode beneath his touch and within seconds she did exactly that. He pressed a finger deep inside her as she climaxed, and captured the cry of her release with his mouth.

As Belle trembled from the aftermath, Eric held her close and eased back to look at her face. Her eyes were shut and she was breathing hard. Her cheeks were flushed and glowing. She had never been more beautiful. Cursing himself, he took his hand from beneath her skirts and pulled the bodice of her gown in place.

Damn my soul to the devil! I never should have touched her, but I couldn't stop myself. How did I let this happen? When the truth comes out about my real identity, Belle will hate me forever. And when Trelane recovers from his injuries and finds out what I have done, he'll cut me down quicker than Cain killed Abel . . . but I'll deserve it for betraying him like this. Bloody hell! Perhaps I should tell her who I am now and just be done with it.

"Belle, I think—"

A loud rapping sound came from the door. "Miss Kingsley, would you like me to bring in the tea tray now?"

Belle quickly sat up and avoided meeting Eric's eyes. "Not in here, Mrs. Tuttle. Ah . . . take it to the ah . . . salon, please. We shall be there shortly."

"As you wish, Miss Kingsley."

Hearing the housekeeper bustling away, Belle hurried to get off of Eric's lap. "I . . . ah . . . really don't know what to say. Forgive me, I've never . . . I'm so ashamed of . . . of . . ."

Eric grabbed Belle and prevented her from moving away. "You've done nothing to be ashamed of, my love. You felt a woman's pleasure. And I was the one who gave it to you."

Belle turned to face him. "Am I . . . am I truly your love?" she asked tentatively.

He nodded and didn't hesitate. "Yes, Belle. I love you with every fiber of my being." Kissing her brow, he drew her into his embrace. "No matter what happens, always remember that I love you."

She rubbed her cheek against his shoulder and sighed. "Of course I shall never forget that. And remember that I love you, too, Trelane."

Pain ripped through Eric far worse than any of the tortures he had suffered during his hellish imprisonment in Venice. *She calls me Trelane. Hell, I would give the world if she would love me instead of my brother. But that's never going to happen. And the sooner I find the person responsible for attacking my brother, the better off we all will be.*

His determination shielded him like armor as he lifted Belle onto the sofa beside him. "I can't stay for tea, Belle. I wish I could, but I only stopped by to tell you that I won't be able to come to dinner this evening. The House has called a special meeting of one of my committees at Westminster. As a matter of fact, what with the discussions, arguments, and debates that will undoubtedly arise, I might not be available to visit you for several days. I hope you understand."

Belle smiled, yet sadness clearly shone in her eyes. "Of course I understand, Trelane. Isn't that what a good politician's wife is supposed to do?"

Eric swallowed against the tightness in his throat and nodded. "Yes, love, exactly that." Closing his eyes, he kissed her brow and gave her a final hug. *Goodbye, my dearest love. The next time we meet, I'll find a way to tell you the truth. Then you will never want to see me again.*

CHAPTER 6

A few days later, Eric sat in his brother's law office wondering how he could get Trelane's loquacious partner to keep quiet and leave him to his work.

Henry paced the room like a proud bantam rooster and chuckled. "I tell you, Trelane, it was the funniest thing I've ever witnessed in court. The senior judge, Sir Malcolm Bostwick, fell asleep in the middle of the prosecutor's rebuttal against our client. His snoring was heard clear up to the gallery. If that cantankerous old goat hadn't found in our favor, I would have sued for a mistrial."

"As well you should, Henry." Eric came around the desk and put his arm on the shorter man's shoulder as he guided him toward the door. "I really appreciate you taking over that case for me.

With all my duties in the House these days, I barely have time to sleep, let alone present a case before the bar.''

"Think nothing of it," Henry preened. "The charges were simple and I thoroughly enjoyed collecting that sizable bonus your client gave me following his not-guilty verdict. If you have any other wealthy nabobs in need, feel free to send them my way. God knows I could use the blunt."

Eric's brow rose. "Having money problems?"

Crossing the outer office together, Henry shrugged. "No more than usual, Trelane. My father's cottage in Redding needed a new roof. Since he's not teaching any longer, he couldn't afford to do it on his own, so I paid for it. Couldn't very well let the place fall down around the old man's ears. He's the only family I have left and it's my duty to take care of him."

Eric thought about what he'd been doing the past weeks and nodded. "I know all about family and the duties that are thrust upon us. But no matter how difficult things get or how high the cost to you personally, you do whatever's necessary to help them."

Henry looked back at Eric as they entered his office. "With all the money your parents have, at least they won't be draining your coffers dry."

"No, but money isn't everything."

"Only a person who has money can say that," Henry snickered, going through a stack of papers on his desk. "Just try living without it and you'll see what I mean."

The memories of what he'd shared with Belle filled his mind and sadness hit Eric full force. *Try living without your soul, Townsend. 'Tis worse than poverty or death, I assure you.*

Shaking off his melancholy, Eric turned to leave. "I'll speak with you later, Henry. I have some notes to go over before Jonathan picks me up for our meeting at Westminster this afternoon."

"One moment, Trelane. I received something this morning that you might find quite interesting. Oh, yes, here it is." Henry held out a document to Eric. "Remember how you gloated over your success at beating down Drummond's price on that house you purchased from him? Apparently, Drummond's not the idiot we suspected him to be. He knew his new bride was about to become an heiress. Her grandmother passed away the morning of your engagement party and left the chit nearly a million pounds in cash and property. The lucky bastard's been out of town on holiday since then. As you can see by this letter, Drummond's asked me to represent him in the transfer of his new holdings."

Eric looked at the paper and nodded, but inwardly he was disappointed. *Well, so much for thinking that Drummond might have been the man responsible for Trelane's attack. The amount of money he lost by selling his house to my brother is a tuppence compared to this.* He handed the letter back to Henry. "Good luck dealing with him. Since Drummond's so wealthy now, you should double your fees."

"Double nothing!" Henry chuckled. "I'll triple

the bill and convince the blighter that he's getting a bargain."

"I'm sure you will. Well, I've got to get back to work."

As Eric was leaving, Henry called to him. "I'm meeting Neville for dinner at Slaton's tonight. We'll probably end up playing cards with some of the other club members afterward. Would you care to join us?"

The mention of Slaton's gained Eric's attention. According to what his father learned recently, a member of the exclusive club was offering a big reward to locate Belle's father. *Perhaps it's time for me to have a look at the place myself. With luck and a hefty bribe to the club's manager, I might find out who else is looking for Sir Francis and why.* "The invitation is quite tempting. If I can get away from Westminster at a decent hour, I will be there."

Henry sat behind his desk and rubbed his hands together. "Wonderful. And bring money with you, Trelane. If I'm lucky at cards tonight, I might be able to provide my father with a new well and cistern before the summer is upon us."

Eric laughed. "Whatever you say, Henry. I hope to see you then."

He was nearly to Trelane's office when one of the clerks rushed up to him with several papers. "Mr. Grayson, I've gone through the rest of the cases you prosecuted when you were working for the Crown and got the information you requested. Many of the men you helped convict are dead. The others, I've listed on these pages with their crimes and where they are located at the present time. Is there anything else I can do for you, sir?''

"No, Robert. This is fine. Thank you for your efforts."

Reading the carefully written list, Eric returned to Trelane's office and closed the door. "Damn! Only three of these criminals have been released from prison. I doubt if any of them could afford to hire men to kill my brother."

"Why would anyone want to kill your brother, Eric?''

Eric spun around to find Alexei Chernoff standing in the room beside the door. "Chernoff, how in the hell did you get in here?"

"The usual way, my friend. I walked in when no one was looking. I am quite good at doing that, you know." Dressed in his customary black attire, Alexei walked past Eric to sit in one of the chairs in front of the desk. "Now, are you going to answer my question? Why would anyone want to kill your brother?''

"Go to the devil, Chernoff! If I had a pistol with me, I would shoot you where you're sitting."

Alexei rolled his eyes and shook his head. "Eric, you really must do something about that wretched temper of yours. Here I am, offering you my aid, and you are threatening to shoot me. That is hardly a way to show one's appreciation."

"Appreciation for what? You were the bastard who got me locked up in Count Orsini's dungeon! If you hadn't betrayed me, I never would have been caught helping Paolo Benedetti escape from his servitude in the glassworks of Venice."

"I did not betray you."

"Oh, really?" Eric scoffed, sitting on the edge of Trelane's desk. "And why should I believe you? In the last ten years, you and I have worked in the same line of business. We're mercenaries who sell our expertise to the highest bidder, if not to the noblest causes. Sometimes we were on the same side, but not always. At least we were honest about our choices and with each other. That is, until Venice. Evidently, we were adversaries there and I never knew it."

Alexei didn't flinch. His pale blue gaze locked with Eric's. "I did not betray you, Eric. Nor would I. Men of our ilk often make sacrifices, but my honor has never been one of them." He placed his right hand over his heart. "I solemnly swear to you that I had nothing to do with your arrest or imprisonment in Venice."

As much as Eric wanted to deny it, his gut instincts told him that Alexei was telling him the truth. "Then if it wasn't you who told Orsini that I was helping Paolo, who was it? Only you and I knew about my plan to aid him. Paolo was desperate to escape, so I doubt he would have mentioned it to anyone."

Steepling his fingers, Alexei nodded. "True, Paolo was quite desperate, but he was also in love. He told Maria Rosario what you were going to do for him. She was the one who turned you both in to Count Orsini."

"But that makes no sense. They were so in love! Paolo wouldn't even consider my plan until I promised to find a way to come back later for her. Why would Maria betray him like that?"

Alexei shrugged. "Mixed loyalties, I suppose. Her father was the manager of Count Orsini's glassworks factory where he was an apprentice. When the old man agreed to teach him the trade of glassblowing five years before, Paolo pledged never to leave Venice. If Orsini discovered that Paolo had left the city with his acquired knowledge, Maria's father and her entire family would have been punished for not stopping him."

Eric's lip curled in disgust. "Being an apprentice in that shop was killing Paolo. Twelve hours a day, six days a week, working in that sweltering shop with those furnaces and molten glass. The constant heat affected his breathing. His hands and arms were badly scarred from burns. Why, the man could hardly stand straight from carrying heavy loads of coal and supplies for his master every day. 'Tis worse than slavery or indentured servitude! Who could fault him for wanting to escape such an existence?"

"Paolo should have thought of that before accepting the appointment and signing his pledge to remain in the city. The art of glassmaking is sacred to the Venetians. Its secrets have been guarded for hundreds of years."

"Yes, I know. Their damned secrets cost poor Paolo his life when he drowned in the canal trying to escape being captured and got me thrown into

Orsini's hellish dungeon for more than a year."
Eric got up and began to pace the floor restlessly.
"Enough talk about Venice. Tell me why you're
in London, Alexei. And what were you doing in
Belle's home the other day?"

"Ah, yes, the lovely Miss Kingsley. You know, Eric,
even with those spectacles, Trelane's betrothed is
a very beautiful young woman."

Eric stood over Alexei and grabbed the lapels of
his fine wool coat. "Stop toying with me, Chernoff!
I want to know what you're up to. Were you hired
by someone to kill my brother?"

"Absolutely not. I am a soldier, not an assassin.
But if I had been contracted for the task, Trelane
would have been dead weeks ago and you would
not be involved in this silly impersonation to trap
the man responsible for the attempt on his life."
Glancing at Eric's hands, Alexei frowned. "Now,
would you kindly stop pulling on my coat? My tailor
spent a lot of time getting those lapels pressed
properly and you are crushing them."

Alexei's remarks about Trelane and his own activ-
ities caused Eric to stumble back in surprise. "How
in the hell do you know about all this?"

Brushing down the lapels of his coat, Alexei
smiled. "I know a great many things, Eric. Some
that would amaze and even shock you. But that's
not why I came to see you. I want to help you find
the man who tried to have your brother killed."

Eric leaned against the desk and crossed his arms
over his chest. "Why the sudden generosity? Obviously you came to England for a purpose. In all

the years I've known you, Alexei, you've never been idle. Won't your present employer be put out if you waste your time aiding me?"

"Not at all. There is no reason why I cannot help you and my benefactor at the same time. As a point in fact, I was working on a task for him when you arrived at the Kingsleys' home and I discovered that you were portraying your brother."

"That's another thing. My brother and I are like reflections in a looking glass. How did you know that I wasn't Trelane?"

Alexei chuckled. "The recognition and the fire in your eyes when you saw me standing beside Miss Kingsley told me all I needed to know. She called you Trelane, so I went along with the charade and kept your secret. My curiosity would not be appeased until I followed you about town these past three days, made some discreet inquiries, and figured out what you were actually doing. Tell me what happened to your brother."

Eric told Alexei about the night of the attack and the full extent of his brother's injuries. "He's recovering, but it will be a while before he is up and about," he explained. "I haven't seen Trelane since he regained consciousness because I've spent most of my recent nights searching taverns and pubs for the brigands who attacked him."

"Yes, I know. That Nag's Head Pub you visited in the East End last night was one of the seediest establishments I have ever seen."

Eric frowned. "You couldn't have followed me in there. I would have seen you."

"I wore a disguise. Do you recall seeing a hunch-backed man sitting at a table by the front door?"

"Now that you mention it, I do. You wore a wide-brimmed hat and had your nose in a tankard of ale. I also remember noticing a strong odor of fish as I passed you."

Alexei grimaced with distaste. "Please, do not remind me. The fellow I bought the clothes from sells herring down by the wharfs. I thought the noxious smell would keep curious people at bay. It worked, but I had to wash my hair and bathe three times to remove the stench from my body. Did you learn anything new last night?"

"No. And it's getting damned frustrating."

"Do you know what the men looked like who attacked your brother?"

Eric shook his head. "Not all of them. But a tall, thin man named Harry was giving the orders. He had a dark beard and a scar high on his left cheek," he said, pointing to a spot on his own face. "Harry was the one who said a lordling was paying them one hundred pounds to do away with Trelane."

"Apparently their employer is a man of means and possibly a gentleman as well. Have you any suspects in that quarter besides Miss Kingsley's father?"

The accuracy of Alexei's statement once again startled Eric. "How in the devil did you know that? I never mentioned a word to you about Sir Francis."

Alexei stood up and put his hand on Eric's shoulder. "Calm yourself, old friend, and stop looking at me as though I am capable of delving into your private thoughts. It was merely deductive reasoning on my part. Why else would you be masquerading as Trelane and not telling Miss Kingsley, unless she had a personal stake in all this? Her father was the obvious choice."

Walking to the window to gaze out onto the bustling street below, Eric sighed. "Forgive my anger. Between my lack of sleep and my inability to figure out what to do next, I'm not fit company for anyone. In answer to your query, there were several men I believed had a motive to harm Trelane. Some he prosecuted and sent to prison, while others, he bested in business deals or political arguments. I simply lack the proof to connect any of them to the crime itself."

"Perhaps the guilty party is a stranger. Someone Trelane has never met."

Eric shook his head. "No. The same gut instinct that convinces me Sir Francis is innocent in all this, tells me that this villain knows my brother very well. It had to be. Who else would have known that Trelane often dismissed his driver and stopped at his government office late at night to work? Just like he did that night after the ball. He was attacked coming out of Westminster Hall, you know."

"Then it stands to reason that the person in question attended the party."

Pressing his brow on the cool glass window, Eric chuckled dryly. "Well, that limits the number to at least five hundred of my family's most intimate friends and associates. Any suggestions which end of the guest list I should start interrogating first,

Alexei?'' When his question went without a reply, he asked, ''What, no more clever suggestions, Alexei? Since when are you so quiet?''

Eric turned and discovered he was alone in the office. Alexei Chernoff was gone. ''Bloody hell! I hate it when he does that.''

There was a knock on the office door. Before he could answer, the young clerk stuck his head inside. ''Begging your pardon, sir, but Lord Chatham's carriage is waiting for you at the curb. The session begins in less than an hour and you wouldn't want to be late.''

''Thank you, Robert. I've got to put on my coat and gather my papers. Tell them I'll be down in a moment.''

Robert nodded. ''Of course, sir. Consider it done.''

Putting his papers in a leather portfolio, Eric looked over at the chair where Alexei had been sitting only a few moments before, and shook his head. *I certainly hope I don't regret trusting Chernoff again. God knows it's a lot easier laughing with the man than trying to kill him.* Something then occurred to him that made him frown. *Bloody hell! Alexei never answered my question. What was he doing at Belle's house the other afternoon?*

''Will there be anything else, Miss Kingsley?''

Belle smiled at Regis Parker, the elderly, white-haired man who ran the stationers' shop. ''Not today, Mr. Parker. I'll take the quills and the bottles of red and black ink with me. If you could have that package of parchment delivered to the house next week, along with the new journal I ordered, I would truly appreciate it."

"Of course, Miss Kingsley." Mr. Parker wrapped the ink and quills in brown paper. "How is your father these days? Needing all these writing supplies, Sir Francis must be working on a book or planning a new expedition. Must be exciting living with such a great man."

Belle pulled on her gloves and fought to keep her smile in place. "Well, you know Papa, Mr. Parker. He's always busy doing something."

Mr. Parker nodded as he tied string around the package. "With his traveling and all, there's not a bit of moss growing under Sir Francis's feet, I imagine."

Nor Paris's or Trelane's either, Belle mused to herself. *I seem to be the only one sitting at home these days. Papa and Paris are God knows where, while Trelane has been too busy to stop by for even a five-minute visit since that debacle with Mr. Chernoff last week. If I didn't receive those sweet little notes from him every morning, I'd begin to suspect that Trelane was out of the country, too!*

The old stationer handed her the package and hurried around the counter to open the door for her. "Thank you for your patronage and take care, Miss Kingsley. Please give my best regards to your father."

She nodded. "I will, sir. Good day."

Belle stepped outside onto the cobblestone walkway. "Now, where did my hackney go? I told the driver to wait for me at the curb." Looking up and down the crowded thoroughfare, she adjusted her spectacles and saw the coach with the dappled gray horse parked on the other side of the street. "Thank goodness he hasn't deserted me. The last thing I need is any more feelings of abandonment today."

She was running across the street when a woman pushing a cart of apples crossed her path and prevented her from reaching the curb. "Sorry, yer ladyship," the old woman cackled. "I didn't see ye comin'."

"That's quite all right, madam," Belle assured her. "I usually suffer from that same affliction myself. Good day."

Belle gingerly stepped around the cart and found herself edging past a group of workmen loading a cargo wagon parked at the curb. Without warning, she was suddenly grabbed around the waist by one of the men and dragged into a nearby alley. She screamed and fought to escape, but her attacker slapped his calloused hand over her mouth and shoved her against a large crate standing beside the building.

"Stop fighting me, Miss Kingsley!" he growled near her ear. "I got me gun and I ain't afraid to use it. We just wants to talk to you for a bit. If you give us what we want, no harm'll come to you, I swears it. Awright?"

Belle looked over her shoulder at him. Nothing

in the bearded man's scarred face or demeanor invoked her trust. She didn't doubt for a moment that he would kill her. *Perhaps if I pretend to comply, he will let down his guard and I can get away.* She nodded and stopped struggling. The moment he relaxed his hold, Belle stomped the heel of her sturdy walking boot onto the man's foot, slammed her elbow into his ribs, and cracked him soundly on the head with her package. The force of the blow caused the bottles to break and sent streams of ink running out of the package. The black and red liquid spattered them both, including the man's eyes.

"You bloody bitch! I can't see! I can't see!" he shouted, rubbing frantically at his face with his hands. "What did you do to me eyes?"

"Oh, my goodness!" Belle dropped the dripping package on the ground and turned to the street. She'd barely taken a step when three men came rushing toward her.

"Get her, boys," her attacker bellowed. "Don't let the chit get away!"

Lifting her skirts, Belle tried to retreat in the other direction, but it was too late. The youngest of the trio, a gangly youth with long legs and dark hair, quickly caught up with her and knocked her down. The impact caused her spectacles to fly from her face and her head to hit the cobblestone-covered ground. Panic and peril were forgotten as Belle fell into unconsciousness from the blow.

* * *

"Where did she go?" Alexei tore off his wide-brimmed hat and the woolen scarf that hid his face and jumped down from the driver's seat on the hackney he'd hired for the day. *I saw Miss Kingsley leave the stationers' a few minutes ago and cross the road in this direction, but I do not see her now. Did she go into another shop?*

Alexei anxiously ran his hand over his long hair that was clubbed back at the nape of his neck. His secret attempt to protect Belle Kingsley without her knowledge was proving far more difficult than he'd originally planned. Tossing his disguise into the cab, he made his way down the street to find her. A cargo wagon hauling a large crate inched past him through the crowded traffic as he arrived in front of the stationers'. He looked in all directions, but couldn't see her. The building across the way was a leather shop that was closed for lunch. A chill ran up his spine. Belle was gone. Someone had taken her.

"By the saints, I have to find her! Grayson will kill me."

Alexei was trying to decide where to look first when an old lady with a fruit cart tapped his arm. "Would ye like an apple, sir? I've nice red apples today."

He shook his head. "No, mother. None today, thank you. I am looking for a young lady who just came out of the stationers' a few minutes ago."

"Was she a pretty lady in dark blue with yellow hair and fancy spectacles?"

Realizing the peddler had seen Belle, Alexei took a handful of coins from his pocket and held it out to her. "Yes, she is the one I am searching for. Tell me where she went and I will pay for every apple on your cart."

The old woman's eyes rounded at the sight of the money. " 'Tis generous indeed you are, sir. But the last I saw o' her was when she was talkin' to the workman over there in the alley," she said, nodding to the opening between the buildings. "Now your pretty lady's gone and the wagon the man was loadin' is gone, too."

He put the coins in the woman's hand. "My thanks, mother."

Alexei ran into the alley and found the broken package seeping with ink on the ground. A short distance away, he saw something glittering on the cobblestones. He hurried toward it and seconds later was holding a delicate pair of gold spectacles. The lens on the left was shattered. He stuffed them into his coat pocket and returned to the street and the apple peddler.

"Mother, the workman who was talking to my lady, do you recall what he looked like?"

The old woman chuckled and shook her head. "My eyes ain't what they should be so I can't tell you what he looked like or the three blokes with him, but I did see that wagon o' his. Had green spoked wheels and a wood crate on it. 'Twas sitting in my usual spot here on the street, lordly as ye please. I was gonna complain, but they drove off.'' Turning her head, she squinted her ancient eyes and pointed. "If you hurry, you can catch 'em. I think that's his rig down by the corner."

Alexei needed no further urging. Running back to his hired coach and donning his hat, he was soon following the cargo wagon through the streets of London. He kept his distance so as not to alert them to his presence. There were four men on the wagon. Three of them were big, burly sorts. The fourth appeared far younger than the rest and was perched on top of the large crate on the bed of the wagon.

Anger surged inside him. *They abducted Miss Kingsley and placed her inside that foul box. When I get through dealing with these miscreants, I will stuff their worthless bodies into that crate and set a torch to it!*

A while later, the wagon pulled up to a deserted warehouse near the river not far from Westminster Hall. Alexei drove past as the men lifted the box off the wagon and carried it inside. Parking the hackney a block away, he hurried back to the building and looked in the windows until he found where the men were. Thankfully, they were too busy tearing off the side of the crate to notice him.

Just as Alexei suspected, Belle was in the box. She was gagged with a scarf and her hands were bound together. A tall, bearded man lifted her onto a chair in the middle of the room. Belle was battered, her clothes were filthy, but she appeared to be all right.

Alexei carefully regarded the men in the room.

I can handle three or four villains without a problem, but I am going to need help if I am to get Miss Kingsley out of there unscathed. He took out his pocket watch and noted the time. *Eric's attending a luncheon meeting with Jonathan Carlisle at Slaton's which is less than a mile from here. How can I go for him and be sure that nothing happens to the lady while I am gone? Dear God, what should I do?*

Returning to the street, Alexei saw a shabbily dressed youth walking toward him. He called out to him. "Would you like to earn fifty pounds?"

The boy, who appeared to be around twelve years old, gaped at him. "Who do you want killed for that much blunt, milord?"

"No one. What is your name, lad?"

"Me name's Tony. Tony Piper. So, what do I gotta do for the money?"

"I need you to go to Slaton's and fetch my friend for me. Do you know where Slaton's is?"

"Aye. Me Pa's a sweep, and a damned good one," Tony boasted. "I helped 'im clean the chimneys in that place last week."

Alexei took a fifty-pound note from his pocket and tore it in half. He gave one of the pieces to the boy. "Go to Slaton's and ask the footman to call Trelane Grayson to the door. Tell Lord Grayson that Alexei needs him and that Belle is in trouble. Come to the back to this building with my friend, and I will give you the other half of this bill. Can you remember the message?"

Tony frowned. "O' course, I can. I ain't stupid. Tell Lord Grayson that Alexei needs 'im and that

Belle's in trouble. But what happens if this bloke don't believe me? I'll have nothin' to show for me efforts."

Alexei took the broken spectacles from his pocket and handed them to the boy. "Give these to Grayson and he will follow you to the ends of the world, Tony. Now get going. We haven't a moment to spare."

CHAPTER 7

"I ask you again, lady, where is the special key?"

Belle shook her head, sending her unpinned hair over her shoulders in disarray. "I have no idea what you're asking for, sir. As I've told you for the better part of an hour, the only key I possess is the one to the front door of my home."

He raised his arm. "For half a pence, I'd smack you again for lying. Now where's the bloody key?"

"You could strike me for free and it wouldn't make a difference," she countered, scowling up at the bearded man looming over her. "I'm telling you the truth. I really don't know what key you're talking about."

"Harry, leave off, will ya," the young, dark-haired man known as Ned called from where he was sitting on top of the crate. "Maybe the chit's tellin' ya the truth. The one you should be wonderin' about lying is his bloody lordship who hired us for this job. Me and the rest o' the boys think he's crazy. Ain't that right, lads?"

The other two men grunted and nodded.

Harry sniffed. "I don't trust that toff as far as I can toss him either, but he owes us money. First he says we beat the man too badly, then he says we didn't do the job at all. I just want to find his damned key, collect what's due, and be done with him once and for all."

"We're wastin' time, Harry. Dealin' with his sort can only get us hung."

"Shut yer trap or get out, Ned. I don't need no boy tellin' me how to conduct me business."

Belle didn't know why her abductors were arguing, and didn't care. In spite of her bravado, she was frightened beyond belief. Her head was pounding and she felt sick to her stomach. But no matter how steep the odds were against her, she wasn't prepared to die. Closing her eyes, she prayed for a miracle.

"What goes on here, Alexei? Where's Belle?"

Alexei held up his hands as Eric rushed toward him behind the warehouse. "Keep your voice down, Grayson. Belle is inside with the villains who abducted her. She's alive and holding her own, praise God. Crouch down beside this broken window and you can see her for yourself."

The sight of Belle bruised and disheveled with her head bowed low caused agonizing pain to rip through Eric. He would have forgotten all about his training as a soldier and crashed through the window to rescue her at that second if Alexei wasn't holding him by the shoulders to prevent him from moving.

"Calm yourself, my friend. If we are to save your lady, we must plan this out carefully or she could be hurt. Did anyone come with you?"

Not looking away from Belle, Eric nodded. "Yes, Jonathan will be here in a moment with his driver and footman. He's loading the two pistols and rifle he keeps in the carriage. I gave your young messenger his reward and sent him home." He glanced back at Alexei. "While we're waiting, would you mind telling me how you knew where to find me and that Belle was being abducted?"

Alexei leaned against the building beside him. "I got into your brother's office last night by picking the lock. That eager clerk of his keeps a record of all your appointments listed on his calendar. As to Miss Kingsley, after you told me about the attack on Trelane, I had a suspicion she might be in danger as well, so I began following her two days ago. This morning I disguised myself as a hackney driver and allowed her to hire my services for the day."

"Belle didn't recognize you?"

Smiling, Alexei shook his head. "No. I have become quite adept at playing roles over the years. Miss Kingsley had no idea who I was beneath the disguise." His face suddenly grew somber. "I believe the man who attacked your brother is the same one who kidnaped her. He has a scar on his cheek as you described and I heard the other fellow call him Harry. He also appears to be the only one inside carrying a gun."

Eric saw the man in question and nodded. "Yes, that's him. He seems to be arguing with his men. Any idea why he abducted Belle?"

"I could not hear what they were saying, but I saw Miss Kingsley shaking her head. Whatever he demanded from her, she adamantly said no." Alexei straightened up and moved away from the building. "Jonathan is here with his men."

"Fine. Now we can get this over with." Casting one more look at Belle, Eric stood up and removed his elegant tailcoat and neatly tied cravat. "I know just the way to do it, too. When I get through with Harry and his cohorts, they will rue the day they first saw this face."

"Harry, I wasn't tellin' you what to do," Ned insisted. "We just don't want to end up on the gibbet cause o' this bloke and that's what the law will do to us for snatchin' a lady. What if his lordship's wrong and there ain't no special key at all?"

Harry frowned and walked back to Belle. "There's a special key, awright. He said he saw it hisself and she had it. I just gotta convince her to give it up to me."

"But Harry—"

"Shut your trap, Ned. If you ain't got the stomach for the job, just step away and leave me to do it." He cocked the hammer of his pistol. Yanking Belle by the hair, he pulled her head back and waved his gun under her nose. "Look here, wench, I'm tired o' playin' games with you. You're gonna tell me where the key is or I'll—"

"Put down that gun and take your hands off my lady, Harry," Eric called out as he entered the warehouse.

Belle saw him and gasped. "Trelane!"

Harry's eyes rounded in disbelief. "Hell, I thought we killed you weeks ago!"

Ned jumped down from the crate and backed away from Eric with the other two men. "We did kill 'im, Harry. Honest we did. I checked him meself. He was all bloody and broken up. Maybe he's a ghost!"

Eric kept walking toward Harry, carefully keeping his gaze averted from Belle's so he wouldn't lose control. "Perhaps I am a ghost come to exact my revenge on the villains who killed me late one night behind Westminster Hall."

"Y-you don't frighten me," Harry chuckled nervously as he put his arm around Belle's neck and pulled her out of the chair. "Ain't no such things as ghosts."

Stopping only a few feet away from where Harry was holding Belle like a shield before him, Eric smiled. "Oh, really? Then how do you explain my undamaged appearance, Harry? My knowing that you'd taken my lady and my ability to find you like this? Divine intervention?"

Harry shook his head. "I don't know and I bloody well don't care. But I'm gonna get outta this place and I'm takin' her with me. Try and stop me, and I'll pull the trigger and kill her, I swear it!"

Eric sighed in mock indifference. "I think not, Harry. You see, unlike the night you and your men attacked me behind Westminster Hall, I haven't come alone. This time, you lads are the ones sorely outnumbered."

"You walk in here bold as brass, not even carryin' a weapon. Why should I believe you?"

Taking a casual pose, Eric looped his hands behind his back and nodded toward the window. "You better believe me, Harry. Because if you don't step away from the lady, my friend out there will shoot you where you stand. And His Grace is an excellent shot, I assure you."

Harry glanced quickly to his left and saw Jonathan Carlisle standing outside of the broken window, aiming the sights of his rifle directly at him. The man's face went pale beneath his beard. "That's the Duke o' Chatham! He's friends of the bloomin' queen! I ne'er said I'd get involved with the likes o' him."

Eric wrapped the fingers of his left hand firmly around the butt of the pistol tucked into the waistband at the back of his trousers and eased it out. He laughed to cover the sound when he pulled back the hammer on the weapon. "Chatham's also my uncle and best friend. Apparently your employer didn't mention that fact to you either."

"See, Harry, I warned you," Ned exclaimed. "That fool lord that hired you's gonna get us all hung for this. I'm not waiting for the constables to arrest me. Come on, lads, let's get outta here."

As his three compatriots ran toward the back door of the warehouse, Harry's temper exploded. "You cowardly bastards!" he shouted. "Get back here or I'll hunt you down and shoot you meself!"

With Harry's attention diverted to the fleeing men, Eric knew it was time to put his battle plan into motion. Pandemonium became the order of the day when he brought his own weapon forward and shot the pistol from the outlaw's hand. The gun hit the floor and went off on its own. Belle screamed and Eric charged at Harry, knocking him away from her. At that precise moment, Alexei and the two coachmen rushed in the back door and grappled with the men who were trying to escape. Pent-up anger and a thirst for revenge fueled Eric as he pounded his fists mercilessly into his struggling opponent until the man was barely moving. He might have killed him then and there if the sound of Jonathan's voice and the meaning of his words had not penetrated his blood-driven rage.

"Eric, come quickly! Belle's been shot!"

Eric turned to see Jonathan kneeling on the floor beside Belle. She was unconscious with blood running down the side of her pale face. "Dear God, no!" he screamed. All else was forgotten as he rushed to Belle and gathered her in his arms.

Alexei hurried over at the same time and held out Eric's coat to him. "Cover her with this and keep her warm while I check her wound."

"Check her wound? Bloody hell, Alexei, she's been shot in the head!" Eric protested. "We have no time for your amateur attempts at patching her up. I must get her to a real physician before she dies."

Disregarding Eric's terse comments, Alexei knelt beside him and draped the coat over Belle. "Her color is good and she is breathing without difficulty. I think she was only grazed by the bullet." He moved the blood-dampened hair away from Belle's temple and dabbed the wound with his handkerchief. "Praise be, it is exactly as I suspected. Miss Kingsley was nicked along the temple by the shot. She may require a stitch or two to limit the scarring and her head might ache a bit, but I am sure she will be all right."

"But how can you say that? She's unconscious. Perhaps the wound is worse than it appears."

"Miss Kingsley obviously fainted. After what she has endured today, it certainly is not surprising. Stop worrying, my friend. Your lady will be fine." Alexei pressed his folded handkerchief against her wound. "Eric, hold this in place to stanch the bleeding. I will relieve Jonathan's driver from guarding our prisoners so he can fetch the coach so you can take her to a physician. The footman has already gone for the constables."

Eric's frown deepened. "Prisoners? Hell, I'd nearly forgotten about them. Did we get them all?"

Alexei stood up and walked away as Jonathan came over with the news. "No, the young one with the dark hair managed to escape during the melee. We did capture the other two and their leader hasn't come to his senses yet. From the looks of him, I'm afraid that won't be happening anytime soon. You gave him quite a beating, Eric."

Cradling Belle against him, Eric kissed her brow. "The bastard deserved it. I only wish I had killed him for what he did to Belle."

"Your sentiments are understandable but hardly prudent, Eric. We need him to identify whoever hired him to attack Trelane."

Eric looked over at Harry and scowled. "He probably doesn't know his employer's real name anyway. Cowards who employ others to do their dirty work seldom reveal themselves totally to their lackeys."

Jonathan nodded. "Rather like the way that person got the manager of Slaton's to act as go-between when he hired the runners to look for Sir Francis. Too bad that manager, George Miller, hasn't returned from his holiday to Bath yet. I'd really like to know who at the club is searching for Belle's father."

"You know, Jonathan, I've been wondering if the person who paid for the attack on Trelane might possibly be the same—"

Belle whimpered and began thrashing about in his arms. "I have no special key. Go away . . . Oh, my head hurts," she groaned.

He gently kissed her cheek. "I know, sweetheart.

Your abductor's pistol went off when it hit the floor and it's shot grazed your temple."

She opened her eyes to look at him. "Oh, yes, I remember. Those foul men kidnaped me and you came to my rescue. Just like a hero in a fairy tale."

"Some hero I turned out to be," Eric scoffed, lifting the handkerchief to check her wound. "You were nearly killed today because I didn't realize you were in danger. I should have known better. I should have kept you safe."

Smiling, Belle touched his cheek with her hand. "Stop fretting. You came when I needed you and that's what matters. However did you know that—" She suddenly winced and closed her eyes. "I wish this incessant throbbing in my head would cease. It reminds me of someone pounding on a large kettle drum."

Pleased that Belle was awake but distressed by her pain, Eric turned to Jonathan. "See if your man's brought the rig around back yet. In spite of Alexei's optimism, I won't rest easy until Justin or someone on his staff examines her."

When Jonathan called out that the coach was at the door, Eric stood up and carried her into the waiting conveyance. He carefully placed her across his lap. "Rest your cheek on my chest and try not to move your head too much, sweetheart," he cautioned. "We don't want your wound to start bleeding again."

Belle sighed. "I like you calling me 'sweetheart.'

In spite of my pain, hearing you say it makes me feel cherished."

Looking down at the top of her head as she nestled against him, so trusting and peaceful, assailed Eric's conscience. *You may think that now, but when you've learned of my deception, Belle, you'll likely despise my endearment. God knows I would give all I possess to make it otherwise, my love.*

A bit of laughter came from Belle's lips. "I suddenly realized that this is the first time I've ever seen you in a shirt without a coat and cravat." Her hand innocently stroked his chest. "My goodness, I never realized how well developed your muscles are, Trelane. All that writing and carrying law books around must be harder work than I ever imagined."

Eric couldn't reply. The only thing he could do was inhale deeply and battle the sensations her touch was causing.

"You know, Trelane, this injury to my head must have addled my thoughts a bit. When I was waking up, the oddest things went through my mind. I could have sworn I heard you talking about yourself as though you were somebody else. Isn't that silly? I also imagined that I heard Mr. Chernoff speaking with you. He even called you his friend." She snickered. "Considering how poorly you treated that man in my house on your last visit, that's not likely to happen anytime soon. One day you really must explain to me why you dislike Mr. Chernoff so much. My curiosity over your attitude toward him is absolutely maddening."

Eric swallowed hard. *Bloody hell! She heard us talking. I want to tell her the truth, but not now. Not like this! Perhaps I can change the subject and find a way to get her thinking about something else.* He cleared his throat. "All this talking and activity mustn't be good for your injury." He cuddled her closer to him with his right arm. "Shut your eyes and rest yourself until we arrive at Justin's office, sweetheart."

"You must be right, Trelane. My wound is bleeding again. I feel blood trickling down my cheek. May I borrow your handkerchief?"

"I have the one I was using before here in my hand, sweetheart. You sit back and let me do it for you."

"This is nice," she sighed as he gently wiped the blood from her face. "You taking care of me. I could get quite spoiled by all this lovely treatment. . . ." Her voice faded for a moment. "What's that mark on your wrist, Trelane? Were you injured in the scuffle with that man?"

Eric tried to pull his hand away, but it was too late. Belle was pushing back the cuff of his shirt, staring at the lightning bolt indelibly marked into the skin of his wrist and inner arm. "Belle, sweetheart, I can explain—"

"Good grief, I told Paris she was being ridiculous when she said you had a tattoo. You would never allow such a thing to be etched into your skin with ink . . . Why, this isn't a tattoo at all!" She ran her fingers over the raised skin. "It's a scar." Belle turned to face him. "The design looks too perfect to have been an accident. How did this happen, Trelane? Who did this to you?''

Eric was incapable of answering. He gazed into her shimmering eyes and willed himself to reply, but all the things he knew he should say to Belle at that moment just wouldn't come out. He was a coward! How could he tell the only woman he had ever loved that he was a fraud and a liar? How would he be able to deal with her hatred and scorn when she learned of his deception? Where would he find the courage to tell her the truth?

As it turned out, he didn't need to say anything at all. Belle sorted out the answer on her own.

''Dear Lord, you're . . . you're not Trelane, are you?''

''Belle, I need to explain—''

Shaking her head, she struggled to get off his lap. ''Of course you're not Trelane. I wasn't dreaming back in that warehouse. I heard you and the others talking. I heard them calling you Eric. You're his twin, the prodigal son who ran away eighteen years ago and never came back. Where's Trelane? What's happened to him?''

The sheer panic in her voice and eyes tore at Eric's heart. ''Please calm down, Belle. I don't think you're up to hearing about this now.''

Desperate, Belle threw herself against the door and grabbed the handle. ''Tell me this instant or by God, I'll leap out of this coach and you can explain it all to the authorities when my body is found on the road.''

''No! Please don't do that, Belle,'' he implored.

"Please, just sit over there and I will tell you everything."

She nodded. When he reached out to help her onto the seat across from him, she slapped his hands away. "Don't touch me! Haven't you done enough of that already?"

The heat of her anger burned far worse than the brand that had marred his skin in Venice two years before. Rather than dwell on his own suffering, he told her about his return to England the night of the engagement party and how Trelane was beaten and left for dead behind Westminster Hall.

"So your mother asked you to pretend to be your brother in an attempt to find the man responsible for the attack on Trelane. Why didn't anyone tell *me* about the charade? I would have done anything to help you find him." Before Eric could reply, Belle figured out the answer for herself. "Your family thought my father was the one who did it! All because Trelane wouldn't approve of his application for his search for the Grail!"

Eric shrugged. "Well, at the time, it seemed to be a plausible explanation. But I—"

"Of all the nerve! My father is a scientist, a man of learning. He would never harm another person, no matter what the cause. How could you even suggest that he would do such a dishonorable thing?"

Eric held up his hands in surrender. "I agree with you wholeheartedly, Belle. But when all this began, Sir Francis seemed the obvious choice.

Once I learned about the close relationship you share with him, I knew he'd never do anything to harm you or the man you were to marry. That's precisely why I've been searching for someone else who might have had a motive to kill my brother. And after what happened to you this afternoon, my parents will have no choice but to agree that your father is innocent."

Belle sniffed indignantly. "How benevolent of them! That still doesn't excuse what their suspicions have put me through. During these past weeks, I've been courted, kissed, and nearly made love to by a stranger. Did you or anyone else in your family ever wonder how that would make me feel?"

Tears welled in her eyes as she turned her flushed face toward the window. "I've been such a brainless twit! Thinking my future husband had fallen in love with me. Me, the mousy little spinster that no man ever looked at twice! How could I have been so gullible to imagine that a handsome gentleman like Trelane would actually love me?"

"Trelane would be a damned fool if he didn't love you, Belle. You're bright and beautiful, and have a lot to offer a man."

Brushing the tears from her face, Belle chuckled derisively at his words. "Oh, yes, I have so much to offer. I'm half blind and require spectacles to find my way around or risk getting lost. I have a father who's as crazy as a loon and a boorish cousin who insults everyone she meets here in England with her uncouth behavior. What a magnificent prize I am!''

"Don't deride yourself like that, Belle. You are an incredible young woman, lovely, intelligent, and far better than most men deserve. My brother isn't stupid. You are a jewel beyond price, and he knows it.''

Instead of comforting her, his comments set off a rage in Belle that caused her to glare at him. "As if I should believe a single word you say, Eric Grayson! You're a liar and a cheat. A man without scruples or moral conscience. If you'd had an ounce of honor inside you, you never would have touched me. That day in my father's study, you would have taken me there on the sofa if my house-keeper hadn't come to the door. How do you think your brother is going to react when he learns that you nearly seduced me? Me, the woman he was engaged to marry.''

The hatred in her eyes made Eric cringe inside. "Trelane will probably want to kill me and I wouldn't blame him.''

"I could not care less what happens to any of you. After today, I . . .'' Her voice faded as the coach pulled to a stop. She leaned over to look out the window. "Where are we? Without my spectacles, I can't see a foot in front of me.''

"My Uncle Justin's medical clinic. I want him to examine your wound and be sure that you're all right.''

Belle sat up and shook her head. "Well, I'm not

going in there. Take me home and I will take care of myself."

"Don't be ridiculous, Belle. You were almost killed by that shot. A fraction of an inch closer and you would have been dead. My uncle is the finest physician in London. Let him see to your injury."

As the footman opened the door, Belle grabbed the handle and pulled it shut. "I'd sooner give myself over to a heathen witch doctor in Africa than deal with anyone remotely connected to you, Mr. Grayson. As far as I'm concerned, you and your entire illustrious family can jolly well go to the devil! Now, take me home."

From her tone and the stubborn tilt of her chin, Eric knew it would be futile to argue with Belle. "I will do as you request, but only if you promise to send for your own physician if your pain grows any worse."

At her brisk nod of acceptance, he gave instructions to the footman and the coach was soon on its way. Though the drive was little more than a mile, Belle's silence made it seem like an eternity. She sat across from him, quietly staring out the window, her hands folded primly in her lap. Although her clothes were filthy and torn and her hair was wildly disarrayed around her bruised face, there was no mistaking the fact that Belle Kingsley was every inch a lady.

A lady who had captured his heart and was stepping out of his life forever. And because of his actions, Trelane's life as well.

That single thought made him do a reckless thing

a short while later. As Belle stepped from the coach with the aid of the footman and walked to her door, Eric called out to her. "I may have lied and deceived you, Belle, but you deserve to know the truth. I love you. I have loved you since I held you in my arms the night of your engagement party in my father's library. It was wrong of me to deceive you and I deserve your hatred, but Trelane doesn't. Before you break your betrothal to my brother, remember he was the innocent in all this. Don't compound my sin by making him suffer because of me. He's a good man, Belle, and would make you a very fine husband. Promise me you won't make any rash decisions before talking to him first."

Belle didn't turn to look at him, but slowly nodded. A moment later, she stepped into the house and closed the door.

Shouting orders to the driver, Eric fell back in his seat. *Well, I'm done with this ruse. No more skulking about in the dark, afraid to be seen going into the house. Once I talk to Trelane, I'll pack my things and be away from here by morning. The sooner I'm gone, the better things will be for everyone.*

It was then that he spotted the coat he'd been wearing that day, lying on the floor of the coach in a wrinkled mess. "Bloody hell! Trelane's blasted coat is ruined. That's one more thing he'll hate me for." While he was brushing off the dark, superfine wool coat, his hand brushed against the bulge in its pocket. "What in the world is that?"

He put his hand inside and drew out the broken

spectacles. A lump formed in his throat as his fingers caressed the delicate gilded frame. He thought about going back to the Kingsleys' house to return them, but quickly changed his mind. He'd lost his heart, the lady, and the yearning to be with his family. This small bit of metal and glass was all he had left of Belle. He would cherish it as he would cherish the memories of her, forever.

CHAPTER 8

The sun was setting like a ball of fire on the horizon as Eric entered the kitchens of his family's home and hurried past the servants preparing dinner. Wanting a chance to speak with his brother alone, he ran up the back stairs to Trelane's room. The sight that met his eyes when he opened the door nailed him to the floor.

Trelane was awake and sitting up in bed. But he wasn't alone. Paris Mackenzie was sitting in his lap and he was kissing her.

"What in the hell goes on here?" Eric shouted, stepping over the threshold.

Paris scrambled off the bed. "We . . . ah . . . we ah . . ." she stammered and brushed down the skirts of her rumpled gown. Obviously at a loss for words, she frowned at Trelane. "Would you kindly answer your brother, Lane? From the look on his face, Eric isn't very pleased to find us together like this."

Adjusting the sling that held his broken arm, Trelane stared at his twin. "What can I say to a brother I haven't seen in eighteen years? Welcome home? Fancy meeting you here? Will you be staying long, brother dear?"

Paris groaned and shook her head. "You're not helping things, Lane. Perhaps I should just go and let the two of you work things out."

She was nearly to the door when Trelane called to her. "Paris, my dear?"

"Yes, Lane?"

He scowled at her. "Would you please stop calling me Lane? It's not my name."

When he winked, her uncertain frown suddenly turned into a smile. "You will always be Lane to me, sir, so stop complaining and accept it." Blowing him a kiss, she hurried out and closed the door.

For several moments the two men didn't speak. Each one simply took the time to study the other. Trelane's brow rose first. "Well, the prodigal son has come home at last. Has Mama offered to slay the fatted calf to celebrate your return, brother?"

Eric walked closer to the bed. "Save your clever repartee for your political cronies, Trelane. I'm not in the mood for it."

"Apparently your time away hasn't done a thing to sweeten your rather sullen disposition, either.

If you have something to say to me, Eric, just get on with it. Who knows? I might not mind hearing it at all.''

His twin's somewhat glib demeanor goaded Eric into losing his temper. "Bloody hell, Trelane! You're engaged to marry Belle Kingsley. What were you doing with her cousin in your bed? Keeping yourself amused during your recuperation? If you weren't already wearing splints on your leg and arm, I would beat the hell out of you for betraying Belle like this!''

"And I would allow you to do it without protest, because I agree with you, Eric.''

Eric glowered at him and folded his arms across his chest. "Oh, really? Why do I find that difficult to believe?''

Trelane smiled sadly at his brother's skepticism. "Well, you should believe it, because it's true. I never intended to betray Belle. She's a lovely young woman and would have been an excellent wife for me. We're good friends and we suit very well, but I made the mistake of falling in love with Paris Mackenzie.''

"You love Paris? But in your journal, you called her the red-haired witch from Philadelphia and said you hated her.''

Trelane shrugged. "At the time, I thought I did. For weeks after she arrived from America that damnable woman plagued me with her taunting and disrespectful ways. She was so unpredictable, I couldn't stand to be around her. Paris fired my anger and challenged my logic at every turn. She could have me ranting and raving in a matter of seconds."

Perplexed, Eric fell into the chair beside the bed. "And you love this woman?"

He nodded. "Oh, yes. You see, Paris evokes emotions in me that no one else ever has. She's brought passion into my life. Though she often makes me shout and scream, she also knows how to make me laugh and cry. It might surprise you to know that she was the one who told me that my jealousy of you was—"

"You're jealous of me?"

Trelane smiled. "Of course I was, twit. You got to go off on your grand adventure while I was forced to stay at home and be the perfect son. Have you any idea how cheated I felt, how pressured I was when you were gone?"

Eric's frown grew deeper. "I asked you to come with me when I ran away from the ship that night in Greece."

Closing his eyes for a moment, Trelane leaned back against his pillows. "Ah, yes. When we docked in Athens, you'd learned that your hero, Lord Byron, had been killed helping the rebels fight for their independence. You were only sixteen, but you wanted to avenge his death and take his place in the battle."

"Are you mocking me?"

Trelane looked up at him. "Not at all. If anything, I admire your courage and wished I'd had your strength of conviction back then. I quickly grew to hate your nobility and independence. Yet in reality, what I hated most was being apart from you."

"You could have come with me."

He shook his head. "No, Eric. The path you chose was your own. Though I didn't know it at the time, mine was here in England. It just took me several years to sort it out. At first I thought being a prosecutor and convicting felons was the thing to do. But the laws are archaic and need changing. That's why I decided to get involved in politics. As a member of Parliament, I could help write new laws and perhaps make a difference in this country."

Eric chuckled. "So when are you going to run for Prime Minister?"

"Not anytime soon, I assure you." Trelane patted his broken arm. "First I'm going to find out who was responsible for this and the rest of my injuries and make them pay. Have you uncovered any new information?"

"No, but something happened that could lead us to the culprit. Belle was kidnaped coming out of the stationers' this afternoon—"

"Good God," Trelane interrupted, tossing back his blankets as he tried to get out of bed, "have the authorities been notified? Did you get a ransom demand for her release? Why are you sitting here and not out searching for her?"

Eric stood up and eased his brother back under the covers. "Calm yourself. Belle is fine. A former colleague of mine, Alexei Chernoff, witnessed the crime and followed them to a deserted warehouse.

He got word to me and together with Jonathan's aid, we rescued her. The men who abducted her were the same ones who assailed you behind Westminster Hall.''

"How can you be sure of that? Did they confess?"

"No. I recognized their leader from the vision I had of your attack while I was sleeping. The others called him Harry. He was a tall, thin man with a beard and a nasty-looking scar, right about here,'' Eric replied, pointing toward the spot on his cheekbone.

Trelane nodded. "Yes, that sounds like him. My memories of that night are still a bit vague, but I remember him with crystal clarity. Mama told me about your visions of me and how my bad dreams in the past few years were actually about you. Strange, isn't it? Even though continents separated us, a part of us kept in touch with one another, just like Mama and Aunt Victoria did when they were younger.''

Eric reached over and took hold of his brother's hand. "Thank the Lord, Mama was here when I woke up that night or I might never have made the connection between my dream and what was happening to you. Losing you after coming halfway 'round the world to set things right between us is just too horrible to consider.''

"Do you really think we can set things right, Eric?''

"We have to, Trelane. As twins, the two of us share things that no one else can. Yet because we were so alike, resentment reared its ugly head and we fought to be individuals. We allowed the differences to keep us apart and that was wrong. I nearly died in that dungeon in Italy before I realized how badly I missed you and wanted to be your friend, Trelane. I'm ready to bridge the gaps between us—are you?''

Caught up in the emotion of the moment, Trelane nodded and had to clear his throat before he could speak. "Of course I am. Welcome home, brother." He gave Eric's hand a quick squeeze before releasing it. "You've grown to be quite the philosopher while you were away."

Eric shrugged. "Coming face-to-face with one's mortality can do that. It's amazing how many things that never occurred to you before suddenly rise to the surface when you think you're going to die."

Trelane let out a low moan as he wearily leaned back against his pillows and shut his eyes. "I know exactly what you mean. I've done a bit of that kind of soul-searching myself these past weeks."

"Are you going to marry Paris Mackenzie?"

If Trelane was shocked by the sudden change of topics, he didn't show it. Without opening his eyes he replied, "Perhaps. I just know that I can't marry Belle while having all these unresolved feelings for her cousin. It wouldn't be fair to her or any of us if I did otherwise."

Eric sighed. "Bloody hell! What am I to do now?"

Frowning, Trelane looked over at him. "What are you talking about?"

"I told Belle the truth today about everything that's been going on since your attack and she was outraged. She was so upset over the deception that she was breaking your engagement. I told her you were the innocent in all this and made her promise not to end things before speaking to you first.''

''Belle was going to cry off as simple as that and you talked her out of it?'' At Eric's nod, Trelane groaned. ''Bloody hell is right! Thanks for your help, brother. When the lady discovers that I've taken up with her cousin, will you load the pistol for her so she can shoot me without a delay?''

''Are you jesting? If I was foolish enough to put a loaded weapon in Belle's hand, she'd likely use it on me. The woman hates me for deceiving her and I can't fault her for that.''

''Well, you'll simply have to convince Belle that she's wrong.''

Eric frowned at his brother. ''Wrong about what? I lied to her. I made her believe I was you. I held her in my arms. I kissed her. I—''

''Fell in love with her.'' Trelane's brow arched at his brother's silence. ''Surprised that I noticed? I would have to be blind and deaf not to. Why else would you be so upset on her behalf if you didn't have feelings for her? You love Belle, don't you, Eric?''

Suddenly feeling awkward, Eric got up and began pacing the room. ''So what if I do? Belle detests me. She won't listen to a word I say, no matter how sincere my intentions are.''

''Then try a different approach, Eric. Court Belle. Send her flowers. Write her letters declaring your love. Show her with your actions how you feel about her.''

''I can't. It would be a waste of time and only get her angry.''

Trelane snickered. ''Well, what do you know? My brother, the fearless warrior, is giving up without a fight. Never knew you to run from a battle, Eric.''

Eric spun around to confront him. ''I'm not running away from anything. I'm simply accepting the fact that—''

''You're accepting defeat without even trying! If Belle truly means something to you, Eric, you shouldn't let her get away. Being so close to death, I've come to the realization that life is too short and fickle not to grab onto happiness when it's offered to you. And if being with Belle would make you happy, then you owe it to yourself to go after her. Who knows? Perhaps under all her fury and righteous indignation, she loves you, too.''

Instead of firing back a denial, Eric stopped to consider what Trelane said. *What if he's right and Belle's anger comes from the fact that she has feelings for me. I'd be a fool if I didn't at least try to reason with her. What's the worst she could do? Shoot me? Hell! Even if she had a gun, she'd never be able to use it on me as long as I've got her spectacles safely hidden in my pocket.*

Trelane chuckled. ''I see that smile on your face. You're not going to give up on Belle after all, are you?''

''No, I'm not. I may have to get on my knees and beg that woman to forgive me, but I'll do whatever it takes. First thing tomorrow, I am going to see her."

"And if Belle refuses to let you in her home?"

"Then I'll camp on her doorstep until she does." Eric wearily sat in the chair again and looked down at his soiled clothes. "Damn, I'm a mess! I really should go to my room and get cleaned up before dinner, but I'm too tired to move. Do you mind if I sit here and close my eyes for a few minutes?"

"Not at all. Stay as long as you like. But can I ask you a question first?"

Letting out a yawn, Eric nodded. "Sure. What do you want to know?"

"You said that Belle was rescued. What became of her abductors?"

Eric ran his hand through his disheveled hair. "In all the excitement I completely forgot about them. Jonathan and Alexei must have turned in all three to the constables by now."

"Then the leader, the one they called Harry, is in custody so he can be questioned by the authorities?"

"As far as I know. But if you're expecting to get information from him, you might have to wait a while. During the melee, I got carried away and beat the bastard senseless."

Shrugging his shoulders, Trelane frowned. "Well, I'll just have to curb my curiosity a bit longer then."

"Don't worry. Whether he gives them the information or not, we will find the man who ordered the attack on you, Trelane."

"Oh, I know that will eventually happen. I was simply wondering about that special key Harry kept asking me for the night he and his men—"

Two words in Trelane's statement grabbed Eric's attention. "Special key? That's what Belle was talking about when she woke up from her fainting spell at the warehouse. They must have been asking her for it as well."

"Then you should thank God that you captured those men before they harmed her. They were quite desperate to find it. The more I denied knowing what they were asking about, the more brutal the beating got. Eric, where are you going?"

Eric stopped at the threshold to look back at his brother. "I just remembered. The fourth man in the gang, a young buck with long legs and dark hair, managed to escape. I almost lost Belle this afternoon because I didn't realize she was in danger. I won't make that mistake again."

"What if she refuses to let you in? Belle can be quite stubborn when she's upset."

"I know, but I've got a friend to help me." Eric pulled his jeweled stickpin out of his pants pocket and displayed it like a trophy. "Ruby, here, is going to get me inside, and then I'll deal with Belle. Wish me luck!"

Only a few moments after Eric left, Paris hurried in. "I passed your brother in the hall. He looked angry enough to chew the bark off a tree."

Trelane held up his arm and waited for Paris to join him on the bed. Hugging her close, he kissed her again. "That wasn't anger, my dear. It was determination. Eric's just gone off to fight the biggest battle of his life. And if I know my brother, he won't accept anything less than an unconditional surrender.''

Paris shivered. ''Then I pity his opponent for crossing Eric. I wouldn't want to be the loser in a battle with him.''

Trelane kissed her again. ''Save your pity, dear heart. In this particular skirmish, there won't be any losers. Both of them will be winners, I assure you.''

''Catlin Eric Grayson, are you leaving this house without talking to me?''

Eric stopped at the foot of the back stairs to look up at his mother. ''I'm sorry, Mama. I've got to go see Belle right away and it's getting late. Can't we talk later?''

Catherine came down the steps and frowned at him. ''Always running in and out with never a moment to spare for me. Any news about your brother's attackers?''

''A great deal happened today, but I don't have time to tell you about it right now. Why don't you talk to Trelane? I told him everything and he has all the details. See you tomorrow, Mama.''

She grabbed his arm. ''Just one moment, young man. Let me have a look at you before you go. Why, you're all dressed in black! I used to do that myself years ago when I was um . . .'' She looked around to be sure none of the servants were nearby to hear her. "When I was working at night and didn't want to get caught," she whispered. "Promise me you're not going to get into trouble tonight, Eric. Your father's still smarting over the fact that I was once an outlaw with a price on my head."

Laughing, Eric kissed her cheek. "Don't worry, Mama. The only thing I'm out to steal tonight is a lady's heart." He turned and hurried toward the kitchen door. "Wish me luck, Mama. I'm going to need it!"

"Of course, Eric, I wish you all the luck . . ." Stopping short, Catherine gasped. "Wait a minute! You said you were going to see Belle and she's engaged to marry your brother. Catlin Eric Grayson, get back here this instant!"

Catherine's demand came too late. Eric was gone.

Belle closed the journal she was working on and put it in the desk drawer. "I don't know why I even tried to finish that tonight. My mind's on a dozen other things far more confusing then transcribing hieroglyphics found in an ancient tomb in Alexandria."

Picking up the letter that arrived while she was out, she smiled. "At least Papa will be home soon. I never would have guessed that he had gone to Dublin." She looked at the worn condition of the paper and the smudged ink and sighed as she set it down. "Poor Papa probably wrote this missive weeks ago and carried it in his pocket until he remembered to post it.''

Belle took the spectacles out of her robe pocket and put them on. ''Thank goodness I was able to find these old things. They're not as strong as I need them to be, but it's better than stumbling around half blind. Tomorrow, I'll see about ordering a new pair.''

While she was cleaning off the desk, an odd thought suddenly made her laugh. ''I can't believe I'm standing here talking to myself like this. Must be a habit one develops from spending too much time alone. Well, I can't worry about that now. I have a few other things that need sorting out first.''

Not the least of which was her thoughts about a certain deceitful man named Eric Grayson. She understood his wanting to find the person who harmed his brother, but what he had done to her was unforgivable. He'd lied and kept secrets from her. He'd kissed her and made her want things that no one else ever had. His gentleness and passion coaxed her into believing that the man she was to marry loved her.

Yet Eric's worst sin of all was something she had done on her own. She'd fallen in love with the treacherous rogue!

At first she tried to tell herself that it just wasn't so. Any tender feelings she had toward him were actually meant for Trelane. They had to be! They'd been engaged for months. Her admiration and respect for her future husband had simply grown into love, right? Wrong! She knew exactly when her feelings began to change toward Trelane. It was the night when she found him in the library in his parents' house.

For the first time, he teased and flirted with her. He took her in his arms and kissed her, unconcerned if anyone saw them. He made her feel beautiful. He made her feel desirable. He made her feel loved.

But as she learned that day, the man in the library wasn't Trelane. It was Eric.

Although she tried to deny it, a part of her wasn't surprised by this revelation. In her heart of hearts, she'd noticed the subtle changes in her fiancé following that fated meeting in the library and chose to ignore them. With an uncommon hint of mischief in his eyes, "Trelane" suddenly began to encourage her to wear the bright, jewel-tone colors that she favored. He'd taken her shopping, been attentive to her needs, and even scolded her for not wearing the spectacles that he himself had forbidden her to wear. Not even Paris's warnings that something was different about Trelane could make her see the truth.

"Well, that kind of blindness can't be fixed with spectacles and I only have myself to blame." Belle turned down the wick on the desk lamp to extinguish its light. "First thing in the morning I'll send a message to Lady Catherine and ask when I can visit Trelane. I can't very well marry him while I feel as I do about that scoundrel brother of his. Drat it all! Eric Grayson certainly has made a mess of my life!"

She entered her bedroom a few minutes later and found the oil lamp on her vanity was lit. "How strange. I thought I doused that light after I took my bath and put on my nightgown. Oh, well. Mrs. Tuttle probably lit it for me before she went to bed." Belle looked at the embers glowing in the hearth. "Too bad she didn't place another log on the fire when she was here. This room's a bit chilly tonight."

Belle put a log in the hearth and prodded the embers with a poker until the wood caught the flame and was burning brightly. When she stood up, the muscles in her lower back tightened and caused her to groan in pain. Taking off her robe, she sat on the chair in front of her vanity to look at her reflection in the mirror.

"I don't know what's worse. The bruises on my face, the swelling on the side of my head, or this blasted backache." As she unpinned her hair, she leaned toward the mirror and frowned. "Obviously being abducted is dangerous to one's health."

A strange sensation of being watched caused Belle to turn around and look about her room. Finding nothing there, she shrugged. "Fine. Now I'm imagining things. I must be more tired than I thought."

Belle brushed her hair, carefully avoiding her injuries, and fashioned it into a loose braid. She removed her spectacles, blew out the lamp, and crossed the room to her bed. Wearing a soft flannel nightgown, she got under the covers and slid her bare feet between the cool sheets. "Br-r-r-r-r," she shivered. "I should have worn some woolen socks to bed. My toes are practically numb from the cold."

"Hello, Belle," a familiar male voice whispered near her ear in the dark.

Before she could scream, Eric put his hand over her mouth and stretched out on top of her, effectively imprisoning her beneath the covers. "No screaming or shouting for your housekeeper, sweetheart. Besides, the poor old woman would likely have a stroke from the shock of finding a man in your bed. I've come to tell you something and I'm not leaving until you hear every word I have to say. If you promise not to scream, I'll take my hand away from your mouth."

His use of brute force and the sight of his cocky smile that she could see in the firelight only angered Belle more. Rather than acquiesce to his demands, she sunk her teeth into the palm of his hand.

"Bloody hell!" he cursed, yanking back his hand. "You bit me!"

"I'll do a lot more than that if you don't get off me, Eric Grayson, and leave my house immediately."

Grinning, he braced his arms on either side of her shoulders. "But I rather like where I am at this minute. Me on top of you, and you trapped under the blankets unable to escape me. 'Tis a pleasant position, indeed."

"I'm going to scream so loud, the constable on

the next block will hear me," Belle hissed, wriggling to escape.

Eric chuckled. "I wouldn't do that unless you're prepared to marry me."

"Marry you?" she gasped.

He nodded. "Of course, that's what the *ton* and proper society dictates when a single gentleman and young lady are found in bed together. If the man marries the lady, all sins are forgiven."

Belle struggled harder to free herself. "Are you insane? No one can force me to marry you! You broke into my house—"

"I broke nothing. The lock on your kitchen door works as well as it ever did. I know how to pick a lock without damaging it."

"So you're careful as well as sneaky, deceitful, and boorish! Congratulations, Mr. Grayson! Now get off me!" she ordered, bucking her hips up against him as she tried to push him away.

Eric closed his eyes and groaned. "Sweetheart, I wouldn't move about like that if I were you. You have no idea what you're doing to me."

Belle felt something hard pressing against the juncture of her thighs and knew enough about male anatomy to realize what he was suggesting. She suddenly went still. "You wouldn't f-force yourself on me, would you, Eric?"

Looking down at her, his smile faded and he shook his head. "Never, sweetheart. I hope you believe me."

In spite of her anger at the man, Belle knew he was telling the truth. At that moment, the fight drained out of her. "I do believe you, Eric, but that doesn't change the fact that I can't trust you about anything else. How can I? In the past weeks you've constantly lied to me and pretended you were Trelane. You may have done it for a noble cause, but your lies have torn my entire life apart."

"I wasn't lying to you this afternoon when I said I love you, Belle."

His softly spoken admission caused Belle's heart to flutter. "You—you love me?"

A sad smile lifted the corners of his mouth as he nodded. "Yes, I do. I can hear the doubt in your voice, but it's true, Belle. I love you. I want you to be my wife."

CHAPTER 9

For several moments, Belle couldn't speak. When she did, her voice was barely a whisper. "You want to marry me?"

Eric nodded. "Yes, I do. Please say you will be my wife."

Belle wasn't sure if she should laugh with joy or cry from confusion. Unable to decide, she settled on simple logic to give her time while she sorted her feelings. "B-but I hardly know you, Eric. Other than you being Trelane's twin brother, you're practically a stranger to me."

"That's easily rectified. What would you like to know about me? I'll answer any question you have."

Questions were suddenly the furthest things from her mind. Eric's boyish grin and the hopeful exuberance in his voice were nearly as distracting as the feel of him pressing against her. "Could we possibly take this conversation someplace else? I'm feeling sore from my bout with the kidnapers earlier and I can't seem to concentrate very well with you looming over me like this."

"I'm sorry. That was thoughtless of me." Standing up, he took her hand and helped her out of bed. "Would you mind if we sat on the rug by the fire while we talked? It can keep you warm and provide me with a bit of light. Better yet, I'll bring the lamp down beside us so we aren't sitting in the dark."

Belle sat next to him on the floor and tucked the hem of her demure cotton nightgown around her feet. "Afraid to be alone with me in the dark?" she teased as he used a piece of burning kindling from the hearth to light the oil lamp.

Tossing the tinder back into the fireplace, he shrugged. "I'm not very comfortable being in the dark these days. Haven't been in quite sometime."

His unprotected tone as he stared into the flames caught Belle totally by surprise. "Why? Do you have a fear of the dark?"

"I used to think so, but not anymore. Being in the dark just brings back memories I would sooner forget."

"Oh! Then forgive me for bringing it up. We can talk about something else."

Shaking his head, Eric sighed. "No. I said I would answer your questions, and you deserve to know the truth. Maybe it's time I stopped running from these feelings and confronted them once and for all.''

Belle patted his arm. ''All right. Tell me what happened.''

Eric nodded, but kept his gaze fixed on the flames. ''About two years ago, I was aiding a young man to escape from a life worse than slavery in the glassworks in Venice. Count Orsini, the Italian nobleman who owned the factory, discovered what I was doing and punished me by having me imprisoned in his dungeon. I suppose I should be grateful. Though it's seldom admitted to, men guilty of my crime are usually put to death.''

She gasped. ''Just for helping someone escape? Why, that's terrible!''

He drew his knees up and wrapped his arms around his legs. ''Death might have been a better alternative than being confined in that cold, damp hole of a prison beneath Orsini's *palazzo* all those months. For days on end I would be left alone, chained to a wall, without food or human contact. Twice a week, a bucket of water and a loaf of bread were brought to my cell so I wouldn't die of thirst or hunger. In the beginning, my host occasionally had me whipped by the guards for his viewing pleasure.

''The pain and physical discomforts were bad, but my years as a warrior had prepared me to handle those. It was the isolation in the perpetual darkness that was pure torture. With nothing to look at or sounds to be heard save the rasping of my own breathing, I spoke aloud to myself to ward off the loneliness. I ranted and raved, and talked about my past. I cried out to my family and cursed God for abandoning me." He shook his head. "I never realized what a social creature I had become or how much I thrived on being with other people until that simple joy was taken away from me."

Belle swallowed hard against the tightness in her throat. "It must have been awful for you, Eric, but you obviously survived. Did the Italian nobleman change his mind and let you go?"

"Hardly. Orsini meant for me to die in that cell. He didn't want me to forget the crime I had committed against him. 'Tis the same reason he had the thunderbolt from his family crest branded on me as well." Eric held out his arm. "The burn festered and took weeks to heal. If the old priest from San Marco's hadn't learned of my condition from one of the guards and brought me the ointment for it, I would have lost the arm or died from the infection. He was also the one who eventually helped me to escape that damned place."

Belle pulled back the sleeve of his shirt to touch the puckered scar. "I'm so sorry you suffered like that, Eric. No one deserves such foul treatment. Especially not someone like you who was only trying to help another human being survive."

Eric turned toward her. He entwined his fingers with hers and brought her hand to his lips. "Thank you, love. Most people would call me a fool. You make me feel almost like a hero."

"You were a hero then, and you're a hero now."

"Some hero!" he scoffed. "I lied to you, Belle. I deceived you."

She shook her head. "You were only doing what was necessary to find the man who ordered the attack on your brother. I see that now and I understand. You never meant to hurt me when you were posing as Trelane."

"Bloody hell! I'd sooner destroy myself before hurting you on purpose, Belle."

She knelt up on her knees and hugged him. "I know. Whatever lies you conjured to carry out your task were unavoidable under the circumstances."

Putting his arms around her, Eric held her close. "God, when I think of the times my conscience tore at my soul these past weeks when we were together, I want to scream in frustration. It was hell for me. I longed to tell you who I was. I wanted you to say my name and tell me that you loved me and not Trelane. All I could think about was how much you were going to hate me when you found out what I had done and I couldn't blame you."

Belle leaned back to cradle his face in her hands. "I don't hate you. How can I, when you're the man I've grown to care for. I love you, Eric. I have never been in love with anyone but you."

"But you were engaged to marry my brother. I thought—"

She put her hand over his mouth. "For a man of action, Eric Grayson, you waste a great deal of time talking. I just said that I love you. Are you going to waste the rest of the night debating the issue like your long-winded brother or will you finally get around to kissing me?''

Laughing, he nipped at her fingers. ''Oh, sweetheart, just try and stop me!''

Eric pulled Belle across his lap and kissed her with all the passion she'd been dreaming of for weeks. Their mouths joined with abandon, their tongues touched and caressed. Sensations she recognized as desire rushed through her as she responded to his kisses. The new feelings intensified tenfold when his hand cupped her breast.

A moan vibrated in his throat as he lifted his lips from hers. ''You aren't wearing anything beneath this gown, are you, Belle?''

Summoning her strength, she looked up at him. ''No, not a thing. Petticoats and corsets aren't usually worn to bed.''

He closed his eyes for a moment. ''I was afraid you were going to say that.''

''Did I do something wrong?''

Eric shook his head. ''Not at all, sweetheart. But if we don't stop right now, I'm going to forget about being a gentleman and make love to you here on the floor.''

When he tried to remove his hand from her breast, Belle put her hand over his and held it in place. ''But what if I don't want you to be a gentleman?''

''Are you saying that you ... that you want to make love?''

Ignoring the surprise on his face and the heat in her own cheeks, she sighed. ''I'm almost seven and twenty years of age. Hardly a girl fresh from the schoolroom. Haven't I waited long enough, Eric? I want to make love with you tonight."

Eric didn't reply. After he gave her a brief, chaste kiss and stood up, she turned away in embarrassment. "I'm such a fool! You're probably shocked and repelled by my bold announcement. No gentleman wants a lady to act like that."

He pulled Belle to her feet and forced her to look at him. "Then you should be glad that I'm not a gentleman. You were being honest, acting like a real woman, and I wouldn't want you any other way."

"But I thought . . . You didn't respond at first, so I supposed . . ."

Eric put his arms around her. "You know, for a passionate young woman, Belle Kingsley, you waste a great deal of time talking."

His use of her own words eased the tension between them and made Belle smile. "So what exactly do you intend to do about that, sir? Lecture me about my faults and tell me how I can improve?"

He shook his head. "Oh, no. You've got the wrong brother if you're expecting that. I'm the man of action. The one who's taking you to that bed to make love with you all night if you're still interested."

Recalling his earlier reply, she laughed. "Oh, sweetheart, just try and stop me!"

Belle leaned up on tiptoe to kiss him. There was nothing shy or reserved about her kisses. They were as open and carnal as the ones he'd given her only minutes before. Without taking their mouths apart for a second, they eventually crossed the room to the bed. It was only when he tried to undo the buttons on her nightgown that Belle felt her courage slipping.

"I'm not as well endowed as most women," she explained, stepping back and nervously twisting the button with her fingers. "I hope you won't be too disappointed."

"How could I possibly be disappointed when God created you especially for me, Belle?"

The sincerity of his statement melted whatever remained of her fears. She freed the buttons on her gown and let it drop to the floor. Her first inclination was to cover herself with her hands, but the appreciative glow in his eyes as he looked at her told Belle that he was pleased. For the first time in her life, she actually felt beautiful.

Eric smiled. "I'm in awe. You are so incredibly lovely."

"Then you don't find me . . . lacking?"

Shaking his head, he gently cupped her breasts. "Oh, no, love. See how perfectly they fill my hands? And they're soft and pink, like plump little peaches enticing me to taste them."

"Taste them?" Belle laughed nervously. "You make me sound like dessert."

"You are, love. And you're all mine because I never share my sweets."

Eric lifted her onto the bed and came down beside her. He tenderly massaged her breasts as he took first one nipple and then the other in his mouth. He suckled on her, until they peaked hard against his tongue and Belle was moaning in delight.

Capturing her mouth with his, he began to stroke the length of her body with his hands. She quivered as the tips of his fingers brushed the curls on her woman's mound. Remembering the way his touch there had brought her pleasure before, she parted her legs and hoped he would do it again.

Belle gasped when Eric touched the very heart of her femininity. He circled it with his fingers, making her quake in response. When she was close to fulfillment, he eased a finger inside her, then two. The sensation was different, but she liked it. After a few minutes of these caresses, he brought her to a loud, shattering climax.

Eric cuddled her close until she recovered enough to open her eyes. He dropped a quick kiss on her lips. "You are beautiful and honest in your passion, just as I hoped."

"And noisy," she added ruefully. "If you hadn't been kissing me at that very moment, I would have awakened Mrs. Tuttle and the neighbors with my screams."

"Well, I couldn't be more pleased. It tells me you enjoy my touch. A man likes to know these things when he's making love to his woman."

Belle smiled at his possessive tone as he sat up and tugged off his boots. She was amazed at how relaxed and unabashed she felt lying there naked, watching him undress. He tossed his shirt aside, revealing broad shoulders and a trim waist. His chest was shadowed lightly with swirls of dark hair. When he stood to remove his trousers, he reminded her of a statue of the warrior god, Mars, she'd once seen in a Roman temple. He was tall and perfectly formed. Beneath his flat abdomen, his manhood stood thick and proud away from his body. But unlike the statue, Eric wasn't made of cold marble. He was warm flesh and rippling muscles that taunted her, inviting her touch.

When Eric took his place over her on the bed, he braced his arms on either side of her shoulders to gaze down at her. "From this moment on, Belle, you belong to me. I won't give you up to my brother or anyone else. Do you understand what I'm saying?"

The uncertainty in his words and his unguarded vulnerability touched her heart. "Of course I understand. I love you, Eric. I don't want anyone—"

Whatever she was going to say was forgotten with his searing kiss. Belle put her arms around his waist and drew him down to her. Sensations, new and exciting, suddenly assailed her being. The coarse hair on his chest tickled her breasts while the head of his shaft rubbed over the throbbing center of her feminine cleft. Heat shot through her each time he moved. Instinctively, she raised her hips toward his and was rewarded for her efforts as his length slowly entered inside her. His movements of shallow thrusting and withdrawal were intoxicating, and caused her to open widely for his invasion.

Eric felt the tremors growing in Belle and was nearly out of control from her response. She was tight and had never been with a man before. He had to be sure that she was fully ready for him and refused to be rushed. But all logic flew from his mind when she moaned into his mouth. The sounds of her growing passion beckoned him like a siren's call. He quickly drew back and lunged forward, rending her maidenhead in one powerful thrust.

Belle gasped in surprise at the discomfort, but quickly recovered. She'd never felt so full, so complete. When Eric tried to pull away, she locked her legs around his hips and refused to let him move. "No, don't go. I'm fine. Please don't stop now."

Eric needed no further urging and began moving in and out of her. He gloried in the feel of being deep inside her. The muscles of her passage clenched around him, hot and moist. He wanted to go slow, but Belle wasn't having any of it. She destroyed what was left of his discipline when she bucked restlessly against him, demanding his response in full return. In a matter of moments, Eric exploded with Belle's cries of fulfillment ringing in his ears.

Eric sighed in contentment. He felt totally exhausted, but happier than he'd ever been. After years of being alone, he'd finally found his own bit of heavenly respite here on earth. The reason for his joy was cuddled against him beneath the bedcovers, warm and naked, stroking his chest with her fingers.

"What's this on your chest?" she asked. "A birthmark?"

Eric didn't have to open his eyes to know she was referring to the crescent-shaped mark on his chest. "Yes. According to Mama, every child born in her family for the past hundred years or so has the same birthmark on the left side over their heart."

"But yours is on the right side."

Looking down at it, Eric shrugged. "I know. Uncle Justin said it was because Trelane and I are mirrored twins."

"Mirrored twins? I never heard of such a thing. You look identical to me."

"To most people we do," he explained. "Think of it this way. If you were facing a mirror, your reflection is the opposite of what you are. That's the way Trelane and I are. For example, he uses his right hand, while I'm naturally prone to use my left."

Belle frowned. "But you always used your right hand to eat and write when we were together. I would have noticed straightaway if you hadn't."

"One of my tutors tried to break me of the habit when I was a boy, so I learned to use my right hand nearly as well as my left. I can eat, handle a weapon, or write with either hand. It's just easier with my left. The location of our birthmark was the only discernable difference between us when we were born to tell us apart. Now, of course, I have the brand on my arm and Trelane has a collection of scars of his own from the attack."

Belle rested her cheek against his shoulder. "Poor Trelane. You said he was recovering from his injuries and that's wonderful. But I feel a bit guilty about us. I really should have talked to him before we ... ahhh ... before we ..."

Eric kissed the top of her head. "Trelane already knows how I feel about you. As a matter of fact, he was the one who insisted that I shouldn't give up on trying to win your heart. If it will make us happy, he wants us to be together."

"How noble of him," she sighed. "I never realized how gallant Trelane could be."

Eric frowned to himself. *Gallant? Ha! Trelane wants to clear the way so he can pursue Paris. Paris! Bloody hell, I haven't told Belle that her cousin has been at my parents' home all this time. Do I really want to explain all that right now? If I do, Belle will just get angry and take out her ill humor on me!*

At that precise moment, his churning stomach growled loudly. Belle giggled and looked up at him. "Goodness, your tummy is making quite an uproar. Whatever you had for dinner doesn't seem to be agreeing with you."

"I was in such a rush to get to you tonight, I never had dinner. As a matter of fact, I missed having lunch this afternoon as well for the same reason. The only meal I had today was breakfast."

"No lunch or dinner? Well, I certainly can't let you suffer like this." Belle tossed off the covers and pulled on her robe. "Get dressed and come down to the kitchen with me. I have a ham, a brick of cheddar, and a loaf of Mrs. Tuttle's rye bread in the kitchen that should solve your problem. If you behave and keep your voice low so we don't wake my housekeeper, there's even some apple pie for dessert.''

As Belle bustled around the room spouting orders, Eric smiled. "Has anyone ever told you that you're a bossy bit of goods, sweetheart?"

She picked up his trousers and playfully threw them on Eric's chest. "Yes. Papa's been complaining about that for years. With his mind constantly on his work, my father would have starved to death long ago if I hadn't made arrangements for the meals and insisted that he eat them. Well, sir, are you going to cooperate or must I dress you myself?" she asked, propping her hands defiantly on her hips.

He laughed. "I can do it on my own, but having your assistance would make the task a great deal more entertaining." Throwing back the blankets, he stood beside her. "Don't you agree, Belle?"

Belle's bravado drained out of her when she looked him up and down, and beheld his naked appearance. "Oh, my! I still can't believe that someone as handsome and as magnificent as you could possibly want me. Perhaps you're the one who needs to wear spectacles."

Touched by her vulnerability, Eric drew her into his arms and kissed her. He reluctantly took his mouth away from hers. "My vision is perfect when it comes to you, Belle. You're beautiful, strong, sensual, and intelligent. Everything I want in a woman, but far more than I deserve. I will spend the rest of my life thanking God that you saw past my flaws and fell in love with me." Doubts, like the early morning fog that hid the rising sun, crept into his mind to shadow his happiness. "You do love me, don't you, Belle?"

Smiling at him, Belle put her arms around his neck and placed a gentle kiss on his lips. "While your vision might not be impaired, I can see that your memory needs work. But have no fear, Eric Grayson. I won't let you forget. I shall gladly remind you every day in thought, word, and deed that I love you, too."

"Another slice of pie, Eric?"

Leaning back in the high-backed wooden chair in the Kingsleys' kitchen, Eric held up his hands and shook his head. "No, thank you, sweetheart. One more bite and I'll surely burst at the seams of my trousers. Your housekeeper is an excellent cook. You must give her my compliments."

Belle closed the pantry door and sat down beside him. "Mrs. Tuttle will appreciate the praise. Papa usually has his nose in a book while he's eating a meal and seldom notices what a veritable feast she has prepared for him. No one likes having their efforts taken for granted."

The melancholy tone of her statement piqued

his interest. "Did your father do that to you as well?"

She smiled sadly and nodded. "Yes, I suppose he did. But I understood. After my mother died, the only thing Papa had to salve his grief was his work. I did all I could to help him. Everything from writing his correspondence to paying the bills to maintaining our home while we were away on one of his many expeditions. I've arranged passage for us on ships, kept records of his findings, and even bartered with camel traders to cross the deserts with them. Not the typical duties for a young lady by polite society's standards, but I managed."

"Sir Francis should have paid more attention to you and your needs, Belle. You were his child, yet you were the caregiver."

Twisting the end of her long braid around her finger, Belle shrugged. "My life wasn't so bad. It was all rather exciting. I've crossed the Alps, seen the Great Wall of China, explored tombs of kings, hunted for buried treasures, and sailed six of the seven seas. Why, I've visited places most people only dream of or read about in books."

Eric reached over and took her hand. "But all the adventure and excitement wasn't enough, was it? Weary and travel-worn, you longed to be home. In a world crowded with strangers, you always felt alone. You hungered for the simple joys of having caring friends and a family nearby. You wanted to be safe, secure, and loved."

Her mouth dropped open in surprise. "My goodness, Eric, you sound as though you've been inside my head, reading my mind."

He squeezed her hand. "I know exactly how you feel, Belle, because I share these sentiments with you. That's why I came home to England."

She frowned. "You were gone for eighteen years, Eric. If you truly felt this way, why did you stay away so long?"

"When I ran off to join the rebel forces in Greece, I was sixteen and filled with altruistic reasons for fighting for a just cause. Defending the downtrodden and oppressed who couldn't fight for themselves." Eric sighed as he was caught up in the memories of his past. "The patriotic zeal fades with time and soon only the side that can afford your price gains your loyalty. A good soldier can accumulate wealth if he's clever, but the cost is too high. The killing was bad enough, but the loneliness was hell on earth. The friend you make today can be killed tomorrow or become your enemy in the battle you take part in the following week. I only realized how wretchedly I had wasted my life when I almost died in that dungeon in Venice. I swore if I ever escaped, I would go home and make up for all the time I had lost."

A few glistening tears slid down Belle's cheeks. "And you will do it, Eric. I'll be here to help you every step of the way."

Eric smiled and winked at her. "I know, love. That's precisely what I'm counting on." Standing, he pulled Belle up beside him. "Well, enough food and talk for tonight. You go up and get into bed while I check the locks on the windows and doors down here. I will join you in a few minutes, sweetheart."

A frown creased Belle's brow as he took her by the hand and led her toward the stairs. "Eric, I . . . ah . . . don't know quite how to say this, but . . . ah . . . shouldn't you be going home now? Although we have . . . ah . . . made love and all . . . and I've agreed to marry you, I don't believe it's proper for you to be here."

"I don't care what's proper or not, Belle. You're in grave danger and I'm not leaving. 'Tis one of the reasons I came to see you tonight."

"Oh, really? And who are you going to protect me from? Yourself?" she giggled.

Eric took her by the shoulders and made her face him. "I'm not jesting with you, Belle. One of the men who abducted you today managed to escape. With his accomplices in custody, he might be desperate enough to come after you again."

Suddenly sober, Belle squinted up at him. "Why on earth would he do that? I told those men that I didn't have the key they were looking for."

"Trelane didn't have the key either on the night they attacked him at Westminster. But that didn't stop them from beating him within an inch of his life."

"Oh, my God! Are you saying those men were the same ones who nearly killed your brother?"

"Yes. So now you know why I'm so adamant about protecting you. Until the authorities capture that last man, I'm not going to let you out of my sight." Eric dropped a quick kiss on her lips before turning her around, and pushing her up the stairs. "No more arguments, love. Do as I say and go to bed. I'll be up soon."

"Fine, I'm going," she scoffed when she lifted the hem of her long robe and climbed the steps. "But I still think you're worrying for nothing. I don't have any silly keys and no amount of threat or intimidation is going to change that . . ."

Eric chuckled to himself as Belle's voice faded when she reached the upper landing. *Hope she finds her room without her spectacles. I wouldn't want to waste the rest of the night searching the house for her.*

After checking all the locks and dousing the lamps and candles, Eric made his way up the stairs. He was aching and tired, looking forward to sleeping with Belle cuddled in his arms, when he felt a draft of cold air on his face. A second later, he heard her scream. Fueled by fear, he raced down the hall and found Belle struggling with a tall man in the center of her shadow-filled room.

"Unhand her, you bastard!" he shouted as he rushed forward and slammed the man in the face with his fists.

Stunned by the force of the blows, the intruder staggered and released his hold on Belle, causing her to fall to the floor. While Eric gathered her in his arms, the cloaked man ran to the open window. Before he could be stopped, he climbed out of the window to the rose trellis attached to the side of the house. The old wooden slats on the trellis creaked loudly and broke beneath his weight. Eric leaned over the sill to catch him, but it was too late. The man yelled as he plummeted to the ground.

Belle came up behind Eric and touched his shoulder. "D-did he escape?"

Eric ducked back inside and shut the window. "No. He's lying on the ground below and appears to be unconscious. But he's not important. Are you all right, love? Did he hurt you?"

Wrapping her arms around his waist, Belle buried her face against his chest. "I'm f-fine, really I am. Just hold me for a moment, p-please. I'm such a dreadful c-coward. I c-c-can't stop sh-shaking."

His arms tightened around her. "You're not a coward, Belle. 'Tis the aftermath of what you've been through. Talk to me, love. Tell me what happened."

"I d-didn't c-come to my room straightaway," she began. "I went to Mrs. Tuttle's r-room on the floor above and told her that I didn't want to be d-disturbed in the morning. The p-poor old dear is so hard of hearing, I had to repeat my orders several times before she understood what I was saying. With you in my bed, I c-could hardly have her come into my room with my morning tea. Why, the shock alone might cause her to have a nervous attack or something far worse—"

"Sweetheart, you're digressing," Eric interrupted, rubbing her back in a soothing manner.

"Tell me what happened when you got to your room."

Belle sighed. "At first I thought the man standing at my vanity table busily looking through my things by candlelight was you, so I crept across the room on tiptoe to surprise you ... but it wasn't you, of course. Had I been wearing my spectacles, I would have realized that immediately, but I am dreadfully nearsighted, you know. First thing tomorrow, I've got to order a new pair of spectacles before I do myself a mischief and—"

"Sweetheart ..."

"Drat! I'm rambling again, aren't I?" She heaved another sigh. "You really must forgive me, Eric. I usually don't act like a whimpering female, but I'm not customarily accosted in my bedroom in the middle of the night by a man who's been searching through my jewelry box and demanding that I give him some damned bloody key!" Belle gasped and put her hand to her mouth. "Oh, my! Wherever did I pick up such language?"

Shaking his head, Eric smiled over her remark. "I know it was rather difficult to see in the dark, but did you recognize the man when you were struggling with him?"

"Oh, yes! It was the tall young fellow the other miscreants called Ned. You were right, Eric. Ned wants that key. He muttered something about making 'his lordship' pay dearly for all he'd gone through to get it for him. Perhaps you can get Ned to tell you who the man is."

Eric kissed her brow. "All right. You stay here while I go outside to check on his condition."

"I will not! If you're leaving this room, I'm going with you." Belle crossed the room to fetch her old spectacles from the vanity table. "Come with me. I'll show you a quick way through the service entrance to the garden. We mustn't let that fellow escape again."

Rather than waste time arguing, Eric followed Belle to the garden. There really wasn't a need to hurry. Ned hadn't moved. He couldn't. The lanky young man in the dirty brown cloak was dead.

Eric set the lantern he was carrying on the ground and tossed the edge of the cloak over Ned's pale lifeless face. "From the looks of him, I think he broke his neck in the fall."

"He was so young. Barely eighteen, I would guess. Now we may never know who was responsible for the attack on Trelane or what the search for this mysterious key has to do with all this." Belle stepped back from viewing the body and felt something crunch under her slippered foot. "What's that piece of paper doing on the ground? It wasn't there earlier. Perhaps it dropped out of Ned's cloak."

Picking it up, Eric held it to the light. "It's a calling card from Slaton's. That's a gentlemen's club not far from the government buildings at Westminster."

"I know all about Slaton's." Belle pulled the top of her robe closed to ward off the wind. "Papa has been a member since I was a child. He often said more laws were discussed over hands of whist at Slaton's than on the floors of Parliament. When we were in town, Papa had a standing appointment to play cards with Lord Beekham and some of his friends every Wednesday evening. On occasion, Trelane's law partner, Henry Townsend, would sit in and play a game or two as well."

Eric stood up and led her back into the house. "So Neville Farnsworth and Henry Townsend were both members of the club and well acquainted with your father. I had no idea they were all so friendly."

"Neville especially. He's also on the board of directors of the Royal Antiquities Society with my father. He helped Papa get the approval and investors he needed for his last three expeditions. Without Neville's assistance, I don't know what my father would have done. He's been a very loyal friend to both of us."

After they entered the kitchen, Eric locked the door and turned to Belle. "I want you to get dressed and pack a few of your things. Once you're safely secured at my family's home, I'll go for the constables, make a report on what happened, and have Ned's body taken away."

She frowned. "I'm not going to impose on your family. My place is here, in this house, until we're married. Now that all four of my kidnapers have been accounted for, I have nothing to worry about."

"But you do, Belle. The man who hired them is still running loose. What's to stop him from going out and employing others to take their place? Or maybe he will come after you himself.''

"I doubt that," she sniffed, folding her arms across her chest. "The man's a coward and I simply refuse to be chased away from my own home by the likes of him. If you can't remain here with me, secure all the windows and locks in this house. You can nail them shut for all I care, but the only place I'm going now is to bed and that's final!''

Eric knew Belle wasn't going to back down. She had a stubborn streak as wide as his own. He didn't want to alarm her with his suspicions about Neville, yet he was determined to find a way to protect her in spite of herself. A possible solution suddenly occurred to him.

"Fine. Stay home, but I insist on bringing a footman here to keep an eye on things while I'm off working on my investigation. If you go out, he can accompany you. The fellow I have in mind is perfect for the task.''

She scowled. "I don't require a burly nursemaid tending to me and following me about, Eric.''

"Humor me, sweetheart." Eric pulled Belle into his arms and hugged her close. "I know you don't like having too many servants around, but your maid is away tending her sick mother and your housekeeper is elderly and half deaf. I'd feel better knowing he is here.''

"Oh, all right," she sighed. "Send your footman here in the morning. But if he gets in my way or tries to order me about, I'll toss him out.''

Eric smiled triumphantly. *Poor Alexei may have met his match with my Belle. Disguised as a footman in a uniform and wig from my father's household might not be enough to fool her. I wonder if we can hide her spectacles for a day or two. . . .*

CHAPTER 10

"What in the blazes happened to you, brother? You look like hell!"

Eric fell into the chair beside his twin's bed and scowled at him. "And a very good day to you, too, Trelane. If you must know, I've been up all night and didn't get a wink of sleep. Then I spent the entire morning dealing with constables, police reports, and outfitting my friend as a footman."

A frown creased Trelane's brow. "You outfitted your friend as a footman? I'm surprised at you, Eric. If the man truly is your friend, why didn't you simply lend him the funds he needed before reducing him to such a menial position?"

"You don't understand. Alexei is doing me a favor, you hapless twit! I'd never—"

"Catlin Eric Grayson, hold that temper of yours," a female voice warned from the doorway. "I put up with the two of you arguing as boys. I certainly don't have to witness it now."

Eric looked over at his mother. "Sorry, Mama. I'm tired and out of sorts, and as usual, Trelane thinks the worst of me."

"Yes, I know. Your brother has a nasty habit of doing that with most people," Catherine replied as she carried in a tray of food and placed it on the bedside table.

"Mother, you're exaggerating," Trelane protested in his own defense. "I'm levelheaded and fair when it comes to my opinion of people."

"Oh, really? And this from the man who once said Paris Mackenzie was a red-haired witch who should be sent back to Philadelphia on the first available ship—"

Trelane sat up from his pillows to glare at Eric. "Did you let everyone read my bloody journal? What I wrote in those pages was personal, not for public knowledge!"

Biting back his grin, Eric shrugged. "Don't blame me. I didn't tell anyone what was in your journal. You must have been talking in your sleep again, like you used to do when we were children."

"Yes, he did," Catherine added with a nod. "Not often, mind you, but just enough to keep things interesting around here. 'Tis the reason I spent so much time in this room when you were recovering from your injuries, Trelane. Had to be sure you weren't telling all the family secrets in your sleep."

Trelane groaned and rubbed his face with his hand. "Dear God, this is awful."

Catherine ruffled his hair. "Stop worrying, son. You didn't break any laws or breach any confidences when you spoke in your sleep. You mostly talked about personal things. Particularly, your interest in Paris."

That remark brought color to Trelane's cheeks. "Now, Mother, you really must let me explain how this happened—"

"You mean how you fell in love with another woman when you were engaged to marry Belle? Don't bother, son. I figured that out months ago when Paris arrived in London." Catherine took the napkin from the tray and draped it across his lap. "You got angry and took offense at everything that lovely woman said just to cover the fact that you were attracted to her. Your father did much the same thing to me when we first met and you know how that turned out."

"B-but, Mother, I—"

"Not another word, Trelane," she continued, placing the tray on his lap and putting a soupspoon in his hand. "Eat your lunch and don't waste a bit of it. You'll need your strength today. Justin is going to remove the splints from your leg and get you back on your feet this afternoon." Catherine then pointed at Eric. "You, sir, come with me."

Eric frowned. "Mama, can't I just stay here for a few minutes—"

"No. There's a lunch tray and a hot bath being drawn for you in your room." She walked past him to the door. "Come along, son. You can visit your brother later."

When she was out of sight, Eric turned to his twin. "Isn't it amazing? We're grown men and Mama still treats us as though we were little boys."

Trelane lowered the spoon from his mouth and smiled. "And we let her do it every time. Now that's what I find amazing."

Eric winked. "I know, but I'm not complaining. It's one of the joys of coming home again." Standing up, he stretched and yawned. "I better catch up with Mama or she'll be back here in a minute, leading me out by my ear."

Trelane took hold of his sleeve and stopped him. "Before you go, tell me what happened with Belle. Is she all right? Did you work things out between you?"

"Well, she understands why I deceived her and forgave me that sin. And there's still going to be a wedding next month—"

"Oh, hell," Trelane groaned. "She means to hold me to our betrothal. I was hoping she would break off our engagement and cancel the bloody thing."

Eric sighed over his brother's high-handed assumption. "Trelane, I said there was going to be a wedding. The only difference is the name of the groom. Belle has agreed to marry me."

"She did? Thank God! The scandal of it all would have damaged my career beyond repair—"

"Catlin Eric Grayson," an all-too-familiar voice called from the hallway. "I'm waiting for you."

Eric patted his brother's arm. "I'll stop by this evening and we can talk then."

Before he could take a step, Trelane grabbed his hand. "You may not believe me, Eric, but I'm very glad that you've come home. I've missed you, brother."

Eric nodded. "I know. I missed you, too."

Watching from the doorway, tears filled Catherine's eyes as her twin sons embraced. She stepped back to give them a moment of privacy and smiled. Joy filled her heart, because her boys had been reunited at last.

Eric came out of the room a few minutes later to find his mother leaning against the wall with tears running down her face. "Mama, you're crying. What's happened? Are you all right?"

Catherine looped her arm through his and began walking down the hall with him. "Of course I'm all right. Can't an old lady shed a few happy tears once in a while? Now enough talk about me—tell me what happened at Belle's house last night."

"Just as I suspected, one of her abductors broke into the house, searching for that bloody key. When we caught him rifling through Belle's bedroom, he went out the window to escape and fell to his death."

"Of all the luck!" Catherine sniffed. "Can't interrogate a dead man. How will we ever find out who those men were working for?"

Eric squeezed her hand. "All's not lost, Mama. The dead man left behind a clue that might help us. It was a calling card from Slaton's. On the way here, I noticed the name of the club's manager was written across the back of the card. Once we locate George Miller, I'm sure we'll be able to get the answers we need."

His mother suddenly stopped walking and pulled him to a halt. "Did you say George Miller?" When he nodded, she frowned. "Your father received word this morning from the runner he hired that George Miller's body was found floating in the Thames a few days ago. Evidently, he'd been shot in the head and the authorities hadn't been able to identify him until now."

"Bloody hell! First Trelane's beaten nearly to death, then Belle's attacked and abducted and her home broken into. Now the man who helped arrange it all is murdered. And for what? A mysterious key that no one has or knows about! Is this damned intrigue never going to end?"

Catherine patted his arm. "I know it's frustrating, dear, but you're too exhausted to think clearly. Eat your lunch, take a long hot bath, and get a few hours' sleep. Once you've rested, we can all sit down together and come up with another plan."

Eric raked his fingers through his hair and nodded. "You're right, Mama. But if Belle comes by to visit Trelane while I'm asleep, wake me up. I won't allow her to leave this house. If this man is as desperate as I think he is to find this cursed key, Belle will need more than Alexei to protect her if she wanders about town."

"Perhaps I shouldn't be telling you this, but Belle won't be coming to visit today. She sent me a note this morning saying that she couldn't find her spectacles and that she would try and stop by tomorrow afternoon if she found them. Eric, why are you smiling? Do you know what happened to Belle's spectacles?"

Eric raised his brows in mocked innocence as he covered the slight bulge in his coat pocket with his arm. "Why would you think something like that, Mama?"

"Because hiding Belle's spectacles from her would be an easy way to make her stay at home, safe and sound, where you want her to be?"

Catherine laughed at the stunned look on his face and pushed him toward his room. "Why are you so surprised? I know a great many things, son. Not the least of which is that you love Belle Kingsley very much. Are you going to be smart and marry that girl before she gets away?"

Eric stopped to gape at her. "How did you . . . Did Trelane say . . . Oh, bother, who cares!" Chuckling, he hugged his mother. "You're right, Mama. I do love Belle and the miracle of miracles is that she loves me, too. We're going to be married next month."

"I couldn't be more pleased. Belle will make you a wonderful wife."

He pulled back to look at her. "Belle's concerned that people might think it scandalous that she broke her engagement to one brother to marry another. If you and father prefer, we don't have to have a large ceremony and reception. We can be married in a small ceremony with only our families in attendance."

Catherine rolled her eyes. "Fiddlesticks! I've waited thirty-four years to dance at your wedding, son. I won't be cheated out of that. And don't worry about scandals. This family hasn't had one since your father married me instead of my twin sister. Trading one sibling for another is nearly a family tradition."

"Thank you, Mama. I'll tell Belle that we have your blessings when I visit her tonight."

"Since you will be seeing Belle before I do, please give this back to her with my apologies." Putting her hand in her skirt pocket, she pulled out Belle's bracelet and gave it to him. "During the engagement party, the clasp broke. Trelane asked me to take it to my jeweler to be repaired and cleaned the next day. Well, you know what happened that night and I completely forget about it. Yesterday, I took it to Mr. Webber to be fixed and the man refused to do it."

"Why? Not good enough quality for the finest goldsmith in London to touch?"

"No, not at all. Mr. Webber started to clean the metal and discovered the piece was at least five hundred years old. He didn't want to be responsible for damaging a valuable antique."

Eric held up the bracelet and frowned. "This little bauble is a valuable antique? It's nothing but a lot of tiny bells on a brass chain." He shook it. "Noisy, isn't it? Are you positive he just wasn't making excuses because he didn't want to repair it?"

Catherine shrugged. "Mr. Webber has always been honest with me before. I can't imagine why he would say such a thing if it wasn't true."

"I can't either, but I only know the man by reputation." Eric stuffed the bracelet into his coat pocket. "I will give it to Belle and let her take care of it." He kissed his mother's cheek. "See you later, Mama."

As the door closed, Catherine smiled. *I told Miles this was going to happen. We even made a wager on it. That emerald bracelet Mr. Webber had on display at the shop will look quite nice on my wrist! The next time my intuition tells me something worth betting on, I'll hold out for higher stakes. I wonder how much a new clipper ship will cost.*

Whistling happily to herself, the former lady pirate went off to find the man she loved to claim her prize.

CHAPTER 11

"Mrs. Tuttle, have you seen Claude?" Belle asked as she entered the kitchen with an armload of books. "Since we have the Graysons' footman here at the house, I thought I'd get him to help me sort out a few things in the study before Papa returns next week."

The housekeeper looked up from the vegetables she was chopping for soup. "The last I saw of him, he was in the front parlor, checking the locks on the windows. Do you want me to fetch him for you?"

"No, he's probably carrying out orders that Mr. Grayson gave him this morning." Setting the books on the table, Belle picked up a piece of carrot from the cutting board and nibbled on it. "I've been too busy searching for my spectacles since the man arrived to take much notice of him. What do you think of Claude?''

The old woman shrugged. '' 'Tis difficult to say. I ask him a question and he shakes his head or nods. Claude's an odd duck, being so quiet and all, but he seems to take his duties seriously. Wearing that fancy uniform and powdered wig, you'd think he was working for Her Majesty at the palace. Too bad about his humped back. He'd probably be quite tall if he wasn't so deformed and bent over like that.''

''Well it's nice to know that the man can find employment in spite of his disabilities.'' Belle popped the rest of the carrot into her mouth and picked up the books. ''I'll put these in the storeroom before I run upstairs to get ready for dinner. I wouldn't want my lord to see me with dirt streaked on my nose or cobwebs hanging from my hair.''

Mrs. Tuttle laughed. ''As besotted as Mr. Grayson is with you these days, he wouldn't notice. The man practically glows with love for you.''

That bit of news made Belle stop and look back at her housekeeper. ''Surely you're exaggerating, Mrs. Tuttle.''

''No, I'm not. Mr. Grayson wasn't always this way, mind you, but in the past few weeks, his feelings for you are clearly etched in that handsome face of his.'' Mrs. Tuttle dumped the vegetables in the kettle on the stove and chuckled. ''I may be old, Miss Belle, but I know love does marvelous things for a person. Why, it even has your Mr. Grayson acting like a different man."

Smiling to herself, Belle hurried away. "If only you knew how right you are, Mrs. Tuttle. If only you knew . . ."

Eric stepped into the Kingsleys' foyer. Before addressing the stooped man locking the door behind him, he looked around to be sure that they were alone. "Where's Belle and Mrs. Tuttle?"

Alexei put his finger to his lips and motioned for Eric to follow him into the study. When the door was closed, he straightened himself to his full height. "Your lady is upstairs and the housekeeper is preparing dinner. Has there been any news?"

Moving to the fireplace, Eric prodded the burning logs with a poker. "Only that George Miller was found murdered. Someone shot him in the head and tossed his body in the river a couple of days ago."

"Oh, yes, he was the manager of Slaton's who hired the runners to find Sir Francis."

Eric sniffed. "I think he did much more than that. The calling card that dropped from Ned's cloak last night had Miller's name written on the back of it. Now we know he was also connected to the group of thugs who attacked Trelane and Belle. My guess is that George Miller was doing these tasks for the same man. One who didn't want to be found, so he killed Miller to protect his identity."

"What about the men who abducted your lady?

Have the authorities learned anything from them?''

"I just came from the gaol. Harry hasn't regained consciousness yet and his accomplices were only strong-arm hirelings he picked up at a pub near the docks. They have no idea who they were working for." Eric threw the poker down on the floor in anger. "Bloody hell! This is all my fault. If I hadn't lost my temper and beaten him so badly, Harry would be awake, telling us what we need to know."

Alexei shrugged. "So you have said many times. But rather than deride yourself, Eric, you must learn from your mistakes and strive never to repeat them."

Eric frowned at him. "Where is all this saintly advice coming from? You're beginning to sound like the old vicar at my family's church."

Alexei chuckled. "Wearing this, I probably look like him as well." Pulling off the wig, he shook out his long, blond hair and scratched his head. "That feels better. I do not know what I dislike most about this disguise. Wearing the padded hump on my back and staying bent over all the time, or hiding my hair beneath this heavy wig."

"I'm sorry about the need to hide your identity. Belle refused to stay with my parents and I didn't want to leave her unprotected. Bringing you to this house dressed as a servant was the only way I could do it without arousing her suspicions—or anyone else's for that matter."

"By anyone else, you are referring to Lord Beekham, are you not?"

Eric nodded. "I have no choice but to think he might be the man we've been searching for. Neville was at the engagement party, he's a member of Slaton's, and was well acquainted with Sir Francis and my brother. I just wish I could figure out where to find this mysterious key everyone is searching for."

Neither man spoke for a few moments. The silence was broken when the mantel clock chimed seven times.

Alexei clubbed his hair back and put on the wig. "Since you will be here for a few hours, I am going to see what I can learn about Neville Farnsworth. Perhaps he has something hidden in his home that will tell us if he is the guilty one in this scheme."

Eric bent down and retrieved the poker from where he had thrown it on the rug. Using his handkerchief, he rubbed away the soot the poker had left behind. "If you're paying a visit to Neville's house, be careful, Alexei. He has a very large collection of antiques and artifacts and a staff of guards to keep them safe. All right?"

When Alexei didn't respond, Eric stood up and turned around. He quickly discovered that he was alone in the room. "Bloody hell! I really hate it when he just disappears like that! Can't he just walk out the door and say goodbye like everyone else?"

At that precise moment, Belle opened the door.

Squinting her eyes, she looked around the room. "Eric, who are you talking to?"

He shrugged and offered what he hoped was a believable excuse. "No one really, sweetheart. Talking to myself is an odd habit I picked up from the months I spent in Orsini's dungeon."

"Poor dear! You mentioned that last night." Dressed in a gown of royal blue velvet, she shut the door and joined him in front of the fireplace. "Well, you won't have to talk to yourself any longer. From now on, I will happily volunteer to be your audience whenever you have something to say."

"Thank you, love." Grateful that Belle had accepted his explanation, Eric kissed her until she was breathless. But his attempt to distract her turned on him when he felt his body responding passionately to her presence in his arms. With a great deal of effort, he reined in his desire and took on a casual demeanor as he pulled away from her. "So how was your day? Get much accomplished, sweetheart?"

Belle looked beautifully flushed and a bit confused for a moment. "How was my day? Oh, yes, my day. Well, it wasn't very fruitful. I still can't find my spectacles and because it was Sunday, I couldn't go out and order another pair."

"Don't worry. Tomorrow, I'll take you to the optician myself. He can make you a new set and repair the ones that were broken when you were abducted. Speaking about repairs, my mother sent your bracelet back to you." Eric took it from his pocket and gave it to Belle. "She apologized because the jeweler wasn't able to fix the clasp."

Belle frowned. "How did your mother get my bracelet?"

"Trelane gave it to her the night of the ball. He asked her to have it repaired and cleaned by our family's jeweler, Fredrick Webber. When Webber realized your bracelet was a valuable antique, he refused to work on it."

"My bracelet is hardly valuable," she scoffed. "I bought it from a junk peddler in a village near *Rennes-le-Château* in France a couple of years ago for a few francs. Either Mr. Webber was trying to avoid working on such an inferior piece, or the poor man's eyesight is even more impaired than my own."

Eric shrugged. "I'm not sure what to think. Webber has a reputation for his honesty as well as the quality of his workmanship. When he began cleaning the metal, he found evidence that the piece was at least five hundred years old."

Belle held up the bracelet and let it dangle from her fingers. "Oh, my! I bought this because I loved the tinkling sounds the bells made. Now you're telling me it might be a five-hundred-year-old antique."

"Too bad your father isn't in town. Perhaps he could tell us if Mr. Webber was correct."

Crossing the room, Belle sighed. "Papa wanted me to toss this bracelet in the dustbin every time I wore it. Even if he was here, I doubt he would give it a second look." She sat in the chair behind the desk and pulled a magnifying glass out of the drawer. "Well, I'm not so closed minded as Papa.

Let's see if I can figure out if my bracelet is a piece of tasteless junk or an irreplaceable historical treasure. Eric, can you move the lamp closer to me and turn up the wick?''

Eric did as she asked and watched quietly as Belle held the bracelet toward the light and studied it.

She nodded. ''Well, I can see where Mr. Webber started to clean the bells. I rather liked the patina of the old metal and never thought to polish . . . Oh, my! What's this?''

''Is something wrong, sweetheart?'' Eric asked, looking over her shoulder.

At that moment, Mrs. Tuttle came bustling into the study. ''Miss Belle, dinner is on the table and—''

Belle shook her head. ''Not now, Mrs. Tuttle. Dinner will have to wait for a while. Please bring me the brass polish, some rags, and one of the small, stiff brushes you use in the kitchen for cleaning the silver.''

''Uh-oh!'' the old woman replied. ''I know that tone of voice. I've heard it from your father often enough. I'll fetch what you need and return straightaway.''

Eric frowned as the housekeeper hurried out. ''Belle, what's the matter? Is something wrong with your bracelet?''

She held the magnifying glass over the bracelet and motioned him closer. ''Look at this, Eric. There are letters engraved on the bells that were cleaned. I suspect each of the nine bells has similar markings. Once I clean them all, I'll read the letters to you so you can write them down for us to decipher."

An hour later, Eric looked at the list he had drawn up and smiled. "A few of these words are in Latin! I recall enough of my lessons to make out a couple of them. *Curators* means guardians. *Sanctus* is easy. That means holy. But the word in between them, *pactum*, escapes me."

Belle set aside the magnifying glass. Chewing on her lower lip, she studied the list. "*Curators pactum sanctus.* I remember seeing that phrase somewhere . . . Good grief! It was in Papa's notes about the Templar Knights."

Eric sat on the edge of the desk. "Templar Knights? Weren't they the ones in those old Arthurian tales?"

Belle crossed the room and began going through the stack of leather-bound journals on the shelf. "The Templars were used as the model for the knights in those stories, but they weren't fictional characters. They were a religious order of warrior monks established in 1118 by a group of nine knights. The order grew in size and power, and fought valiantly in all the Crusades," she explained, opening one of the journals to peruse its contents.

"Warrior monks? That title seems a bit contrary. Monks are men of God, sworn to uphold the church, not go to war and kill other men."

Belle set down the first journal and picked up another. "They only killed Saracens or infidels. Believing God was on their side, the Templars were fearless warriors. They were the first to enter the battlefield and the last to retreat. Also referred to as the Poor Fellow Soldiers of Christ, their courage and dedication to Christianity and their cause were legendary. The order prospered for nearly two hundred years."

"Really? What happened then?"

"Pope Clement the Fifth and the French king, Philip Le Bel, were envious and fearful of the Templars' power, so they worked together to destroy them," Belle said, flipping through pages. "The order was abolished by papal decree in 1312, and their leader, Jacques de Molay, was sentenced to die for heresy. When he was burned at the stake, it was rumored that de Molay cursed his accusers to join him in death within the year. True to his curse, Pope Clement died within the month and King Philip in a dreadful hunting accident several months later."

Eric frowned in disgust. "Bloody hell! A noble group of warriors brought down by the church and politics. It doesn't seem fair that they were torn apart like that."

Not looking up, she shrugged. "Many people believe the Templars are still very much alive. Following the papal decree, the remaining members of the order banded together and fled to France and Scotland. Today, they've reportedly become a secret sect of members and knights sworn to uphold the laws and doctrines of the Templars."

Eric regarded Belle as she began going through a third journal. Flushed and excited, she seemed quite within her element. "You appear to know a great deal about the Templar Knights, sweetheart."

"Thanks to helping Papa with his research, I know a little about many things. The Templars just happen to be one of them." Suddenly, looking up at Eric, she smiled. "I found it! Right here in Papa's notes." She carried the journal to the desk and pointed out the words with her finger. "*Curators sanctus pactum.* It means 'Guardians of the Holy Covenant.' "

"Guardians of the Holy Covenant? What has that to do with the Templar Knights?"

Gazing back at him over her shoulder, Belle winked. "Quite a lot if you believe that the Templars found the most sacred relics of the Christian faith during the Crusades and kept them hidden from the rest of the world. Those treasures include the Ark of the Covenant that contained the Ten Commandments Moses received from God and the Holy Grail itself."

Eric stepped away from the desk and began to pace the room. "Now that you mention it, I do remember hearing such things about the Templars. But I thought it was a lot of nonsense. Just an old tale someone contrived to glorify their exploits."

"Many historians and archaeologists like my father don't think it's nonsense at all. They're convinced that Templars did indeed rescue these relics from the Holy Land and hid them for over five hundred years in Europe." Belle turned her attention back to the journal on the desk. "According to Papa's theory, the Templars who escaped to Scotland in 1312 brought the Grail with them and placed it in a secret vault beneath the floor of a chapel located just north of the border with England.''

"But if the Templars had the Holy Grail, why did they hide it? Having such an important relic might have strengthened their cause."

Belle shook her head. "The Templar Knights would never employ it for their personal gain. Their purpose was to hide the Grail until such time that a more enlightened society could make better use of its virtues."

Turning the page, she frowned. "I never read this section before. From the date on the entry, it appears that Papa added it to the journal a few days before he left London." A moment later, she called to Eric. "You won't believe this. It's about *special keys* unlocking the mysteries of the Templars."

The mention of a "special key" brought Eric back to the desk. "That's what those men who attacked you and Trelane asked for. What does your father say about a special key in his notes?"

"Not a great deal, but he does make reference to the fact that many Templars took precautions to hide what was theirs from outsiders by the use of a special key. Only one of their own would recognize the significance of the key if they saw it." Turning the page, she leaned closer to it. "Isn't that odd? These strange little marks and numbers look like the ones on the last two bells."

"What are you talking about? When you were reading off the letters on the bracelet, you never mentioned a thing about strange marks or numbers."

Belle sighed. "Since I couldn't readily identify what they were, I thought it best to concentrate on the letters first." She pointed down at the page. "Have you ever seen markings like this before?"

Eric looked at the page. "Those appear to be longitude and latitude markings that you would find on a map."

"Are you sure?"

"Positive. Because my family owns so many ships, sailing is a large part of our lives. My parents taught me how to read charts and maps when I was barely out of leading strings. Give me the magnifying glass and the bracelet. If the markings are longitude and latitude positions, I'll know it."

As Eric took her place studying the piece under the light, Belle got up to stretch her muscles. "How was I to know what those marks were, anyway?" she admonished herself. "Papa never allowed me to touch his precious maps. He didn't want me to strain my pretty eyes or overtax my feminine brain."

Jotting his findings on a sheet of parchment, Eric chuckled. "Don't be too harsh on your father, Belle. Most men don't realize that women are just as intelligent as they are. In fact, females are usually smarter. Being around my mother and older sister, Diana, convinced me of that years ago." He put down the pen and turned to Belle. "Well, I was right. These are map positions. As a matter of fact, there are two distinct locations shown here. Though I don't have a map to confirm it, one of them appears to be in southern Scotland."

Belle's face went pale. "My word! You don't think . . . Can it be . . . ?"

"The locations of the Holy Grail and the Ark of the Covenant?" Eric finished for her. He suddenly looked at the bracelet in his hand and closed his fingers angrily around it. "Bloody hell! This is the key they've been searching for."

"My bracelet is a key?"

He shook his head. "No, the *inscription* on your bracelet is the key. The key to finding the secret treasures of the Templars. This bracelet is what those men were hired to find the night they attacked my brother. And when they didn't find it on Trelane, they waited a couple of weeks and came after you."

Belle gasped. "Dear Lord, you must be right. My bracelet broke during the party and Trelane put it in his pocket. We were surrounded by dozens of people at the time. Any one of them could have been responsible for what happened to him."

"Not just anyone, sweetheart. It was a man who knew antiquities and recognized the true value of this bauble. He was a friend, someone who knew my brother's habits, and was a member of Slaton's."

Coming to his side, Belle put her arm around Eric's shoulder. "You know who it is, don't you?"

He shut his eyes for a moment. Eric knew Belle would be very upset by what he was about to say, but he had no choice but to be honest with her. "I think it's Neville Farnsworth."

As expected, Belle jerked back as though she had been struck. "I-I can't believe it! How can you even suggest such a vile thing? Lord Beekham is one of Trelane's oldest and dearest friends."

"I have no choice. All the evidence points to him. Neville was at the ball and witnessed what happened to your bracelet. He also knew that Trelane often stopped at his offices at Westminster before going home. And if that wasn't telling enough, Neville Farnsworth is a voracious collector of rare and expensive artifacts."

"Many people do that," she protested. "Lord Beekham has a high regard for such things. He's my father's strongest supporter and they both serve as directors for the Royal Antiquities Society."

Eric arched his brow. "But unlike your father, Neville's interest in antiques and artifacts isn't based on a love of history, Belle. In fact, he boasted to me that he does it strictly for the profits. If he possessed a piece of the Templars' legendary treasure, he could sell it to the highest bidder and be set for life."

"But how can Lord Beekham be the one who hired those thugs to attack your brother? You've been with him countless times since that night and he thinks you are Trelane. Wouldn't he have acted suspicious or at least surprised when you turned up unscathed after those men supposedly carried out his orders?"

"Maybe Neville thinks they attacked the wrong man or lied to him about doing it at all."

Belle frowned. "One of my abductors, the bearded one named Harry, mentioned something about their employer saying precisely that. At the time I didn't understand what they were talking about, but it makes perfect sense to me now. Couldn't this Harry identify the man who hired him?"

"He might if he regains consciousness. I'm afraid the beating I gave Harry for hurting you was a bit too severe. The physicians don't know if he's going to survive."

Shivering, Belle moved to the fireplace and held her hands toward the flames to warm them. "I don't want to believe it, but you may be right about Neville Farnsworth. But without proof, we can hardly show up at his door and accuse him of such things."

Eric knew more than the chill in the room was bothering Belle. He joined her in front of the hearth and took her in his arms. "Don't worry, sweetheart," he said, kissing her brow. "Perhaps I will just turn over all the evidence to the magistrate and let the authorities deal with him."

"But what if we're wrong, Eric?" Belle pulled from his embrace to look at his face. "What if Neville is innocent? Then the person really behind this plot would be free to come after me again. I don't want to live in fear for the rest of my life."

"You won't, love. I would die before letting anything happen to you."

She stretched up on tiptoe and kissed his lips. "While I appreciate the sentiment, my gallant warrior, I wouldn't want to lose you, either." A moment later, a smile curved Belle's mouth. "I think I know of a way that we can find the guilty person and end this mystery once and for all."

Looking at her face, his eyes narrowed. "Why do I suddenly get the feeling that I'm not going to like your suggestion?"

"Because you worry too much." She patted his cheek. "Now promise me you won't interrupt until you've heard everything I have to say."

Eric folded his arms over his chest. "Fine. You have my word."

"Your parents will have to hold another party."

"Another party? But—"

Belle put her hand on his mouth. "You promised. All right?" As he nodded in agreement, she took her hand away and continued. "Your parents will have to hold another party. We will limit the guest list to family and members of Slaton's who attended the ball two months ago. During the party, I will wear my bracelet so we can see if anyone takes a special interest in it. I don't relish being the bait in this trap, but there's no other way to do it." A frown creased her brow at his silence. "Well, aren't you going object and tell me that my idea is insane?"

Eric shook his head. "Can't do that because I agree with you. We'll have to take special precautions to protect you, of course. But your plan should work."

Overjoyed at his approval, Belle threw her arms around his neck and hugged him. "Thank you so much for not fighting me on this, Eric. It shows that you have confidence in me and consider me your equal. Your honesty is quite refreshing. And after all the disappointments and deceptions I've had to deal with lately, I don't know if I can handle any more lies."

Belle's remarks struck Eric's conscience with the force of a lightning bolt. Holding her as he was, she couldn't see his face and he was grateful for that. He would have wagered a thousand pounds that she'd be able to see the guilt he was feeling in his eyes.

"You know, sweetheart, occasionally lies are necessary. Especially when you're trying to protect someone."

"Stop worrying about that, Eric. As I've told you before, I understand that you were helping your brother and I've forgiven you." She sighed and hugged him closer. "But please don't lie to me ever again."

Eric grimaced. *Bloody hell! When Belle finds out how I got Alexei to disguise himself as "Claude" the footman and didn't tell her about it, she'll have my head. Perhaps if I make my confession now and explain how I was only doing it to protect her, she'll find it in her heart to forgive me this one last lie.*

He eased from their embrace to look at her. "Belle, there's something I need to tell you—"

"Miss Belle," Mrs. Tuttle called from the corridor, "it's getting late. When would you and the gentleman like me to serve dinner? The soup is hot and I just took a fresh batch of biscuits from the oven.''

"Put it on the table, Mrs. Tuttle. We'll be right there.'' She turned her attention back to Eric. "I'm sorry for the interruption. Now what was it you were trying to say?''

Gazing into Belle's expectant face, Eric felt his courage slipping. "Let's have dinner first. Talking about important things is always better on a full stomach.''

She looped her arm through his as they walked toward the dining room. "This certainly has been a day for surprises and making plans. I still have to come up with a reason for the party.'' Belle sighed. "I really wish Paris were here. She is so clever when it comes to figuring things out.''

The mention of her cousin's name reminded Eric of another deception Belle didn't know about and one he had been carefully avoiding. But not any longer. The time for truth had come. "Well, sweetheart, the day isn't over yet and I've got another surprise or two for you. But before I tell you about them, have you ever heard the old adage about not killing the messenger . . . ?''

CHAPTER 12

Seven days later, Belle stood at the viewing window in the salon overlooking the Graysons' ballroom, wondering when she had lost total control of her life. A few months before, she'd been happy, looking forward to getting married, and making plans for her future with her new husband. Now she was angry, resentful, and alone.

Wiping a tear from her eye, she snickered to herself. *I know very well when it happened. The moment I fell in love with Eric Grayson and put my trust in him. He's a rogue and a liar, and I'm far better off without him. As soon as we uncover the villain who's been after my bracelet, I'll never have to see him ever again.*

The door opened behind her. "There you are,

cousin. I was looking all over the house for you. Why are you hiding in here all by yourself?''

Belle adjusted the fit of her spectacles and turned to face Paris. ''I wasn't hiding. I merely needed a bit of privacy so I could sort out my thoughts before I dressed for the party. Why don't you join me for a few minutes so we can talk? You've been so busy helping Trelane with his exercises and recovery since I arrived a week ago, we've hardly seen one another. How did Trelane do with his walking today? Is his mended leg still giving him a lot of pain?''

''In spite of his complaints, Lane's getting better and stronger every day. I think he moans and groans over his discomfort just to garner my sympathy.'' Paris joined her at the viewing window and looked down at the activity in the room below. Eric was sitting at a table, addressing a large group of men clustered around him. ''How are things progressing with the plans for tonight?''

Belle shrugged. ''How would I know? The moment Lady Catherine heard my idea to catch the man responsible for Trelane being attacked and my abduction, she took over the plan as though it were her own.'' Heaving a sigh, she walked to a nearby sofa and sat down. ''I really shouldn't complain because she's been so kind, but Lady Catherine is far too stubborn and autocratic to suit me.''

Paris nodded and sat beside her. ''She does have that way about her. Likes to give orders even more than I do.''

"And she's getting worse. Besides moving me into this house and assigning guards to protect me, Lady Catherine had a new gown made for me. When it arrived this afternoon, she told me in no uncertain terms that I had to wear it to the party. I tried to reason with her, but the woman refuses to take 'no' for an answer."

"What's wrong with the gown?"

"Nothing, really. The gown is quite lovely. It's the height of fashion and made from the finest quality of silk I have ever seen in my life. And before you ask, it fits me perfectly."

Paris frowned in confusion. "So what's your objection to wearing it?"

Belle sighed. "The gown is ruby red."

"You love the color red and you always have. With your complexion and blond hair, that particular shade would look beautiful on you."

"That's exactly what Lady Catherine said. But I still don't want to wear it."

"Now, let's see if I understand all this. One," Paris said, counting off on her fingers, "the gown was a gift that didn't cost you a penny. Two, it's lovely and made of incredibly expensive silk. Three, it fits you perfectly. And four, the color is becoming on you." She shook her head. "This makes no sense, cousin. What aren't you telling me?"

Belle nodded toward the viewing window. "Ruby red is *his* favorite color."

Paris chuckled. "So, that's the way of it. Eric likes ruby red, so you won't wear the gown because you don't want to please him."

"Hearing you say it that way sounds rather child-ish, I admit. But I can't help the way I feel."

Paris put her arm around Belle's shoulders. "Honey, I wish you would get past your anger and accept the man's apology. Eric loves you so much—"

"That he lied to me. After saying he would never do anything to hurt me ever again, he lied to me, Paris."

"He had his reasons, honey."

Belle shook her head. "I can't accept that. Eric knew I was worried about you. But did he tell me you were here? No. Not even when the truth about him deceiving me all those weeks by pretending to be his brother came to light. And do you know what his excuse was for that? He didn't want to get me upset." She sniffed indignantly. "Upset would have been better than the rage I felt when he finally told me how you'd been imprisoned in his parents' home for over a month."

Paris drew her arm back and looked a little uncomfortable at that particular remark. "Impris-oned is such a harsh word. It's true, they forced me to remain here the first day or two, but I quickly discovered that I didn't want to go. And as he recovered, Lane and I grew close. Oh, we still ar-gued and teased, but another emotion surfaced between us."

Belle smiled and patted her hand. "You fell in love, Paris. There's nothing wrong in that. I never had those feelings for Trelane. He deserves to be loved and you do, too. I couldn't be happier for you both.''

"What about you and Eric? You love each other so much."

Belle's smile suddenly faded. "Love isn't enough for me. Call me a fool, but I want trust and honesty as well. Eric doesn't know the meaning of those words."

"Aren't you being a little hard on him?"

Belle shook her head. "No, I'm not. Besides keeping your whereabouts from me, he led me to believe that Alexei Chernoff was his enemy. Turns out the man is one of his most trusted associates."

"Alexei Chernoff. Is he a tall man with long, pale-blond hair? Rather good-looking, with broad shoulders, dresses all in black?"

"That certainly sounds like him. Has he been to this house recently?"

Paris nodded. "Oh, yes. He came by last week with Eric. I saw the two of them going upstairs to the servants' quarters together. Later that day I overheard several of the maids cooing over him. Something about his deep voice sending chills up their spines."

Recalling her own reaction to the mysterious man, Belle sighed over the memory. "That was Alexei. No doubt about it."

"You sound very interested in this man."

Belle frowned at her cousin. "Well, I'm not. He just happens to have a way of speaking that catches your ear like a beautiful song. So melodious and rich. If you ever get the chance to hear him speak, you'll know what I mean.''

Paris sniffed. "I'm still trying to figure out what he and Eric were doing up in the servants' quarters."

"Getting a footman's uniform and a wig for Alexei."

When her cousin scowled in disbelief, Belle explained how Eric had brought Alexei to her home disguised as the humpbacked "Claude" to protect her.

"And if that wasn't bad enough, Paris, Eric stole my only pair of spectacles to keep me from leaving the house."

Paris arched her brow. "It sounds like Eric loves you, Belle. Be honest with me, cousin, and set your anger aside for the moment. Are you absolutely sure that you want him out of your life?"

The sound of Eric's voice drew Belle back to the viewing window. Watching him was both pleasant and painful for her. She longed to run downstairs and throw herself in his loving arms, but she couldn't. He'd lied to her. Made a mockery of her trust. What would stop him from doing it again?

"Belle, you didn't answer. You love Eric. Do you really want him out of your life?"

Belle shrugged as tears coursed down her cheeks. "I don't know, Paris. As God is my witness, I swear I really don't know."

Paris shook her head. "Well, if you ask me, you're the one who's doing all the lying now, cousin."

* * *

". . . and Fraiser, have six armed guards patroling the rear wall in the garden. If anyone tries to escape that way, I want them stopped no matter what." Eric set down the paper he was reading from on the table and turned his attention to the other three dozen men around him. "Ten of you will be dressed as servants and footmen, while the other twenty will be attired in formal clothes so you can mingle freely with the guests. But unlike them, there will be no drinking of spirits. I want you all clear-eyed and alert. Remember, Miss Kingsley, the lady you're going to keep a close watch on tonight, has blond hair and will be wearing a bright red gown and gold-framed spectacles. Now, go with Fraiser to the servants' wing, get your assignments, and be back here ready to work in two hours."

As the men began to leave, Eric saw Jonathan Carlisle hurrying into the ballroom toward him. "Did you find Chernoff?"

Jonathan sat in the chair beside him. "No. I went to the Savoy where he's been staying, but no one has seen him in nearly a week."

"Bloody hell! Of all times for him to disappear. I could have used a man of his talents tonight."

"You've already hired a small army to protect Belle. How much difference could one man possibly make, Eric?"

"A great deal when the man is Alexei Chernoff. He and I served together in many campaigns over the years. People who knew of his abilities called him 'Smoke' because he could drift in and out of places without being detected. By the time an enemy knew of his presence, he was already gone. I was counting on him to help me watch Neville tonight.''

''You mean here in the ballroom?''

Eric shook his head. ''No. When Neville sees the bracelet on Belle's wrist, there isn't a doubt in my mind that he will try to get it. If he doesn't attempt to steal it himself, he'll go out and hire someone to get it for him just as he did before. I wanted Alexei to follow him when he leaves this house to arrange it.''

Jonathan frowned. ''I still can't believe that Neville Farnsworth had the audacity to order an attack on your brother. They've been friends for as long as I can recall. You haven't told Trelane about your suspicions, have you?''

Eric shook his head. ''Not yet. After discussing the matter with my parents, we decided to wait. Until Neville makes his move to get the bracelet, we have no real proof of his guilt.''

''But are you sure he's the one? Neville Farnsworth has always been a materialistic bounder buying up and selling off the choicest artifacts like a tradesman, but I never took him for a man who could betray a best friend.''

''When compared to the amount of money that would be made by selling a piece of the Templars' treasure, friendship is a cheap commodity, Jonathan.''

The Duke of Chatham nodded. ''I know. But for

your brother's sake, I just wish it were someone other than Neville.''

Eric picked up a list from the table and handed it to him. "Fine. You look at these names and tell me who else could have done it. These men are all members of Slaton's who attended the ball in February. Now, the man we're searching for has to know about history, artifacts, and Trelane's working habits. Who on this list would know that my brother stopped at his office at Westminster nearly every night on his way home?''

Leaning over the list, Eric pointed. "There's Lord Mumford. Though he's a PM like Trelane and works on a few committees with him, Mumford is deaf and nearly blind, so it can't be him. Then we have you, of course. While you knew of my brother's habits, you've got more money than Croesus and Mama said you never were any good at your history lessons, so that eliminates you as a suspect. Oh, yes, then we have Henry Townsend, Trelane's humorous but hardworking law partner. More of a buffoon than an intellectual—''

"Enough, Eric!" Jonathan tossed the list at him. "You've made your point most admirably and I agree with you. The only man on that blasted list who fits the criteria we're looking for is Neville Farnsworth. I'm just grateful that you'll be here when all this comes out. Trelane's going to lose his best friend. Perhaps having his brother at his side will ease the blow for him.'' Jonathan stood up. "I'm going home for a hot bath, a shave, and a change of clothes. I'll be back as soon as I can to help you.''

Alone and bone-weary, Eric got to his feet and gathered his papers. *I wish I could be here for Trelane, but unless Belle can forgive me, I'll have to leave England. I can't remain here and not be able to hold her in my arms and love her. Whoever said love conquers all must have had me in mind. I've survived assassins, imprisonment, and battles on four continents during the past eighteen years, only to be brought down by a gentle, soft-spoken beauty who captured my heart.*

An odd feeling that someone was watching him caused a ripple of awareness to rush through Eric. Looking around and finding himself the only person in the room, he shrugged off the sensation and hurried out of the ballroom.

The Graysons' palatial ballroom hardly resembled a trap that evening.

The floor was polished to a high sheen. Dozens of vases filled with colorful flowers added a festive glow while their scent, subtle and alluring, wafted in the air. A group of musicians played softly in the corner as servants rushed about with trays of refreshments through the well-dressed crowd.

It was amid all this perfection that the ''appointed'' guest of honor stood with the Graysons in the receiving line, grumbling to her cousin after being introduced to the latest arrivals.

''Why me?'' Paris hissed, fussing with the skirt of her purple velvet gown. ''All this curtseying and pleasantries is making me ill! Couldn't you have told everyone that it was your birthday instead of mine? You know I can't stand being polite to these people."

Belle sighed as she adjusted the chain of the bracelet on her gloved wrist. "If you're referring to British aristocrats and politicians, cousin mine, you'd best get over it. Especially since you'll soon be married to one of them."

Paris glanced quickly down the line to where Eric was standing with his parents, chatting with an elderly couple, before she replied. "I hate to correct you, Belle, but I am not marrying Trelane."

"Why not? I thought you were in love with him."

"I am, but . . . but . . ." Paris rolled her eyes. "Trelane hasn't gotten around to asking me yet."

"He will. Just wait and see."

Paris gasped. "Belle, do you know something that you're not telling me?"

Winking at her, Belle turned to greet the next couple. "Good evening, Lord Quentin, Lady Mary. My, my, you do look fetching in that gown, Lady Mary. Is it new?"

A short distance away, Catherine Grayson was struggling to retain her composure and failing miserably. "Son, when I get my hands on that overpaid rag peddler, Madame Renoir, she will regret the day she was born!"

Keeping his smile firmly in place, Eric patted her back. "Keep your voice down, Mama. We mustn't let the guests know that anything's amiss."

Catherine sniffed. "Plenty is amiss around here

and it's all her fault!'' she whispered to him. ''When I picked out that fabric for Belle's gown, Madame Renoir swore there wasn't another bolt like it in London. Ha! At least twenty women have arrived at the house tonight wearing that blasted ruby red silk! Not counting Lady Mary. The woman resembles a ship in full sail in that color! Have you ever seen so many ruffles and flounces? Why, it must have taken three bolts to make that gown alone.''

''So, I've noticed, Mama. But there's little we can do about it now.''

Snapping her fan open, she waved it briskly in front of her heated cheeks. ''Perhaps not. But tomorrow morning, I'm going to visit that French tart and make her wish she had never crossed the channel to peddle her wares—''

''Catherine, my dear, is something wrong?''

The countess turned to her husband. Her face was a mask of innocence as she replied, ''Of course not, Miles. Whatever gave you that idea?''

''I thought you might be upset by the fact that so many ladies have arrived wearing red this evening. I know you contrived to have Belle stand out from the crowd, but now she'll merely blend in with all the rest.''

Catherine cast a quick glance at Eric before she looked at her husband. ''Well, we shall just make the best of things. Thank the Lord, Belle is wearing her new gold spectacles tonight. If naught else, that will set her apart from the others.''

Miles regarded the crowded ballroom and frowned. ''My love, I thought we were keeping the guest list to a conservative level to eke out a villain. I vow the crush wasn't this bad at Her Majesty's reception last week at the palace."

"Yes, I know. Quite a few people who weren't on the invitation list came anyway. I didn't want to create a scene by questioning them, so I said nothing."

Miles laughed. "You've never let that stop you before, Cat."

She leaned toward him to whisper. "Need I remind you, sir, that we have more than two dozen guards disguised as guests interspersed throughout this crowd and another ten dressed as servants? With so many strangers flitting about, I wasn't sure who was who."

Eric pulled out his pocket watch and frowned. "Where in the blazes is Neville? Nearly everyone else has arrived. I thought he'd be here by now."

"Patience, my son," Miles assured him. "He will be here."

"I hope so, Father. I sincerely hope so."

Belle saw the concern etched in Eric's face and longed to console him, but she couldn't. At least not yet . . .

"You're doing it again," Paris scoffed in a husky whisper. "Instead of just staring at the man, why don't you say something to him? You're hurting, he's in pain, and you both want to be together."

Running her fingers over her bracelet, Belle shook her head.

Paris heaved a sigh in disgust. "You are so stubborn! Eric tried to reach out to you when we came downstairs, but you refused to budge an inch."

"I have no idea what you're talking about."

"Yes, you do! An hour ago, Eric told you how beautiful you looked tonight and your answer was to shrug off his words, and stick me between the two of you in this receiving line. I've never seen a man so crestfallen in my life. How can you be so cruel to him?"

"He lied to me about Alexei and you—"

"And you're whining like a spoiled child! He did it to protect you, Belle. No other reason. Eric loves you and you love him. Bury that wounded pride or you're going to lose him forever."

The walls of Belle's resolve began to crumble. Paris was right. She was acting like a child. Eric loved her, flaws and all. Instead of trying to make her fit into some mold of perfection that society would accept, he encouraged her to think, to wear what she liked, and to be her own person. He treated her like an equal, not a possession. No one else had ever done that for her before.

Watching Eric as he spoke to his father, tears filled her eyes. After finding such an incredible man to love and share her life her with, how could she allow her stupid pride destroy it all? "You're right, Paris. I don't want to lose Eric. But there's no time to tell him now. Once this party is over, I'll set things to right."

"Good! It couldn't happen soon enough to please me." Paris wiped the tears from Belle's cheeks with her gloved fingers. "You look a bit weepy, little cousin. What you need is to splash some cool water on your face before anyone sees you like this and I could use a drink. Lady Catherine," she called out in a moderated voice to her hostess. "I don't wish to be rude, but how much longer must we remain in this receiving line? No one's arrived in quite some time."

Catherine nodded. "I was just thinking that myself. Why don't you and Belle go inside? We will join you in a few minutes."

Eric frowned as Belle turned to walk away with Paris. "Remember what I told you, Belle. Stay together and don't leave the ballroom. And if anyone takes a special interest in your bracelet, be especially careful."

She surprised Eric by looking back and smiling at him. "Whatever you say, sir. You'll not get an argument out of me." She punctuated her statement with a quick wink of her eye.

His attention stayed firmly fixed on Belle as she entered the ballroom. For the first time in a week, hope began to pool inside him. Perhaps things were going to work out between them. He prayed it was true, because the alternative of losing her was simply too painful to consider.

The sound of familiar voices coming toward him jerked Eric back to the matter at hand. Pasting an amused smile on his face, he turned to greet the newest arrivals.

"Neville, Henry," he said, acknowledging each

with a nod. "I was beginning to think that you two weren't coming tonight."

Neville shook his head. "Don't blame me. Henry insisted that we stop at his tailor on the way to pick up his new waistcoat, so I agreed. He simply failed to inform me that the man's shop was clear on the other side of the city."

Henry snickered. "I did tell him, but Nev was too busy gloating over the Etruscan urn he stole from under Lord Weston's nose this afternoon to hear me."

"I stole nothing," Neville insisted. "I paid a fair price for that piece. If Weston wanted to bid on the urn, he should have arrived on time for the auction."

Trelane's corpulent partner chuckled. "He would have if someone hadn't gotten the clerk at Sotheby's to change the order of the program, putting the urn on the block in the first position instead of the last."

"B-b-but I didn't . . . I never—"

Henry waved his hand in dismissal. "Calm yourself, Nev. I was merely jesting with you, old boy. Forgive me. At this moment, I must pay my respects to our charming hosts." He bowed his head respectfully to Miles. "Good evening, my lord. I am truly honored to be a guest in your home."

The earl patted the younger man on the shoulder. "As always, we're glad that you could join us, Henry. We haven't seen enough of you these days. How have you been?"

Henry smiled. "With Trelane serving in the

House, I've been kept quite busy at the firm, but I don't mind. It's good to know that our country is benefiting from my partner's outstanding efforts." He bowed before Catherine and kissed her hand. "My lady, you are a vision of incredible loveliness." Leaning close to her ear, he nodded toward Miles, "Just remember, dear lady, when you're ready to abandon wealth and nobility for youthful exuberance and undying adoration, I'll be waiting for you."

Catherine laughed as he stepped back and comically wagged his eyebrows up and down at her. "Henry, you are still a scamp! We've missed having your mirth in this household. You really must visit more often." At that moment, she spied his colorful vest. "Is that the new waistcoat you picked up this evening?"

"Yes, it is," Henry preened, opening his dark blue tailcoat to show it off. "Shantung silk from China. I usually don't wear ruby red, but when Madame Renoir showed me the fabric, I knew that I had to have it."

"The witch must have a warehouse filled with the stuff," Catherine muttered.

"Beg pardon, my lady. Did you say something?"

"You did say Madame Renoir? The dressmaker whose shop is on Park Street?"

Henry nodded. "Yes. Her husband, Pierre, is my tailor."

Catherine frowned at Eric before she spoke to her husband. "Miles, is one of our ships going to France anytime soon?"

"As a matter of fact, *Torie's Pride* is leaving for Marseilles the day after tomorrow. Why? Do you fancy a quick trip to the continent, my dear?"

She sniffed. "Not for me. But there's a little something I might like crated and delivered across the Channel as soon as possible."

Eric understood the implications of his mother's words all too well. "Now, Mama, don't do anything rash."

Catherine didn't respond. Wearing a beatific smile, she took Henry's arm. "Come along, Henry. You can escort me to the dining room so we can partake of the buffet supper together. I have something to consider and I always think better on a full stomach."

As they walked away, Miles looked at Eric. "What's that all about?"

"Nothing that won't keep until morning. But if Mother sidesteps the issue as she usually does, don't let her put anything on that ship without inspecting it first." Before his father could ask another question, Eric decided to put their plan into action and turned to Neville.

"Why don't we all go inside and join the celebration? I've yet to give Paris my good wishes for her birthday."

Neville frowned as the three of them entered the ballroom. "Good wishes, Trelane? I thought you didn't like the woman."

Eric shrugged. "Let's say I'm getting used to having her around. Besides, it pleases my future wife. And I'll do whatever's necessary to make my lady happy." He stopped on the edge of the dance floor to look around. "Where can they be?"

At that precise moment, Jonathan hurried up to them. "Good evening, gentlemen. Trelane, I need to speak with you."

Searching the room, Eric shook his head. "Can't it wait for a minute? We're looking for Belle and Paris."

Jonathan touched his arm. "It's about the '*smoke*' problem we discussed earlier. The man you wanted to handle the situation tonight is in the foyer." Jonathan turned to Miles and Neville. "Sorry about the interruption, but Trelane's been having a great deal of trouble with the bedroom chimney in his new home and you know how he is about delays."

Eric realized what Jonathan was saying. Alexei had arrived and was waiting to see him. "Father, why don't you and Neville stay here until I return? I'll just be a few minutes."

Eric and Jonathan had only been gone for a moment when Neville saw Belle and Paris on the far side of the room. "My lord, isn't that Miss Kingsley and her cousin over there beside the punch bowl?"

Miles frowned. "Why . . . ah . . . yes, I believe you're correct. But maybe we should wait until Trelane returns before seeking them out. He'd never be able to find us in this crowd."

"Of course he will. Besides, I'm parched and could do with a bit of liquid refreshment. Let's hurry before we lose sight of the ladies."

The earl sighed over his inability to keep Neville

away from Belle without arousing his suspicions and followed him across the room.

"Good evening, Miss Kingsley, Mrs. Mackenzie," Neville announced as they arrived at the refreshment table. "You ladies certainly look lovely tonight."

Neville's sudden appearance nearly caused Belle to drop her spectacles as she wiped the lenses with a napkin. She quickly recovered her composure and smiled at him. "Thank you, Lord Beekham. It's kind of you—"

"Bella, my girl! There you are at last!"

"Papa?"

Before she could react, Belle was spun around. Her spectacles flew from her hands as she was instantly enveloped in her father's arms. "Of course it's Papa!" Sir Francis chuckled. "Forgive me for being away so long, Bella. I have so much to tell you."

Neville and Paris hurried to retrieve her spectacles that skittered across the floor, but not before one of the footmen, carrying a beverage tray, stepped on them. The servant lost his footing, sending filled wineglasses in all directions. Red wine showered all over the front of Paris and her gown. Miles rushed to her rescue.

"A thousand pardons, my dear. Are you all right?"

Paris wiped the splattered wine from her cheek and neck with her gloved hand. "I usually prefer to drink my wine rather than wear it, my lord. But it will wash off."

Miles frowned. "On your skin perhaps, though I don't hold out much hope for your gown. Come with me, my dear. Maybe the housekeeper can help you get those stains out before they set in."

As the earl led Paris toward the kitchens, Neville brought the spectacles to Belle. "I'm afraid they're beyond repair, Miss Kingsley. The lenses are shattered. Do you have another pair?"

"My old spectacles are in the library," she sighed. "The way I'm going through these, I should have the oculist make them by the dozen."

Neville held them out to her. "The frames don't appear to be too badly bent. Maybe your man can use them again."

"Perhaps. I'll send them to Mr. Edmund's shop in the morning." The bells on her bracelet tinkled loudly as she reached for the spectacles. "Thank you for getting them for me, Lord Beekham."

Belle then noticed that Neville was staring oddly at her bracelet. A frown marred his brow. "Is there anything wrong, sir?"

Neville shook his head. "Not at all, my dear. Just thought about something I need to take care of."

Before she could get him to explain further, Sir Francis broke into their conversation. "Bella, my girl, I'm sorry about ruining your spectacles. I was just so excited about seeing you and my new project, I got carried away with myself." He slapped Neville on the back. "When the members of the Royal Antiquities Society hear of my next expedition, they'll be begging to invest in it."

"Oh, really?" Neville chuckled. "Has another

possible hiding place for the Holy Grail or the Ark of the Covenant suddenly come to light?''

Sir Francis scowled at him. ''Bah! Now you're teasing me, sir. Most people don't believe those blasted things exist, so finding backers to fund such a search is an exercise in futility.''

Belle reached over and patted her father's shoulder, causing her bracelet to jingle loudly. ''Calm down, Papa. Rather than go through all that, why don't you tell us about this new expedition? That's what we really want to hear about, isn't that correct, Lord Beekham?''

Turning to Neville, Belle saw he was once again looking at her bracelet. A shiver of apprehension crept up her spine. *Good grief! Neville must be the man Eric has been searching for! He seems to know a lot about my father's work and now he's fixed his attention on my bracelet. I wonder where Eric is? I've got to get word to him about this.*

Unaware of her concerns, Sir Francis began to explain the details of his new expedition to Belle and Neville Farnsworth. ''Pyramids, much like those found in Egypt, have been located in the Americas. A team of explorers from Dublin will take on the site in Peru, while I will head up a group that will handle the ones in Mexico . . . .''

While Sir Francis spoke, Belle noticed how Neville's eyes would often dart to where she held her hands, folded at her waist. His interest in her bracelet was obvious and making her quite nervous. She looked around, hoping to locate Eric or one of his parents, but without her spectacles, she was unable to see more than a few feet. Frustrated, she decided to do something about that.

"Papa, forgive me for interrupting you, but I've got to put these broken spectacles away and get my old pair." She kissed his cheek. "You carry on with what you're telling Lord Beekham about your exciting new expedition and I'll be right back."

Sir Francis nodded. "Of course, dear girl, of course. Neville and I will wait here until you return."

As Belle made her way through the crowd, she heard her father relating the details of his upcoming trip and couldn't help smiling. *That's the way to do it, Papa. Keep Neville your captive audience for me. Once I get my spectacles, I'll find Eric and let him decide how best we should proceed with this.*

In the salon above the ballroom, a man stood at the viewing window like a sentinel in the darkness, watching her. "Leaving the room by yourself is not a good thing, Belle," he murmured. "Any manner of man could make use of your error in judgment. Yes." He nodded. "Any man indeed."

Closing the viewing window, the man hurried out of the salon.

CHAPTER 13

Eric returned to the ballroom more than a little annoyed. "Bloody hell, Jonathan! Where did Alexei disappear to this time? I rushed out to see him the very moment you told me he was here and now he's nowhere to be found!"

"I don't know what to tell you, Eric. Chernoff made it sound important that he talk to you right away. I can't understand where he could have gone or why."

"Alexei lives by his own rules and always has. Half the time I've known him, I was never quite sure if he was friend or foe."

Standing near the center of the ballroom while he searched the crowd, Eric sighed. "God knows I certainly didn't want to leave Belle in this crush with Neville running about freely on his own. Thank the saints my father is staying right beside Neville for me.''

"I don't think so.'' Jonathan pointed across the room. "Isn't that your father over there by the French doors talking to Catherine? I don't see Farnsworth anywhere near them.''

"Bloody hell!'' Eric elbowed his way through the crowd, leaving Jonathan trailing behind in his wake to apologize to everyone he roughly crashed into as he passed them. "Father, where is Neville Farnsworth?''

Catherine braced her hands on her hips. ''That's precisely what I asked him. But your father doesn't know. I did my part by keeping Henry amused while you two cornered Neville so you could glean information from him, and now you can't find the fool man!''

Miles frowned at his wife. "You're acting as though I lost sight of Neville on purpose, Cat. I was doing quite well until one of the guards disguised as a footman dropped a tray and showered Paris with red wine. The poor woman was positively dripping in the stuff when I led her into the kitchen so the housekeeper could help her clean up.''

That bit of news got Eric's attention. "If you took Paris to the kitchen, who is with Belle? You didn't leave her alone, did you?''

"Of course not,'' the earl replied. "Her father arrived and he was talking to her, over there by the punch bowl. As a matter of fact, Neville was with them when I left the room with Paris.''

Eric and Jonathan were taller than everyone else in the room, so it was easy for them to peruse the crowd. "Bloody hell! I don't see Belle, Sir Francis, or Neville anywhere."

Jonathan shook his head. "Neither do I. But isn't that Fraiser, the man in charge of your guards, coming toward us wearing the major domo's uniform? Perhaps he knows where Belle is."

"Yes. It's him." Eric grabbed Fraiser by the arm and led him to a nearby alcove. "Where's Miss Kingsley? I don't see her in the ballroom."

"She must be here, my lord. My men would have reported to me if the blond lady in the red gown and gold spectacles had left the party."

Eric's eyes narrowed. "Are you sure? The room is filled with women in red gowns."

Fraiser snorted. "Yes, but few of them have blond hair and Miss Kingsley is the only one wearing spectacles. My men and I are professionals, sir. We know what we're doing."

Jonathan rested his hand on the nettled man's shoulder. "Forgive my nephew's anxiety and don't be offended, Mr. Fraiser. He's simply worried about his lady's safety. We can't seem to find her and we obviously need someone with your expertise. Could you possibly speak with your men and have them begin a thorough search of the room for Miss Kingsley without alarming the rest of the guests?"

Fraiser bowed respectfully. "Of course, Your Grace. I'll report back to you posthaste."

Eric scowled at Jonathan as the security man rushed away. "You really do have a gilded tongue.

Though I'm not sure if it was your title or your sugar-sweet tones that got Fraiser to hop to your bidding."

The Duke of Chatham winked. "It's a bit of both, Eric. Now, let's see if the two of us can find Sir Francis and Neville Farnsworth."

Belle entered the library and practically fell into the chair behind the desk. "My goodness! After being in this house for the past week, I didn't think I could get lost so easily. As soon as I can catch my breath, I'll return to the party before Eric discovers I am gone."

Opening the side drawer, she took out her old spectacles and put them on. As she had done several times in the past week, she sat back in the chair for a moment to look at the library. The Graysons' cozy, book-laden retreat would always hold a very special place in her heart. This was where she had first met Eric. Where he had kissed her. Where she had fallen in love with him.

Surrounded by the memories of that fateful night, Belle smiled and accepted the fact that no amount of anger or disappointment would ever destroy her love for Eric. He would drive her insane with his secrets and his overly protective nature, but she would be patient and understanding. And it would be well worth the effort. They loved each other very much and they were meant to be together.

Another memory of yet another night filled her

mind and Belle felt herself blushing. *Perhaps after I accept Eric's apology and tell him how much I love him, I can convince him to spend the night with me. Even if someone locks my door to protect my virtue, Eric can always employ his friend Ruby to let himself into my room. Making love will surely make our reunion complete.*

The mantel clock chimed the hour, shaking Belle from her reverie. "Oh, dear, it's getting late! I'd better get back to the party before Eric panics and sends the army out to find me." Standing up, she brushed the wrinkles from the skirt of her gown. The action caused the bells on her bracelet to jingle. "Soon I will know if this noisy bit of bait can really catch a villain."

Belle turned as the door opened and Henry Townsend stuck his head inside. "Well, another familiar face at last! Did you get lost as well, Miss Kingsley?"

She smiled. "It's easy to do in this house. Especially when I don't have my spectacles on. I thought you would know the Graysons' house after all the years you've been friends with Trelane."

Henry stepped into the room, chuckling. "You would think so, but it's worse than a maze for me. All these floors, different staircases and corridors. Never been good with puzzles myself."

"I don't mind puzzles if I can see what I'm doing." Belle touched the frames of her spectacles. "Without these, I'm as blind as the proverbial bat."

Henry nodded, his usually merry face suddenly sad and tinged with melancholy as he leaned back against the door. "At least the spectacles can help you. My father has been blind for over a year now."

"Oh, that's too bad. Being totally blind must be quite a burden."

"It is when you consider that he spent his entire life reading books and the crudely written papers of his students. He taught history and Latin at Cambridge University. That's where Trelane, Neville, and I met and became friends."

Belle heard a metallic click and couldn't quite place the sound for a moment. When she noticed that Henry's hands were still behind his back, she realized that Trelane's friend and law partner had just turned the key in the lock. It was then that she became aware of one more thing: Henry was staring intently at her bracelet.

Dear God, it's never been Neville Farnsworth at all. Henry is the one who wants the "key" to the Templars' treasure. He's locked us inside the library and blocked the door with his body. How can I get away from him?

Belle smiled as she eased her way toward the French doors to the garden. "So the three of you became friends at Cambridge. I didn't even know that Neville attended university."

"Most wealthy families expect it of their sons. If he hadn't been born rich, Neville would have likely been a professor of history like my father." Henry sighed. "We were quite an unlikely trio back then. Two sons of money and affluence and me, the charity case."

"What do you mean, 'charity case'?"

"Because my father was on staff at Cambridge,

I was allowed to attend school there. If not for that, I never would have gotten an education."

"Don't be so hard on yourself, Henry," she said, inching closer to the garden doors. "You may have had humble beginnings, but now you're one of the most successful barristers in all of England. Why, your client list boasts some of the most powerful families in Europe, if not the world."

Henry shook his head. "But that's only because Trelane Grayson was my law partner. And it's *Lord* Trelane Grayson," he said, emphasizing the title. "The brother of Viscount Ryland, son of the Earl of Foxwood, and nephew of the Duke of Chatham. Quite a pedigree for a barrister . . . a blue-blooded barrister. And that's what the aristocrats want. A barrister who is one of their own."

The door was less than a foot away as she gave him her most encouraging smile. "Perhaps that's why they came in the beginning, Henry, but you've more than proven your expertise. Especially now that Trelane's serving in the House of Commons and Parliament. Without you there, working hard and taking excellent care of your clients, the firm of Grayson and Townsend would have fallen into ruin months ago."

Henry looked down and shrugged. "Maybe you're right. But it's not enough. I'm not Trelane's social equal nor will I ever be. Only great wealth and prestige from an outstanding accomplishment could even the differences between us. And soon, all that will be mine."

Belle used his momentary distraction to make

her move. She grabbed the knob on the French door and twisted it. Before it turned, Henry pounced upon her with a speed that was frightening and totally unexpected for such a heavyset man. He wrapped his arm around her neck and pressed the barrel of a gun against her head as he dragged her away from the door.

"Such pretty words and sentiments, but I knew exactly what you were doing, Miss Kingsley. Don't scream for help, my dear, because I'm desperate enough to shoot you to get my key back."

"Your key?" she rasped, struggling to breathe against the pressure he was applying to her throat. "If you're referring to my bracelet, Henry, it belongs to me. I bought it from a junk peddler in France."

"But it was mine first. I paid a fortune for it in *Rennes-le-Château*. Minutes after I bought it, I was robbed by a common pickpocket. I chased the little bastard to an open-air market. By the time I caught the boy, he had gotten rid of it. I strangled the brat and tossed his body in the river."

"You killed a child for a piece of cheap jewelry?"

Henry tightened his arm around her throat. "Don't take me for a fool, Miss Kingsley. I know that piece is the key to the Templars' treasure."

"How did you discover that?" she rasped.

"An old manuscript written by a medieval knight reported to be a Templar was found at an abbey in that area of France and brought to my father to translate several years ago. But his eyes were already failing him, so I pored over the Latin in that text for months and eventually learned how this knight had engraved the map settings for the secret locations of the Grail and the Ark of the Covenant on those bells. Once I discovered where the knight was buried, I hired a grave robber to get it for me. When I saw it on your wrist at the engagement party, I knew God had finally given me back what was supposed to be mine."

Henry released the force of his hold on her neck and rubbed the barrel of his pistol on Belle's head. "Now, give it to me."

Belle's fingers were shaking as she tried to unfasten the clasp while he kept talking near her ear.

"I actually held it in my hand for a moment at the party when the link broke. But Trelane was determined to have it repaired for you. I hired a gang of thugs to rob him of it later that night behind Westminster. They swore they had beaten him bloody when he wouldn't turn the key over to them, but they obviously lied or hurt some other man because Trelane stopped to see me the next day, very healthy and unscathed." Henry sighed. "Truth be told, I'm rather happy my old friend hadn't suffered after all."

Belle freed the bracelet and held it out to him. "Take it, Henry. It belongs to you. I won't tell anyone, I swear it."

Snatching the bracelet, Henry cocked the hammer on his pistol. "I'm sorry, but I don't believe you. The only way to save myself is to shoot you and make it look like a robbery. Farewell, Miss Kingsley."

The garden doors crashed open and Belle gasped at the sight of her rescuer entering the library. "Eric! Help me, Eric!"

Henry yanked Belle in front of him like a shield, keeping the gun at her temple. "Why are you calling Trelane by that name?"

"Because that is my name, Henry. I'm Eric Grayson, Trelane's twin," he said, adjusting the sleeves of his formal black cutaway coat as he calmly walked toward them. "Surely, Trelane has mentioned me to you over the years. My saintly brother usually refers to me as the prodigal son of our family."

"Of c-c-course he mentioned a brother," Henry stammered as he backed up. "B-but why are you here?"

"Because I've been masquerading as my brother to trap the person responsible for attacking him. He nearly died that night. It's too bad one of Trelane's closest friends is guilty of such a heinous crime."

Henry shook his head. "I don't believe you're Eric. This is some kind of jest. I've known Trelane for over fifteen years and I would bet my life that you are he."

Suddenly, the door to the hallway silently opened behind Henry and another man, identical to the first, entered the library. He was dressed exactly like his twin and he was smiling. "And you would have won that wager, Henry, because he is Trelane. I am Eric Grayson."

Henry's eyes nearly bulged from their sockets as he looked from brother to brother in stunned amazement. "By the rood! There *are* two of you!"

Belle used his confusion to her advantage. She slammed her elbow forcefully into his chest, causing him to lose his hold on her and his gun. Henry reached to grab her, but Eric was quicker. Spinning the shorter man around, Eric slammed him in the jaw with his fist, sending Henry crashing to the floor.

Trelane picked up the gun. "Well done, brother! Knocked him out with a single blow. One of these days you must show me how to do that."

Eric usually would have appreciated praise coming from his brother, but he was too busy taking Belle into his arms and kissing her to notice anything else. Easing away from her a moment later, he tenderly stroked her cheek and gazed into her eyes. "Are you all right, sweetheart?"

Smiling at him, she nodded. "I'm fine. Truly I am now that you've come to my rescue again. How did you know I was in here with Henry?"

"As much as I'd like to take all the credit, it was my brother who told me where to find you. Trelane was watching the festivities from the viewing window and saw you leave the ballroom. Since he knew about our plan to use you and your bracelet as bait to find the culprit—"

Belle looked at Trelane. "Who told you about the plan? It was Paris, wasn't it? I knew she couldn't keep a secret."

Trelane grimaced from the stiffness in his leg and leaned his hip on the edge of the desk. "Paris told me nothing. I knew something was afoot and spied a bit on my own. When I overheard my brother talking to Jonathan in the ballroom earlier today, I decided to include myself in the scheme. Identical clothes, sneaking about in the shadows, watching without being seen. It was fun pretending to be my brother for a change." He suddenly frowned. "But you know, Belle, I was really quite put out when I learned how everyone knew what was going on but me."

"Forgive us, Trelane. We were only trying to protect you."

Eric cupped her chin and made her face him. "Exactly what I was trying to do when I didn't tell you the truth about Alexei and Paris. Can you forgive me now?"

"Only if you agree that we won't ever keep secrets from each other. No matter how noble the reason."

He dropped a quick kiss on her lips. "Never again, I swear it."

Henry began to moan on the floor.

Looking down at him, Trelane sniffed. "Well, it appears my old friend and partner is waking up. Shouldn't one of us send for the constables?"

"That will not be necessary, my lord. They are already here."

Trelane jerked with surprise when he found Alexei standing behind him. "My word! I didn't hear you come in."

"And you never will," Eric sighed. "Trelane, this is my associate, Alexei Chernoff. He's been helping me take care of Belle and find out who was responsible for attacking you."

Trelane set down the pistol and extended his hand to Alexei. "Good to meet you, sir, and thank you. I appreciate all you've done on our behalf. Did you say the constables are here?"

Dressed in his customary black attire with his silvery-blond hair flowing across his shoulders, Alexei shook his hand and nodded. "Yes, my lord. They are waiting in the garden with the guards Eric hired for the night. I brought them in that way so the other guests would not be alarmed by their presence."

"Excellent. Bring them in. The sooner we get this man out of my family's home, the better."

As Alexei went outside, Henry struggled to sit up. "I'm sorry, Trelane," he whimpered. "I-I never meant for you to be hurt. You were my friend."

"A friend? I don't think you know the meaning of the word, Henry. A real friend isn't envious or deceitful of his companions. I heard what you said to Belle about Neville and me. When we met you at school, we offered you our friendship and trust. I considered you my equal and even asked you to be my law partner. But evidently that wasn't enough for you."

Henry shook his head. "You don't understand.

My father is a brilliant man, a wonderful teacher, and he was paid only a pittance for his efforts. Now he's blind and reduced to living in poverty. If it wasn't for my support, he'd starve to death. I didn't want to end up like him.''

"That doesn't give you the right to break the law, Henry."

Henry snorted. "Why am I even trying to explain this to you, Trelane? You were born to wealth and affluence. You can't possibly know what it's like not to have money or respect.''

"Respect is something earned, Henry. It's not a birthright or something inherited along with a title,'' Trelane countered. "Greed is what drove you to this. Greed for money, power, and respectability. In the name of greed, you betrayed me, inflicted pain on others, and committed a murder to cover your crimes. May God forgive you for all you have done, because I cannot.''

After the constables took Henry Townsend away, Eric found Belle standing alone in the garden, gazing up at the stars. He came up behind her and wrapped his arms around her waist. "What are you thinking about, sweetheart?''

She leaned back against him and sighed. "Many things. You. Me. Our future together. It's rather ironic that we actually have Henry Townsend to thank for the way things worked out. If not for him, I would be marrying your brother in three weeks' time instead of you.''

"I doubt that. Once I kissed you in the library the night we met, you were mine forever. I never would have let you marry Trelane."

Belle turned in his arms until she faced him. "Oh, really? What would you have done? Kidnaped me before I got to the church?"

He hugged her close. "Whatever it took, sweetheart. I fell in love with you the moment we met and in my heart of hearts, I knew I could never let you go."

"Good. Because I feel exactly the same way." She stretched up on tiptoe and kissed him until they were both breathless and throbbing with need. Pulling away slightly, she looked up at him. "I don't want to wait until the wedding to make love with you again. Isn't there some way we can be together tonight?"

"It depends. Are you staying here or going home with your father?"

Belle frowned. "Darn! I forgot Papa's home. He'll expect me to go back to the house with him."

Eric chuckled. "No, love. That's perfect. It's a damn sight easier sneaking about in your family's house instead of mine—there are a lot fewer people to contend with." He kissed her. "You go home with your father. I'll be there within the hour. There's something I need to take care of before I can go anywhere."

She was nearly to the house when she turned back to him. "Eric, should I leave the kitchen door unlocked?"

Patting his ruby stickpin, he shook his head. "Don't bother. I have a friend who can help me."

Belle laughed. "Oh, yes. I forgot." She blew him a kiss. "See you in an hour, my love."

Eric closed his eyes for a moment and inhaled the cool night air. Contentment filled his being like a welcome tonic. The pains of his past were a far distant thing now. Fears of the darkness had disappeared. Loneliness and despair would trouble him no longer. Loving Belle had cured his ills and welcomed him home at last.

His eyes suddenly opened. He knew he wasn't alone.

"Welcome back, Alexei. When you sent in the constables and didn't return, I wondered how long you would stay away."

Eric turned to find his compatriot standing a few feet away. Alexei smiled. "So, you knew I was here. Is that why you sent your lovely lady home?"

"No. You and I have a few matters to discuss privately. And I have a gift for you." Eric took Belle's bracelet from his pocket and gave it to Alexei. "This is what you came to England for, isn't it?"

Alexei's brow rose. "Why would I want a lady's bracelet, Eric?"

"It's not a bracelet. It's a mantle clasp, the one you asked Belle about the day you appeared at her home. When I heard Henry saying it was found in a medieval knight's grave, the pieces of the mystery began to come together in my mind. Why have you gone to all this trouble to retrieve this clasp? Are you hoping to find the treasures for yourself?"

Shaking his head, Alexei smiled. "No. Personal gain is not my interest. I came to retrieve the clasp because it was my duty to do so."

Eric frowned. "Your duty? Are you working for someone?"

"In a manner of speaking, yes. I work for God."

"God?" Eric's jaw suddenly dropped. "Bloody hell! You're one of them. You're a Templar Knight!"

Alexei nodded, his face serious yet serene. "Yes, I am a Templar. Sworn to protect and defend the secrets of our holy order."

"But you can't be one of 'them.' Templars are monks and monks are men of God. You're a soldier. I've seen you fight."

"Like the nine men who founded our order, I am a soldier. It is the way I make my living. But I am a man of God first."

Pacing a few steps away, Eric dragged his fingers through his hair. "You know, I often wondered why I never saw you with a woman. I thought you were shy or perhaps you didn't—Well, never mind what I thought. Obviously I was wrong. Knowing what I know now, it makes sense."

Alexei chuckled. "You are a good man, Eric Grayson. Honest, brave, and with great integrity. That is why I chose to be your friend. Sometimes you doubted my intentions, but it was my actions and my need for concealment that fueled those doubts.''

"Such as what happened in Venice. I thought you had betrayed me. You call me a good man and I . . .'' A bit of a long-forgotten memory entered Eric's mind. He turned to face Alexei. "You were the one who came to me in the dungeon dressed in a priest's robe and saved my life. I was burning up with fever, begging for death, but you said no. That I was a good man, worth saving.''

Alexei nodded. "And you are, Eric Grayson. Never forget that.'' He gave Eric the mantle clasp. "Return this to your lady, with my blessings.''

"But the locations of the Templars' treasures are on this.''

"Not any longer, Eric. I received word this morning that my brothers have moved them far from harm.''

Eric looked down at the chain and bells in his hand. "Will the Templars ever share their treasures with the rest of the world?''

"It is not our treasure. These gifts from God belong to all mankind. We are but the caretakers. And until the people of this earth can appreciate the bounty of His goodness, the Templars will continue to carry out their duties as they have in secret all these centuries.''

When Eric tried to slip the mantle clasp into his pocket, it fell to the ground under an evergreen bush. He bent down to pick it up. "Alexei, could you at least tell me what the Grail is? Is it really the cup of . . ." The question died on his lips as he turned and found that Alexei was gone.

Rather than be disturbed by his disappearance, Eric smiled with knowing acceptance. "Godspeed to you, Alexei Chernoff. If the Almighty is indeed merciful, we shall meet again, my friend."

CHAPTER 14

When Eric opened the door to Belle's bedroom nearly three hours later, she tossed her spectacles on top of the vanity table and threw herself into his arms. "Thank goodness you're here. I thought something awful had happened. I was about to get dressed and go out looking for you. Did you have problems getting into my house?"

He shook his head and gave her a quick kiss. "No. The trouble I had was getting *out* of my family's house. Bloody hell! I've never had so damned many people trying to tell me what to do."

Belle helped him remove his coat and hung it in the closet. "Well, why don't you sit in the chair by the fireplace and tell me all about it? From the tone of your voice, I can see you're quite upset about this."

"Upset, annoyed, and shocked beyond belief is more like it! Who in the blazes did they pick on while I was gone these past eighteen years?"

"Keep your voice down, Eric, or we'll have my father and Mrs. Tuttle to contend with as well. And I would prefer not hearing from them at this hour, thank you very much." She ushered him to the chair and pushed him into the seat. "So, tell me what happened."

Before he could open his mouth, Eric was out of the chair and pacing the length of her bedroom. "What happened is that my family has gone completely over the edge! First, my father and Jonathan cornered me in the library. While you and I were talking in the garden, the two of them were deciding my future. My future! Father demanded that I take over the family's shipping business with my older brother James and Jonathan insisted that my talents would be better put to use working for the government."

Belle sat wearily in the chair he'd abandoned. "What kind of work does Jonathan have in mind for you?"

"With my experience dealing with conflicts in foreign countries, he thinks I could help the War Department or, possibly, the diplomatic corps. He even offered to put in a good word for me with the queen if I was interested in becoming an ambassador." Eric shuddered. "Me, an ambassador? Not bloody likely! I told Jonathan he had the wrong brother."

"Well, Trelane is better suited for—"

"And don't even get me started on my brother!" Eric snapped. "After all I did for him, you wouldn't believe what that high-handed cretin said to me!"

Belle leaned her elbow on the arm of the chair and rested her chin in her hand as he passed her. "I won't know unless you tell me. Go ahead, I'm listening."

"When I went to my room to change out of Trelane's clothes, I found my saintly brother waiting for me. The good barrister tore into me again for keeping secrets from him. Said I should have told him about my suspicions regarding Neville and allowed him a say into what had to be done. Here, I was so concerned about how badly he would feel about being betrayed by a friend, and the ungrateful clod attacks my noble intentions like an angry dog!"

"Trelane's a proud, independent man, exactly like you. How would you have felt in his place?"

Eric sighed, his face a mask of grudging acceptance. "All right, I'll concede to that point. But not the rest of it. He can bloody well go to the devil with his damned advice!"

Belle rolled her eyes as he walked stiffly past her again. "Dare I ask what Trelane suggested?"

"He wants me to go back to school! Said I should use the brains God gave me, and attend the university." A bark of harsh laughter left his lips. "I'm a thirty-four-year-old man, not an eager lad just out of Eton, for crying out loud!''

''What course of study did he suggest that you pursue?''

Eric shook his head. ''You'll never believe it! He wants me to study law so I can be his new partner. Me and Trelane partners! Hell! We'd argue so much, there would never be time to deal with the courts or our clients. Why would my brother even suggest such a fool thing?''

''Because he needs you, Eric.''

That statement made Eric stop in his tracks. He wheeled around to face her. ''That's insane. Trelane doesn't need me.''

She nodded. ''Yes, he does. After what transpired with Henry, Trelane is going to be hard-pressed to put his trust in anyone. He knows you're honest and intelligent. But more than anything, he knows you would never betray him.''

''Of course I wouldn't betray him. He's my brother and I love him. But I can't be a barrister. The first time a judge didn't find in my favor, I would lose my temper and be held in contempt for hitting the man.'' He walked back to where she was sitting beside the fireplace and sighed. ''I'm honored that Trelane thought of me, but he would be better off with someone else as a partner.''

''Did you bother to tell him that?''

Deep in thought for a moment, Eric stared into the flaming hearth. ''No. But I will tell him tomorrow.''

His softer tone of voice gave Belle hope that the

brunt of his anger was spent and now they could proceed with "other things." She stood up behind Eric and comforted him by rubbing his back. "Well, none of this has to be decided tonight. Take your time, consider your options, and I will support whatever choice you make."

Eric turned and took her into his arms. "My mother told me you would do that. She also said I should discuss everything with you first, that it was 'our' life that I'd be deciding on, not just my own."

"I always thought Lady Catherine was a very intelligent woman."

"She is that, but being preached to by one's mother in the middle of the night on the back stairs can be quite aggravating!"

Feeling his tension returning, Belle sighed to herself. *So much for "other things."* She rested her cheek against his chest and hugged him close. "Am I correct in assuming that Lady Catherine caught you sneaking out of the house tonight?"

"Yes. And it's not the first time. I swear that woman can read my mind."

"It's not that, Eric. You and your mother are kindred souls. You're both stubborn, strong, protective, and extremely free-spirited. Lady Catherine probably sees a great deal of herself in you."

"That's precisely what she said. But it still doesn't mean that I should be pleased when she makes me sit with her on the back stairs in the middle of the night and reprimands me like a naughty little boy."

Belle chuckled. "Oh, it couldn't have been that bad."

"You think not? Mama waved a finger under my nose and informed me that I wouldn't be traveling the world anymore. Like a bloody tyrant, she stood there and told me my place was home in England, and that's where I was to stay!"

A frown of uncertainty creased Belle's brow. "But why are you so upset about that? Just last week you told me you'd had your fill of going from country to country, and didn't want to leave England ever again. Have you changed your mind?"

Eric kissed the top of her head. "Not at all, sweetheart. I just resented my mother telling me what I should or shouldn't do as though I were a child. And if that wasn't bad enough, she slapped me for swearing in her presence again."

"Well, I wasn't going to mention it, Eric, but you do cuss quite often. Comes from too many years of being in the constant company of men, I suppose. If you're not careful, I'm afraid our baby's first words are going to be 'bloody hell'."

"Our baby?" He jerked back to look at her face. "Belle, are you saying that you . . . that we . . ."

"No!" Belle felt her cheeks burning. She buried her face against his chest. "At least, not yet . . . I hope."

Eric laughed and gave her a reassuring squeeze. "Oh, sweetheart, either way makes no difference to me. I love you and I want us to have children together. Though I must admit that I'd like to have you all to myself for a little while. Do you think me dreadfully selfish for saying that?"

Gazing up into his clear blue eyes, she smiled. "How can I, when I find myself thinking much the same thing? I'm glad you came tonight."

"I am, too. But after the way I've been carrying on, with all my ranting and raving, I wouldn't blame you if you tossed me out on my ear."

Belle shook her head, tossing her hair away from her neck. "Oh, no, that would be an awful waste of time and energy."

Eric's smile dissolved into a grimace as he gingerly touched the bruises on her throat with his fingers. "Damn! I should have killed Henry Townsend for hurting you like this. When I think of how close I came to losing you tonight, I could—"

"But you didn't lose me, so stop worrying about what might have been." She pulled his hands away from her neck and kissed them. "I could think of far better things for us to do. Like this." She placed his hands inside her robe to cup her bare breasts.

Without warning, the door was suddenly flung open and Sir Francis came rushing into the room, reading from a stack of papers in his hand. "Bella, my dear, I saw the light under your door and knew you'd be awake."

Eric snatched his hands away and hid them behind his back as Belle gasped and pulled the top of her robe together. "Papa, this isn't a very good time—"

Sir Francis looked up from his papers. "Oh, Eric's here. Good, good. I could use his opinion on my travel plans. Have you ever been to Mexico, my boy?''

"Well . . . ah . . . no, sir, I haven't,'' Eric replied, casting a quick look at Belle. "I spent a few months in South America about seven years ago, though. Why do you ask?''

"Just trying to figure out how long the voyage will take. Well, I can look into that tomorrow.'' Sir Francis held up one of the papers. "I'm also making a list of the supplies we will need for our trek through the jungle. We wouldn't want to forget anything.''

The words "we" and "our" caught Eric's attention. Before he could question his future father-in-law, Belle took the old man to task. "Papa, I told you that Eric and I wouldn't be going on the expedition with you.''

Sir Francis frowned. "Why not, Bella? I've postponed the departure date to the day after your wedding. That should give you more than enough time to get ready for the trip.''

Eric could see the anger building in Belle and decided to rescue Sir Francis from her wrath. "As much as we would love to accompany you on this wonderful adventure, sir, I won't be able to leave England for at least two years. Maybe more. My father has asked me to take over his position at Ryland Shipping while he tends to family business elsewhere with my mother. He's depending on me, sir, and I can't let him down. I trust you will understand.''

"Oh, of course, of course. A lovely woman, that

mother of yours. Can't blame your father for wanting to be with her." Sir Francis began walking to the door. "Perhaps the two of you will be available for my next expedition, wherever that happens to be. Good night."

Eric was about to breathe a sigh of relief when the old man turned around and waved his papers at them. "By the by, thought you both should know I'm putting the house in your names as a part of your wedding present. Plus a tidy little sum for sprucing it up a bit. I'm rarely here and a house should be lived in. Well, I'll see you two in the morning. 'Night, Bella, my dear. Eric."

Sir Francis was nearly out the door when he looked back at Eric and his daughter. "I would strongly advise you to lock this door in the future. You never know who could drop by and spoil your fun."

"But, Papa, we didn't . . . I mean . . ."

He shook his tousled head of pure white hair. "No explanations are necessary, my dear. I was young and in love once myself. I'm just grateful that Eric didn't try to use the trellis outside your window. I weakened it some thirty-odd years ago when I crept into this very room to visit your mama before we were married and I never got around to having it repaired. A person could get killed using that old thing. Well, blessings to you both. Good night."

Belle locked the door behind her father and turned to Eric. "My father actually climbed a trellis so he could sneak in here to be with my mother before they were wed? I don't know whether I should be mortified or laugh about this."

Eric pulled her into his arms. "Take joy in it, sweetheart. Evidently your parents were very much in love and unable to wait to be together either."

"But what would your mother and father have to say about it if they knew?"

He chuckled. "Nothing much, considering my mother gave birth to James and Diana less than six months after they were married. Now, are we going to spend the night discussing our families and their tawdry pasts or would you like to make love with me?"

Belle smiled. "I thought you would never ask—"

Eric captured her mouth with his. When he pulled her tightly against him, the lump in his trouser pocket poked Belle painfully.

"Ouch!" she cried, stepping back to rub the aching spot. "What's in your pocket? A handful of jagged rocks?"

"No. In all the excitement, I forgot to give you this." He took out the mantle clasp and handed it to her.

"Oh! My bracelet! I wondered what became of it. I thought the constables might have kept it to use as evidence against Henry."

Eric shook his head. "They won't be needing it. When I last saw Townsend, he was babbling about making a full confession and throwing himself on the mercy of the courts. Not that he deserves any. He murdered George Miller and hired those thugs to attack Trelane. The leader of the gang regained consciousness earlier tonight and gave the authorities a description of Henry Townsend that fits him perfectly.''

"Murder, betrayal, assault, and kidnaping. He went through all that to get my bracelet and the secret locations of the Templars' treasures.''

"It's not a bracelet, sweetheart. It's a mantle clasp. The one Alexei Chernoff came to see you about a month ago.''

She frowned up at him. ''What has your friend Alexei got to do with this? Is he trying to find the Grail and the Ark, too?''

Eric smiled ruefully and shook his head. ''No, love. Alexei was sent to retrieve the stolen mantel clasp to prevent anyone else from using it. As surprising as it may seem, Alexei Chernoff is a Templar Knight.''

Belle gasped. ''You're telling me that I wasn't wrong. That the order still exists?''

"Yes. Alexei said the Templars were the caretakers of the treasures God gave to mankind. And until the people of this earth can appreciate the true worth of his gifts, the Templar Knights would continue to carry out their duties as they have in secret for over five hundred years.''

"But if this mantle clasp is genuine, why did he return it to me?''

"The clasp is real, but the secret is safe. Evidently, other members of the order moved the treasures to new hiding places. Since you loved the piece, Alexei wants you to have it as a keepsake.'' Eric put his arm around her shoulders and began leading her toward the bed. "A devoted monk or not, I think my friend has a soft place in his heart for you, Belle."

"Now you're beginning to sound jealous."

"I'm also possessive as hell and I won't apologize to anyone for saying so."

Belle put the mantle clasp on the night table and turned back to Eric. She began unbuttoning his shirt. "Well, I'll just have to do my best to soothe your worries and tell you every day how much I love you. Do you think that will help?"

He smiled. "Words are nice, but a special lady once told me I was a man of action."

"Are you really? Couldn't prove it by me. Here I am, all bathed, powdered, and bare beneath this robe, ready to make love, and you're—"

"Just getting started."

Eric drew Belle into his arms and tenderly kissed her. As their tongues touched and caressed, joy filled his heart. The fear of losing her was gone. She was here, safe in his embrace, tasting like forever. Nothing had ever felt so good, or so very right. Without breaking the kiss, he pushed the robe off her shoulders and eased her down to the bed.

"You are so beautiful, I can hardly believe you're mine," he whispered as he tossed his shirt aside to lie down beside her. "I'm going to kiss every inch of your body just to remind myself that it's true."

Belle shivered with excitement as Eric made good his pledge. With his hands, lips, and tongue, he lovingly touched and caressed her. Her arms, breasts, and neck were treated to his tender ministrations. Even her fingertips were adored and nibbled on and drawn into his mouth, one by one. A restlessness she didn't understand caused her to move her hips from side to side by the time he'd journeyed down one leg and was halfway up the other. But Eric knew precisely what to do to relieve it.

Eric parted the lips of her womanhood and kissed her moist, pink flesh. Then his tongue probed her, licking the tiny, sentient nub hidden there. She gasped and wanted to beg him to stop, but the sensations were too good, her needs too great to let modesty interfere. It felt wonderful, frightening, and intense all at the same time. When he suckled on it and thrust his fingers inside, her orgasm exploded. Crying out with her release, she collapsed sated and content on the bed.

A few moments later, Belle opened her eyes to see Eric stretching out, naked and aroused, beside her on the bed. She turned toward him and kissed him as she ran her hands over his large, powerful body. When her questing fingers wrapped around his manhood, it was his turn to shiver with need. He moaned into her mouth as she stroked his hardened flesh.

Knowing her touch was bringing him pleasure gave Belle a newfound confidence in herself as a woman. Still holding him, she began kissing his chest and laved his nipples until they were taut beneath her tongue. She was about to kiss her way down his flat abdomen when Eric suddenly pulled her hands from his hardened flesh and pressed her back against the bed as he loomed over her.

"But, Eric, I wanted to taste—"

Eric silenced her with a quick kiss. "Next time, love. I can't wait a second longer. I need to be inside you now."

In a single motion, he entered her—deep, hard, and sure. Belle arched up against him, wrapping her legs around his hips as she met his thrusts with equal fervor. Time was forgotten as the two lovers rushed fast and hot to a shattering climax.

Her cries of release were music to Eric's ears as he went over the precipice of passion and felt his seed flood her womb.

The sun was coming up as Eric cuddled Belle in his arms. He was exhausted, but too filled with plans and dreams of the future to sleep.

Things had certainly changed for him in the past few months. He'd come back to England—bitter, world-weary, and alone. His taste for war and adventure had soured. The search for home and family had seemed like an impossible quest. But not anymore. The answer to his prayers, and his needs, was sleeping happily in his arms.

As if sensing his unrest, Belle reached up and patted his whiskered cheek. "I love you, Eric," she whispered in a drowsy voice. "We'll be happy together, I promise."

"I know, sweetheart. There's not a single doubt in my mind."

And miracle of miracles, there wasn't.

With a smile on his face, Eric fell asleep.

CHAPTER 15

Three weeks later . . .

The cream of English society had come together for what was to be the wedding of season. The long-estranged son of the Earl of Foxwood was marrying the daughter of one of the country's most honored scholars and explorers. Besides being an advantageous pairing for them both, it was bandied about town that theirs was indeed a love match. Invitations were highly valued. Ladies in their springtime finery—pastel gowns and elaborate bonnets adorned with yards of tulle and satin flowers—and gentlemen attired in handsome suits and top hats filled the pews of the old church, eager to witness the event.

But what should have been a dignified ceremony held a couple of surprises for the bride and groom. . . .

". . . and do you, Belladonna Marie, take this man to be your lawfully wedded husband?"

Eric looked at his bride and laughed out loud. "Belladonna?"

Belle poked him in the ribs with her elbow. "This isn't funny," she hissed, so the wedding guests wouldn't hear her. "My Mama loved plants and she thought the sound of that name was quite beautiful. It probably never occurred to her that the plant was poisonous."

He smiled and kissed her cheek. "Being named after a toxic plant isn't the worst thing in the world, sweetheart. Believe me, I know."

Belle frowned with curiosity. "What do you mean—"

The archbishop cleared his throat. "May we please continue?"

Instantly chastened, the couple nodded as the cleric repeated the question to the bride and she made her proper response.

"And do you, Catlin Eric, take this woman—"

Belle giggled out loud. "Catlin? Did he say your name is Catlin?"

Sighing, Eric nodded. "Now you understand what I meant about your name not being so bad. Do you think it was any easier for me being named after my mother?"

Looking back at his mother, Eric winked and then asked the archbishop to continue with the ceremony.

Sitting in the front row of the church, Catherine Grayson, Countess of Foxwood, was glowing with happiness. Her prodigal son had come home and found love at last. And by the end of the week, his twin would be married as well.

Miles squeezed her hand. "You are positively beaming, my love. I thought ladies usually cried at weddings."

"Not this lady, darling. I have every reason to celebrate. I never thought Eric and Trelane would ever get married. That they've fallen in love with two incredible young women only adds to my joy."

Miles shook his head. "Even after all these years, you're such a romantic, my love."

Looking up at her husband, Catherine smiled. His dark hair was thick with silver and lines creased his noble face, but she still thought he was the handsomest man in the entire world. "Of course I'm a romantic. Being happily married to you all these years, English, how could I be anything else?"

Miles brought her hand to his lips and kissed it. "Perhaps, but you were the one who brought love into my life and taught me of its worth, Lady Cat." He tucked her hand into the crook of his arm. "Now let's be quiet and listen to the ceremony before the archbishop turns his scowl on us."

Catherine nodded and tried to turn her attention

back to the couple before the altar, but her gaze drifted to her brother, Jonathan, who was sitting at the end of their row.

"Miles, at the reception, I want you to talk to Jonathan. He's nearly thirty-six and it's past time that he finds a wife. As the Duke of Chatham, it's his duty to get married and produce an heir."

Rolling his eyes, Miles snickered. "Use that logic on your brother and he'll balk for sure. No man wants to get married because it's his duty. Especially not an independent man like Jonathan."

"Once Jonathan's settled in and married, my obligations to this family will be complete and I can rest easily."

"I don't think so."

Catherine frowned at his ominous tone. "Whatever do you mean?"

"What about Sarah?"

"Our youngest daughter is fine and in no rush to get married. Thanks to you, her mind is filled with books, school, and her never-ending search for logic."

Miles nodded toward the row behind them. "Oh, really? Take a look back there and tell me what you see."

Pretty and petite, blond-haired Sarah was sitting between two very handsome young men. She was smiling and chatting with both of them. From the frowns and muttering being exchanged by the two fellows, it was obvious that they were vying for her attention. When one reached over and shoved the other, Sarah looked positively delighted.

Miles chuckled. "It looks as though our problems are just beginning in that quarter, my love."

Closing her eyes, Catherine sighed. "Bloody hell!"

To my Readers:

I hope you enjoyed meeting Lady Cat's sons, Eric and Trelane, and their ladies, Belle and Paris. If you'd like to see what happens next in this family saga, I invite you to read the next book in my *Reluctant Heroes* series, THE RUNAWAY DUKE, being released in October 2002.

When Jonathan Carlisle goes off to contemplate marriage, he finds himself the victim of a kidnaping. He's injured in his escape and wakes up being nursed back to health by a lovely young woman named Melanie. Secrets abound and problems plague, but love cannot be denied.

I love hearing from my readers. If you'd like a bookmark or my current newsletter, send a SASE to me at PO Box 16434, West Palm Beach, FL 33416.

Forever yours,

Susan Grace

COMING IN AUGUST 2002 FROM
ZEBRA BALLAD ROMANCES

__A FALLEN WOMAN: The Brides of Bath
by Cheryl Bolen   0-8217-7249-X $5.99US/$7.99CAN
Since her husband's tragic death, Carlotta Ennis had hoped to attract a
wealthy husband in Bath. Instead she made the ruinous mistake of loving
a rake who was willing to seduce her, but not marry her. Now she is certain
no decent gentleman will ever marry her . . . until James Rutledge returns
home from the war and offers his hand . . .

__A DANGEROUS FANCY: American Heiresses
by Tracy Cozzens   0-8217-7351-8 $5.99US/$7.99CAN
Lily Carrington's ambitious mother had set her sights on a titled marriage
for Lily. As honorable as she was beautiful, Lily vowed not to disappoint
her family—even as she became the pawn in a sordid plot of seduction
by the Prince of Wales himself . . . and found herself falling in love with
a most unlikely hero.

__KING OF HEARTS: The Gamblers
by Pat Pritchard   0-8217-7255-4 $5.99US/$7.99CAN
Wade McCord, a U.S. Marshal, poses as a gambler at a stagecoach stop
to smoke out a notorious outlaw gang. But he never counted on his
burning desire for Lottie Hammond, a woman who may be in league with
the outlaws. Wade knows Lottie has secrets, but he also knows that the
time has come for him to gamble his heart on the promise of love.

__ON MY LADY'S HONOR: . . . And One for All
by Kate Silver   0-8217-7386-0 $5.99US/$7.99CAN
Sophie Delamanse envisioned a dull marriage to Count Lamotte, one of
her twin brother's Musketeer friends. Her life took a tragic turn when the
plague comsumed her family. Her brother promised that Lamotte would
come for her, but when he never arrived, Sophie vowed to go to *him*—
disguised as her brother—and make him pay for his dishonor.

Call toll free **1-888-345-BOOK** to order by phone or use this coupon to
order by mail. *ALL BOOKS AVAILABLE AUGUST 1, 2002.*
Name _____
Address _____
City _____ State _____ Zip _____
Please send me the books that I have checked above.
I am enclosing $ _____
Plus postage and handling* $ _____
Sales tax (in NY and TN) $ _____
Total amount enclosed $ _____
*Add $2.50 for the first book and $.50 for each additional book. Send
check or money order (no cash or CODs) to: **Kensington Publishing Corp.,
Dept. C.O., 850 Third Avenue, New York, NY 10022**
Prices and numbers subject to change without notice. Valid only in the
U.S. All orders subject to availability. **NO ADVANCE ORDERS.**
Visit our website at **www.kensingtonbooks.com.**

BOOK YOUR PLACE ON OUR WEBSITE AND MAKE THE READING CONNECTION!

We've created a customized website just for our very special readers, where you can get the inside scoop on everything that's going on with Zebra, Pinnacle and Kensington books.

When you come online, you'll have the exciting opportunity to:

- View covers of upcoming books

- Read sample chapters

- Learn about our future publishing schedule (listed by publication month *and author*)

- Find out when your favorite authors will be visiting a city near you

- Search for and order backlist books from our online catalog

- Check out author bios and background information

- Send e-mail to your favorite authors

- Meet the Kensington staff online

- Join us in weekly chats with authors, readers and other guests

- Get writing guidelines

- AND MUCH MORE!

**Visit our website at
http://www.kensingtonbooks.com**